DRIVETIME

James Meek was born in London in 1962 and grew up in Dundee. He is also the author of the novels *We Are Now Beginning Our Descent* (2008) and *The People's Act of Love* (2005), which won the Royal Society of Literature Ondaatje Prize, was longlisted for the Man Booker Prize and has been translated into more than twenty languages.

He now lives in London. He has worked as a journalist since 1985, and his reporting from Iraq and about Guantánamo Bay won a number of British and international awards.

Also by James Meek

McFARLANE BOILS THE SEA (1989)

LAST ORDERS (1992)

THE MUSEUM OF DOUBT (2000)

THE PEOPLE'S ACT OF LOVE (2005)

WE ARE NOW BEGINNING OUR DESCENT (2008)

DRIVETIME

JAMES MEEK

CANONGATE
Edinburgh · London · New York · Melbourne

Published in Great Britain in 2008 by
Canongate Books Ltd, 14 High Street,
Edinburgh EH1 1TE

First published in 1995 by Polygon, 22 George Square,
Edinburgh EH8 9LF

1

British Library Cataloguing-in-Publication Data
A catalogue record for this book is available on
request from the British Library

ISBN 978 1 84767 029 8

Typeset by Palimpsest Book Production Ltd,
Grangemouth, Stirlingshire

Printed and bound in Great Britain by
Clays Ltd, St Ives plc

www.canongate.net

For Yulia

PART ONE

One Friday evening in late summer Alan Allen walked from his lodgings to a university in the town of Edinburgh to try to stop the authorities throwing him off his course of studies. On the way, by the railings of a bridge, he stopped and looked at the moon, which had been at the edge of his vision all the way. It was full, the colour of resort hotel concrete, its dry seas dark like lichen. When it cracked open, a blood-red yolk would drop down on the park, spreading slow like honey over the grass and trees.

A woman came up behind him. Gregor! Is it Gregor? she said.

I'm not Gregor, said Alan.

Gregor! Gregor Ferguson, the councillor, the young one.

You've got the wrong person.

Gregor Ferguson, the young one, you must know him, it's you, is it not? From our ward.

I'm a student, said Alan.

Yes, you're a student. And a councillor. Listen. The woman looked up and down the street and pulled a folding cardboard theatre from inside her coat. She tapped it on the railings. It opened out. She set it on the ironwork, holding it there with one hand. It was patterned on a theatre of the previous century, coloured red and gold, with printed curtains, tassels, fringes, boxes, lamps and masks; someone had covered it with muddy watercolour paint and sprayed it with graffiti. The woman took out five cardboard actors on strips. A black ballpoint pen had been used to try to update them. They still looked like pirates. They had cutlasses. Their eyepatches had been made sunglasses.

I'm needing rehoused, right, said the woman. I've got four kids and just the two bedrooms.

A cardboard partition came down dividing the stage in two.

One of the kids has got asthma.

There was a highpitched coughing and one of the pirates jumped up and down and keeled over. The woman tilted the theatre so the stage was in darkness. She went on talking, making the sounds of destruction. They've been breaking in – kkkkh! pppgggghhhh! while I was away staying at my sister's and there's no light – ccchhhsss! there's no water – ppppwwwwhhhhgggg! they've taken everything, they've taken the taps off the sink, tschsss, they've smashed the glass in the windows, pwwwhcchhh . . . they've ripped out the meters.

Maybe the police.

What do I care who did it, them or the other mob?

said the woman. I need rehoused. I've been all over the place, all your offices, it's mental. She looked into the blackness beyond the proscenium. It's dark in there. Have you ever lived in the dark?

I'm not your councillor, said Alan. I've got to get on. It's late.

The woman let go the pirates, gripped his arm and looked up at him. They said to ask young Gregor, the councillor, she said. I'm at my wit's end, son. If your own councillor can't help you who can?

Alan jerked his arm back sharply to free himself from the woman. She fell down with a bump on her arse. She kept a hold on the theatre, which was dunted on the ground. Her pirate children slithered from the stage and flew off the bridge into the void.

Sorry, said Alan.

Help us up, then, said the woman. You ought to be more careful.

Alan pulled her to her feet. I didn't mean to do that. I'm not a councillor and I'm late.

You should've been more careful, son, you know it.

Yeah, I know it. Alan walked away.

Son! called the woman. Give us a hand a second.

Alan came back. The woman gave him the theatre to hold while she looked through her handbag. She took out a cigarette and lighter. She lit the cigarette and lowered the lighter. Alan handed the theatre back to her free hand. The woman took the cigarette from her mouth with the free hand and moved her other hand towards the theatre. The lighter was still lit. The theatre caught fire. The woman let go. Alan was holding something half-cardboard, half-torch. He flung it over the bridge and it dropped flaming into the nether regions.

The woman drew on the cigarette, lifted it from her lips between cleft fingers and fired beams of smoke from her nostrils. That's what happens, she said. I'm telling you, that's what happens. She rubbed her buttock, frowning. You've really fucked my rumty-tumty, d'you know that?

Sorry, said Alan. He turned round and left her.

At the university Alan went into a seminar room on the third floor of a tower block. It was half full. Standing on his own in front of a broad bare table was the reader Robert Bewick from the town of Cleveland, a bigger than average man in jeans and a brightly coloured sweater. He was reading his work in a slow voice, raising or lowering the pitch slightly for dialogue.

The boat knocked against the side of the pier, he read, and standing there on the old timbers Frank and Meonie felt it thudding through the soles of their feet.

Frank, said Meonie, gripping his wrists tightly with her small warm hands, it don't make no difference to me if you get on that boat. I knew you were always wanting to even when the joint was going fine and the folk'd come all the way down from Boston to hear the band. You don't want to feel bad now the band's gone home and your sister's near torched the place. I guess there's an art in leaving, and maybe now's the time.

Frank looked serious. Not wanting to break Meonie's hold on his wrists, a pleasant sensation, he bent down and touched her forehead lightly with his own.

You got it wrong, he said. It's the boat that stands still and us, we're the travelling ones. I guess I just want to be still for a while. You can travel well enough on your own. Look after Danny for me, and the Briar Rose. And Frank climbed down into the boat. Before Meonie could think of anything to say he was gone and there was nothing left but the sound of the water slapping against the pier and the steady agitation of the crickets.

Bewick looked up and closed the book. People clapped. Alan clapped a couple of times and started to chew his lip.

The professor stood up. Alan bit a chunk out of the corner of his mouth, tasted blood and went blind and deaf for a second.

. . . that marvellous reading as much as I did, said the professor.

At the back of the room, a six-foot man wearing a long black winter coat and a disgusted expression clicked his tongue loudly.

There's a short time left for questions, said the professor.

Yeah, said the tall one, standing up. He had a blue Adidas sports bag in one hand. I'd like to ask Mister Bewick whether the education system is elitist.

I don't know, said the writer. You have great buildings and some fine teachers.

You're incorrect on that last item, Mr Bewick. The teachers are in the way.

He made scissors of two fingers in his free hand and passed them across his face, snipping. In the silence you could hear the patting of the flesh of the fingers as the blades closed. Cutouts. Me on one side. Knowledge on the other. Teacher in the middle. Snip snip.

You don't have to go to college to learn, said the writer. But it does give you time to learn. It gives you time to think. I wasn't a great scholar at college but I read a bunch of books, made some friends and learned a whole lot about how to do nothing.

People laughed. The professor laughed loudest. He exhausted his lungs trying to blast out a deep authoritative chuckle.

Yes, said the professor, pointing to a fair-haired girl with round silver glasses who was gripping the edge of her seat with her hands and inclining her whole body towards the writer, smile to the wind.

Why are there so many marsupials in your stories? she asked.

Alan had never read anything by Bewick. He folded his arms and looked round. The student with the sports bag had left. Alan got up and walked out of the seminar room.

After about ten minutes the audience came out. The professor wasn't among them. Alan waited a moment and went back into the seminar room. There was no-one there. There was another exit. Alan went through and along a short corridor to another door behind which he could hear the professor and the writer talking.

If I had a knife, I could show you how we used to do it in the town of Marseilles, said the professor. Hands flat on the table, fingers spread out. Fast, like that. We never nicked a finger.

I've got a jackknife, said the writer.

The professor laughed nervously. He said: Let's finish our drinks first.

The writer cleared his throat. Yeah. So. Is there much hunting round here? I mean can you go after deer at all, do you need a licence?

You can go stalking.

Stocking? What's that? Like laying up deer for the winter, that kind of thing?

Alan opened the door and walked into the room. The professor and the writer stood next to a long table covered in a white cloth and an expanse of tiny full sherry glasses. In the silence that followed him coming in, Alan counted the number down each side and multiplied them to reach the following result: 840 sherry glasses, minus the two the professor and the writer were holding, 838. A good method of detecting the early stages of earthquakes. There was nobody else in the room.

Hi! said the writer.

Hi.

Help yourself to some sherry, said the professor.

Thanks. Alan picked up a glass and stood watching the men from a distance of several yards.

I'll have another one, said the writer.

Alan tried to detect the slightest tinkling of glasses which might indicate a tremor taking place in the earth beneath. There was none. His scalp crinkled with fear and he could hear nothing but sustained Jacques Cousteau scuba exhalations from the writer and the professor.

Why are there so many sherry glasses? expressed Alan.

We like to treat our guests well, indicated the professor. Did you enjoy the reading?

I didn't see all of it.

Too bad, said the writer.

Alan floated towards the two forms. Would the janitor get the bulk of the sherry or were there caterers involved?

I'm one of your students. Alan Allen.

Of course. The professor probed a piece of Alan with his hand. We're always glad to see you here.

Yes. I was wondering if there was any way you could let me back in. It's important for me. I'd work harder. I'd work differently. I'd work.

The professor said nothing for a while, he looked at Alan. The writer was looking round the room like he was about to deliver an estimate to paper it.

Alan looked down at the easy to clean industrial grade carpet tile in imperial khaki, a thousand miles below. After several years he lifted his head and stared into the professor's cheek. Please, he said.

The panel's already made its decision, said the professor, there's nothing I can do.

Where does that leave me?

You can look for a job, can't you? I'm sure one of the teacher training colleges. You were a teacher, weren't you, Bob?

Never, said the writer. I got a master's degree and a doctorate and went straight into contact sports from there.

Alan focused on the bridge of the professor's nose. In case of emergency, strike nose to release blood. Alan had a chronic congenital condition. He'd been born without any fists.

He took another sherry glass and drank half.

Yes, he said. He put the glass down and floated towards the door. The tall student was coming in, striding.

You're Alan, he said. You don't remember my name. He nodded towards the professor. Know what he's doing? He's standing in my light.

I was asking about getting back in, said Alan. But it's finished.

Bollocks. This'll sort them out, said the student, unzipping his sports bag and taking out a baseball bat. He walked past Alan.

How d'you want it, professor, comedy or tragedy? he said. He was gently bouncing the big end of the bat in his cupped left hand. The professor had put down his sherry glass.

We can talk this over with your director of studies, he said.

No! shouted the student.

He dealt the sherry glasses three blows with one-handed strokes of the bat. The crack of the bat on cloth-covered wood was like the knock that wakes people from their final night's sleep to face something they've spent their life avoiding. A fragment of glass spun through the air and clicked against one of the buttons on Alan's jacket. The student approached the professor with both hands on and swung at his ribs. The professor dodged.

You were a boxer, weren't you, Bob? the professor gasped.

Referee – referee! said the writer, stepping back, taking out a small pad and starting to take notes.

The student caught the professor a glancing blow on the hip. The professor staggered and grunted but stayed upright.

Please! he said in a low voice.

Oh fuck, said the student, wrinkling his nose, and took aim for a big swipe. The professor closed his eyes, turned his face downwards and clenched his hands between his thighs, shuffling away slowly. The bat caught him at the end of its curve, striking him with a faint, deep sound on the base of the neck. Jesus Christ, below the shoulder! the writer shouted. The professor didn't cry out. With his eyes still closed and his face still turned downwards he half-fell against the window ledge.

It won't help you, he muttered, and started coughing.

It's already helped me, said the student, clenching his teeth and shivering.

I've been in fights before, in the town of Paris.

What the fuck does it matter where they were? screamed the student, swinging the bat back and hitting the professor's jacketed shirted ribcage with every third word. Is your fucking violence more intellectual as well?

The professor cried out.

Maybe that's enough now, said the writer.

That wasn't a fight, said the student, putting the bat back into the sports bag and zipping it up. It was putting him right where he's been going wrong. He looked at the writer.

Don't think I'm stopping because of you, he said. You're a writer. But me and him – he nodded at the moaning clothes on the floor – we're readers. He turned and caught Alan's eye. Alan looked away, left the room and went downstairs.

In his wallet were banknotes worth 28, a Visa card, a cash dispenser card, a cheque card with a limit of 50 and a condom in red foil.

In different pockets he had 3.97 in loose change, a chequebook with six cheques, a driving licence and a receipt for 49.99 from the Debenhams store. There was 445.67 in the current account and a 300 limit on the Visa card. He owed them 240. He was due a 200 deposit from his landlord when he left the lodgings. He owed his parents 200 but he could let that one go for a while. To get a car, insurance, petrol, run away from the credit card collectors, crank up the overdraft – you were talking what, 1,000 realisable over a week.

Later that night Alan entered a callbox, put a .50 in and dialled his parents' number. He could still catch them before they got the accordion out.

The door of the phone box opened behind him and a hand took him firmly by the fringe, pulling him outside. He let go the receiver and it smacked against the glass panel. He was tugged out of the box by the hair and walked slowly backwards. It was a good chance to scream, something he hadn't done for fourteen years or more. He blew it.

The hand let go of his hair, took him by the lapel of his jacket and shoved him round. It was a boy in a black and purple shellsuit. The boy had amazingly good skin, not a pluke in sight.

What? said Alan.

Gregor Ferguson, said the boy. Is that you?

No!

The boy stared at him with his smooth heavy face, not blinking, not relaxing his grip.

How? he said.

How d'you mean, how? I'm someone else.

Two other boys came up on either side of Alan.

Fucking cunt beat up my mother in the street. Supposed to be a fucking councillor, she goes up and asks him about getting rehoused and he goes mental and next thing she's lying in the gutter.

That's terrible.

Terrible for her. Terrible for you. Nemo me impune lacessit.

I'm not him. I'm not a councillor. I'm Alan Allen.

You look like a student.

I was one.

Nemo – d'you know who I am?

No.

I don't know myself sometimes. It begins with a D and . . . ends with a D. But when you live in a house without any light, how do you know who you are? You – you come home at night and you get the loan of a neighbour's mirror and lights to look at yourself and – then you go into the house and go to bed in the darkness, and you go to sleep, and then you wake up, and then . . . how do you know . . .

You could get a candle, said Alan.

A candle? screamed D-D.

Staaaaaaaanleeeeeeeeeey! wooed the other boys like Oliver Hardy. Alan heard the click of metal on metal.

We don't lacessit nemo impune us, said D-D, shaking Alan back and forward. Nemo! He let go of Alan's jacket and put his hands to his own neck. His face darkened and he made a coughing, choking sound. His mouth opened and his eyes squeezed shut. His torso quivered as he struggled to breathe.

Not afuckinggain, said one of the boys.

Where's his fucking sniffer?

D-D opened his eyes wide and collapsed onto the ground, gripping his throat with both hands like he was strangling himself. The boys were burrowing into his shellsuit. They pulled out an asthma inhaler and pushed it up his nose. Just the touch of it must have given his lungs some kind of jolt because he managed to inhale.

NEMO! he shouted, and fell back, coughing his windpipe red raw.

Alan went back into the phone box and picked up the receiver. It was dead. His hand was shaking. He put the receiver back on the hook. The coins went rattling into the machine. No change.

He went on to the Threshers shop and bought a bottle of Cabernet Sauvignon from the region of Plovdiv for 2.50 and a couple of ring-pull cans of white table wine from the region of Burgos for a single each. They threw in the carrier bag.

Your list, said the guy behind the counter, handing Alan a yellow sticky note. Alan looked at it. It said:

freezer bags
vaseline
Sauvignon Blanc
hamsters (2)
cream eggs
batteries (HP2)

Not mine, said Alan.

The guy shrugged. Alan crumpled the note and stuck it in his pocket.

Have you got cream eggs? he said.

The guy shook his head. Nor hamsters, he said, licked his lips and sniffed.

Alan's way led across a park. Taking the most direct line he left the lighted pathway and strode over the grass. The clinking of the bottle and the cans and the plastic rustle of the bag got to him. He screwed up the neck of the bag and held it tightly in his fist so the things inside were immobilised. The noise of traffic was remote, there was the flick of grass blades as his boots went through them and the thud of his soles on the earth like the blows of a bat on a man's chest. He started to run towards the trees at the far side of the park. It was a steady pace he could keep up forever, as long as the turf lasted. The trees got no nearer. He sprinted forward, legs kicking out and shoulders working out of time, till he felt a pain in his lungs and he was sucking in more air than he could cope with. He slowed down and walked the rest of the way.

Alan went down the steps to the basement flat where Malcolm Tummel lived with his girlfriend Paula McInnes. The place was roomy but smelled a bit of rot or damp or some such. Paula opened the door. Hi, she said. She shouted down the hall: Malcolm! It's your other lover.

Oiled up and ready, said Alan.

You big poof, said Paula. He's in the kitchen, cooking up some Cantonese shite as usual.

How's it going?

As well as can be expected, thankee kindly sir, what with my rheumatism and the ague. Paula hirpled off into the bedroom.

Alan went to the kitchen. Malcolm was chopping ginger and garlic. Hello! he said.

Hi. What d'you want, red or a can of white?

Cans, eh? Let's see what that's like.

Alan told Malcolm the violence of the evening while Malcolm brought the rice to a state of dry tenderness and steamed the vegetables. By comparison, the stir-fry was easy; the only danger was that the light oil or the onions would burn before the other ingredients were cooked. Malcolm knew what he was doing, but there was the risk you'd leave off stirring at the wrong moment and all would be lost. This time the beef in aniseed sauce came out fine. There wasn't too much of it, though, maybe ten bits of meat, or worse, nine or eleven.

Is Paula not eating? said Alan.

She had some cheese on toast earlier on.

Alan cleaned out the first bowlful in a few minutes. Three chunks of meat left.

You have the two, said Malcolm.

Are you sure?

Go on.

Thanks. Sometimes he drafted plans to murder his friend, he was so fucking saintly.

I should give you something for this, he said.

Don't be stupid.

I don't often cook for you.

You will.

How d'you get the rice so dry? said Alan.

It's rinsing the grains beforehand, and getting the proportions of rice to water right, so it all boils away at the right time. Malcolm shrugged. Luck.

They went through and watched the TV news. There was an item about arson in a community theatre and a protest meeting of residents in Gregor Ferguson's ward. There was an interview with the residents' leader. They were sick fed up of being treated like dirt by the council, and now old people were literally being kicked into the gutter. We want the police to investigate Councillor Ferguson, she said, and urgent action on the state of our homes, or there'll be trouble.

They had Councillor Ferguson in the studio. I totally deny these allegations, he said, which are clearly part of a police-inspired provocation aimed at exploiting the already tense situation in this deprived area.

D'you think I look like him? said Alan.

You might if you had a beard and were a foot shorter, said Paula.

And glasses, said Malcolm.

Does anyone want a lift through to Glasgow? said Alan.

Why're you going there, anyway? said Malcolm.

It's a better place for me than here.

Why?

Life is sharper. People there are hard and cool. I want to be like them.

Ice is hard and cool, said Paula.

Hard and cool but warm, I mean, said Alan.

Nothing's hard and cool and warm. Except Prince's penis, said Paula.

I don't see what difference it makes, Edinburgh or Glasgow, said Malcolm. All this difference thing is music hall shite. How's moving somewhere else going to change your life? It's still streets and shops and people on top and people on the bottom. You find a few friends and the rest you don't know. And then the novelty wears off.

I'm not bothered. I want to go, and I'm going. At least I'll know where I'm going.

We all know where we're going eventually, said Malcolm.

Later Alan went by himself to a party in another part of town. Some guy he'd never seen before showed him into the kitchen. Alan placed his red wine firmly on the table, found a plastic cup, went to the sink, rinsed it out, dried it carefully, picked up a bottle of rosé from the region of Guarda, examined the reproduction of an 18th-century shepherd and shepherdess on the label, sniffed the contents and poured a full measure into the cup. He would drink this one cup, no more.

He had on a black jacket, a black cotton shirt with embroidered pockets, a bootlace tie with a steel ram's head fastener, pale blue jeans, pointy black ankle boots, black socks and tartan boxer shorts. He didn't know the clan.

He took a big swallow of wine, sweet, tepid and oily, and looked out into the hall. A man with not much hair and a massive jaw was talking to a pale, scarlet-lipped woman wearing fingerless black lace gloves. He was propped up against the wall with one hand and leaning over her. His jaw was about the size of her face.

Alan poured himself another glass of the pink stuff. He held up the bottle. All right if I take this through? he said. Nobody cared. Alan took the bottle into the hall and stood next to the man and the woman. They stopped talking and looked at him.

Fancy a refill? he said to the woman, glancing at the man.

That's kind of you, said the man. His voice was deep enough to make your breastbone vibrate. He held out an empty china mug with a picture on it of Lord Snooty and his pals. The woman smiled.

Watch him, she said. Back in a minute. She went off.

Alan poured wine into the mug. The man held it steady. Alan felt him watching the flow. He waited for him to say something. He didn't say anything. Alan filled the mug up to the brim.

How come you gave me so much? said the man.

You didn't say anything.

If I was lying on the road, and you were driving towards me, and I didn't say anything, would you run me over?

The man shook his head and smiled. It was a big smile; six inches at least it must have been. A relative of the host, or recruiting for the kind of sex you only read about, or would like to.

How are you fixed for cash? said the man.

Not too hot, said Alan. You?

I'm rich, said the man.

How rich?

Rich enough. I own an estate. In the region of Lothian.

Big?

Three miles, north to south; two miles, east to west; a mile deep.

Deep?

Deep.

Inherited?

Won. With my own sweat. And the sweat of my honest employees. We worked for thirty years to make it out of nothing.

What happened to the others?

They're on the dole.

The two men drank draughts of wine.

McStrachan, said the man.

Alan, said Alan.

It'll be something to see when it's finished, said McStrachan. Fountains, a lake, a grotto, canaries.

Canaries?

Canaries or peacocks. In fact, peacocks, almost certainly. It's just you know how they are, they scream all the time, and in enclosed spaces. And they take longer to react to the gas.

Yeah, said Alan, not listening, looking round to see where the pale woman went. He couldn't see her.

I have enemies, said McStrachan. Bureaucrats and speculators and lawyers, trying to claim what's mine. I'll win. But they're cunning. They tell me my estate's burning and can't be put out. Or that it's not profitable. Profitable!

Is it profitable? said Alan, switching back in.

No. It will be. I've got other interests. Business. An estate is a pond, but trade is a spring. That was Daniel Defoe. A good man. Never had the taste of coaldust in his mouth but a good man all the same. How about you?

I'm going to the town of Glasgow.

Why?

To look for work.

Yes, there are lots of people who don't work because they don't want a dirty job with low wages, aren't there, said McStrachan. That's why I lost so many people. And then some people who aren't poor have an ambition to be.

I don't.

You do. But it's not so easy. How are you getting to Glasgow?

I'm buying a car.

There you go.

Are we not allowed to have spare cash?

That's always been my understanding. Listen, you can do a job for me.

No thanks.

There's this antique down south I need picked up. It's an egg painted to look like the moon.

A hen's egg?

Yes.

Have you got a picture of it?

For God's sake, you know what the moon looks like, don't you?

Only one side of it!

That'll do. I'll give you the address and some money.

I'm not going that way.

McStrachan put the mug down on the floor. From his blazer pocket he took a red and black lacquered pen and a notebook bound in old red leather.

I'm taking the northern route.

Look. Here's the address. Here's my phone number. Here's the money. McStrachan held out two 50 notes.

Alan took the piece of paper with the address on. It said: The Elms, Little Screwing. Alan handed the piece of paper back.

What?

You know what.

What? said McStrachan, clenching the mighty jaw.

There's no such place.

How do you know?

I would have heard about it. It would have been on the TV shows.

It was.

And in the papers.

It has been. McStrachan shook his head. Alan took a step back as the jaw swung round. McStrachan looked straight at him and stuck the jaw out. No wonder you're unemployed, he said. You don't know what the moon looks like and you've never heard of the classic joke place name.

Alan laughed. He stopped when McStrachan didn't. Come on, he said, I know you're making it up.

Arrogant and ignorant, the worst, said McStrachan. Astonish me. Next thing you'll be telling me they really did drop an atom bomb on the town of Hiroshima.

Alan said nothing.

Well?

Well what?

How do you know they did? Were you there?

I've seen film of it.

Where?

On TV.

When?

I can't remember. Loads of times.

When, exactly? On what channel? What was the name of the cameraman? Did you see a sign saying This Is Hiroshima? Did you see the radiation?

I saw a lot of people with radiation injuries.

Oh, you're a doctor, are you?

No.

I'll tell you what you remember. You've got a fuzzy black and white two-dimensional picture in your mind of something that looks as if it might once have been a city, somewhere. Other pictures of a bright flash and a mushroom cloud and a big silver plane. Some memory of people you assume are from Hiroshima gathering at a shrine somewhere. Hearing a lot of people say the phrase The atom bomb on Hiroshima, but not exactly when or who.

Look, I don't need your work, or your money.

That's not what you said a minute ago.

I need work and money but I don't need your work and your money.

Unemployed arts student, said McStrachan, and walked heavily away.

When he had gone Alan knew he had been an idiot for not taking the money from a rich man. Yeah, and to be an idiot, a good notion. To be simple-minded, to be ignorant, to admit your ignorance to everyone, not by shrugging your shoulders or shaking your head but by saying in a clear voice: I don't know. Then everyone would stop talking, the words would stop, and people could get on with it. Thought and action would be one and the same thing. Among the idiots all you would lose would be all this fucking conversation and these statements. An end to would, could, should and might. In the land of the idiots all you'd hear would be chopping wood, trout frying, waterfalls, snarling engines and the moans of lovers.

I don't know.

What? said the pale woman with the fingerless gloves.

Anything, said Alan, lifting his head out of his chest, straightening his shoulders and pushing himself off the wall. He clasped the empty cup with both hands.

You came back, he said.

Uhuh. Is the wine finished?

Yes. I'm an idiot.

Don't worry, I'm used to people talking to themselves.

I really am an idiot, I know nothing.

It's the booze, said the woman, grinning. She had an oval face and flickering eyes and barely detectable freckles. She put out her hand and tapped the fastener on his bootlace tie with a fingernail, like a fragment of flying sherry glass clicking against a jacket button. Sheep, she said.

Isn't it a ram?

You know something.

Alan panicked and started chewing the rim of the plastic cup silently.

I see you coming out of the language lectures, said the woman. You always look as if someone's about to be kind to you. My name's Deirdre.

Alan.

I know. Her tongue moved inside her cheek, she fiddled with her glass and swivelled to and fro.

I'm leaving this place, said Alan, relieved with a vision

of him in the car alone under the mountains, gliding through rainclouds.

How d'you mean? said Deirdre, peering confused and unhappy at him. With the unhappiness and her freckles he lost the vision. A cold, tingling wave made him shiver and he had an immediate hard-on.

I'm going to the town of Glasgow. I need to get away from here. I'm buying a car and moving out altogether.

Drastic, said Deirdre.

The main thing is to be moving, said Alan.

Do you want to see my flat? said Deirdre. It's near here.

Sure.

It was warm on the street. Alan took off his jacket and slung it over his right shoulder. His limbs had become loose and separate, like they'd melted a bit, he tried to co-ordinate them, watching himself, shaking his head. He looked at Deirdre. She smiled. What if he had to meet her parents? Terrible to inflict elocution lessons on a daughter, scarred for life. Sitting round the table, four of them, mute, then the mother stretching out her hand offering him a heavy casserole full of boiled potatoes, too heavy for her thin old wrist, the wrist trembling, the casserole shaking, everyone roaring, the casserole crashing into the crockery. No problem because the two of them would get up from the table and go to a private room and swiftly undress each other, their mouths wetly merge. And there was that professor lying there with a ruptured spleen or something, after slipping Alan the gift of sexual attraction. What a beauty.

What're you thinking? said Deirdre.

I forgot.

How can you forget? Tell me something.

All memories, facts and the five jokes Alan knew left him. He retained rules, recipes, songs, how to tie his shoelaces, how to drive and the shape of the jokes – like there were these three factors in a situation, the first factor said in this situation I'd obvious, the second factor said I'd bit less obvious, the third factor said I'd totally unexpected, taking the situation to be another situation altogether, me being thick.

I like your gloves, said Alan. His mouth had gone dry.

I got them from a catalogue. I love warm evenings. I should go and live in Paris.

Alan shifted his jacket from the right to the left and put his arm on Deirdre's shoulder.

It's hard to keep in step, he said. She laughed, lifted her hand and toyed with his fingertips.

So what is it you do? said Alan, like he cared.

I'm a nurse.

Would he come to love this woman? Should you have sex before love? Of course!

D'you mind if I go in here and get some chips? I'm starving, said Deirdre.

Go ahead.

D'you want some?

No. I'll wait out here.

Deirdre went into the chip shop, pulling off the gloves.

Alan took a few steps from the entrance. There was

a callbox on the corner. He could still catch his parents before they left for the bran store.

A sound came from behind the callbox, like a fingernail tapped on a steel fastener, like a glass fragment clicking on a jacket button. A human tooth bounced over the pavement. Alan couldn't tell if it was incisor or canine.

A man came out of the darkness after the tooth. He was covering his mouth with his sleeve. Luckily he was wearing a dark jacket. Or was it luck?

D'you want me to pick it up? said Alan.

The two of them looked down at the tooth.

What, d'you think they'll reinstall it? said the guy through his sleeve.

Put it under your pillow, you'll get some cash.

Yeah, and it gets deducted the following fortnight. The tooth fairy passes on claims.

The guy put his heel on the tooth and twisted it, like he was planning to crush it on the paving stone. There was a sound of enamel squeaking on concrete.

Oh, Jesus, stop! said Alan, putting his hands on his ears.

Eh?

Stop. The guy stopped. I've got this problem with imaginary tortures, said Alan.

At least they're imaginary. The guy looked over his shoulder. Aggro in our time, he said, unbelievable.

Should you not get to the infirmary?

Infirmary? Yeah. But infirmary, you know, doctors, police, reporters.

It seemed the guy was a councillor, Gregor Ferguson by name, who'd been the victim of some kind of student game, no offence, he was a student himself, but you know what happens. There was this student wandering round the town, looking like him, yeah? and one of the constituents, like really well known in the community, right, went up to him with some complaint, stupid bitch, though she was a good woman, really great, and she had plenty to complain about, Alan didn't know the state of their houses, it was just she was such a fucking pain in the arse, so anyway this student made out like he was listening, then he just said That'll teach you to vote for the revolution, darling, and pushed her into the gutter. So her sons'd come looking for him, Gregor Ferguson. And they'd found him.

Alan shook his head and looked through the window into the chipper. Deirdre was near the head of the queue. She turned, serious, like she was going to check he was still there. When she saw he was watching she smiled, bent her head forward and waved.

Yeah, said the councillor. It's a great laugh, then people get hurt.

I guess the student didn't mean to push her into the gutter.

You would say that, wouldn't you, you'd take his part. Do you know him?

No!

No. If he was a man he'd come forward and take the shit himself. The trouble with some people is they think they're saving themselves for something special.

Someone comes up to them on the street and they can't listen to her cause they're too fucking busy. And it doesn't matter cause when they leave college they're going to give crateloads of cash and a couple of years to charity, and vote for the party of kind people, and stand in the bar and spend three hours talking to their pals about the situation, and one day they're going to do something totally fucking excellent that'll help a thousand people instead of hearing an old woman out for a few minutes. But somehow it never gets done. Cause they can't put Listened Patiently To Old Woman For A While on their fucking Curriculum Vitae.

I know what you mean, said Alan.

Do you fuck know what I mean.

A sound of joints cracking came from the darkness beyond the phone box. Councillor Ferguson, said a low, emphatic, patient voice. Councillor Ferguson. A couple of other voices joined in.

Come on, councillor.

Councillor Ferguson.

You're not finished.

Councillor.

We're waiting for you.

Ach, said the councillor, taking a few steps in each direction, still with his arm over his face. He went a bit closer to Alan.

If you meet him, watch out, he said. A man who can't tolerate being bored for five minutes by a stranger in trouble isn't going to lift a finger to save your life.

The councillor walked back into the darkness. There

were words too low to hear. Deirdre came out of the chipper with a big poke of chips, steaming from the open end. She was smiling and chewing a bulging mouthful at the same time. She held out the bag. Alan bent his head to sniff up the hot sauce vapour and took a couple of crispy ones. As they walked away Alan heard a sound like a football kicked hard into the branches of a tree, and a grunt. They left the tooth on the pavement, with the white curving mark it'd made when it scraped over the concrete paving slab.

Deirdre's flat was on the third floor of a wide-staired tenement block. There were pot plants on the stair. Deirdre edged the key into her lock notch by notch and turned it. The draught excluder stroking the carpet, the withdrawal of the key, the click of the tongue of the Yale as the door closed behind them, the rustle of their sleeves, the creak of a floorboard, caused Alan to laugh out loud.

Shhh!

What? whispered Alan.

The other people might be here.

Alan followed Deirdre into the lounge. Big fronds on every side, shiny and green. Pine and books. Not a flat to throw up in. Alan chose the right hand side of the settee, hard by the armrest. Deirdre put a record on and turned the volume right down. It sounded like Aretha Franklin but it was so low you couldn't tell.

The people I live with are strange, said Deirdre. She sat down on the armrest next to Alan. They go to bed early, like ten o'clock.

Is that strange? said Alan.

I think so.

Deirdre picked at a knot of thread on the settee with the nails of her thumb and index finger. She was looking intensely at the white wall opposite. Alan put his hand on her shoulder.

There's an idiot on your shoulder, he said.

Deirdre let herself slide off the armrest into Alan's lap. She still wasn't looking at him. Alan put his arms round her and kissed her on the cheek. He leaned towards her mouth but she kept her head turned away. He stroked her breast. Her breathing was louder. Alan put his left hand under the hem of her skirt and ran it along her thigh. Nothing happened. Alan's erection was painfully compressed. Events tended towards a centre. Alan moved his left hand up as far as it would go and fumbled with some elastic. His fingers went paddling through wiry hair and found a cleft, and a moist, complex topography. He rubbed cautiously. Deirdre stiffened.

Why won't you kiss me? said Alan.

I want to. I can't. It turns me on.

Don't you want to be turned on?

No.

Alan pressed his fingers further in. No idea which juicy bump was which. Deirdre drew a quick breath and stretched her legs out. A woman was not a clarinet.

They rolled off the settee onto the carpet. Alan returned his fingers quickly to the place. He liked it, Deirdre didn't seem to mind, he wanted her to be grateful.

There's something I have to tell you. I have a boyfriend, said Deirdre. Are you angry?

No, said Alan. The boyfriend might be. He might be entitled to be.

He's not here, said Deirdre. He won't be back tonight.

Alan wanted her to stop talking. He plied the fingers, deeper still.

You are angry, she said. Alan withdrew. He wasn't angry. He was surprised at her.

You might know my boyfriend. He was a student as well. He's in some trouble just now. Do you want me to tell you about it?

No. Alan got up and sat on the settee. Deirdre went away and came back after a while with coffee. She'd changed into a dressing gown. Alan spent what seemed to him a long time sucking Deirdre's breasts.

That's one reason to have babies, she said, with her eyes closed and a big grin on her face. That feeling of having your nipple sucked.

One time they went still, mainly naked on the settee and with the main light blazing on them, waiting for somebody moving around in the hallway to go back to bed.

I don't like it here, said Deirdre.

When Alan was leaving Deirdre kept hugging him and saying I'm sorry, I'm sorry. He wasn't sure what she meant. He walked home. He sniffed the savoury scent on his fingers along the way. Maybe try it with lemon next time.

Alan had asked a friend about cars. The friend said:

A thousand'll get you a hundred miles before something goes wrong. A tenner a mile – what kind of a transport arrangement is that? Then you got the petrol and all the other rubbish. If you were a fly sly wily handyman you'd know what to look out for and be able to fix it if it broke down but if you're not! Christ you've got to be daft, once your insurance and tax come off what've you got left? A tyre goes and you're down at Kwik-Fit with the wily smiley man in the blue overalls who's chewing the Wrigley's Spearmint Gum and juggles with spanners all at the same time. Then it's the battery and you're down at Halfords for a new one sealed in plastic in a plastic bag with the receipt thank you, call again. And that's you fucking stony broke, running on empty. Get help.

The lure of the road. You know that long straight stretch on that country road on a hot day in August with no-one around? God talk about virtual reality. A guy was killed there last month. He was on a bike. A Honda. He was doing wheelies at 90. They buried him with his head in his helmet and his helmet still embedded in the tank. They couldn't separate them.

The only difference between the auctions and the dealers is that at the dealers the cars are waxed and polished and cost four times as much. All right you get a six-month guarantee maybe but what use is that if after six months the two half-cars they've welded together fall apart when you're tanking along the bypass in the rain? Exactly. So between the auctions and the dealers you've got a private sale. What a gamble!

Alan didn't pay any attention. The seller was on the edge of town, half an hour on the bus, then a ten-minute walk along Baltasound Crescent. All the streets began with Bal. There was a Balquhidder Prospect, a Balnaguisich Drive and a Balrog Close. The developers had proposed the list to the council and the council had accepted it.

Brakes, handbrake, tyres, wipers, lights. He could check the lights at least. Whether they went on or not. Here was the problem. Your car broke down. You knew fuck all about cars. Not to make assumptions, but which was the better place to break down, outside the pub or outside a conference of child psychiatrists? Worse: your ten-year-old daughter broke down. Outside the pub, or outside a conference of child psychiatrists?

Alan found the house, a semi with a garage attached. A guy answered the door.

I've come about the car, said Alan.

Mm-hm, said the guy. Mm-hm. Mm-hm . . . You've come about the car, haven't you?

Yes.

I thought so. The guy smiled. Come on then. He came out and led Alan to the garage, tossing the car keys in the air and glancing back over his shoulder.

Bit special, this door, he said, winking. He squatted down and unlocked it. He hauled it open. It wanted oil.

Stiff, said Alan.

The guy smiled. Titanium, he said. Expands in the heat.

Oh.

Only four dozen people in the world have garage doors like that.

Yeah?

The car was there. It was intact. Alan saw it would be his. It was twelve years old. Like an overpriced malt whisky. Only 78,000 on the clock, so they said, it could have been round once already. Alan kicked one of the tyres. He didn't know why.

I'll tell you one thing for free, said the guy. You know the difference between real ex-SAS men and piss artists? The real ones never talk about it, that's what the difference is.

Alan tried the driver's door. It was open. He got in. It smelled strongly of stale bread, slightly of petrol.

The guy came up and knelt beside him. It's ex-police, he said. Got some contacts there, can't speak about it, but they muck about with their motors. First time I took it out on the motorway, I was trying to find fourth gear, and suddenly the gearstick kind of clicked, and – whoah! I was overtaking Porsches. It doesn't work now, of course, I asked them to take that mechanism out, it was too dangerous.

Right.

I'm sorry I can't tell you about Ulster, but rules are rules. That's just the way it is.

That's OK. Can I start it up?

If you're ready for it.

Alan turned the key. The engine made a sound like the Queen Mother with a fishbone stuck in her throat and began turning over, loud but steady. Exhaust fumes seeped out into the sunshine. Alan pressed the throttle. It had a light touch, the engine went straight to warp 10 with a ripping noise from behind. He tried the clutch, a hard action, and went through the gears, first you had to ram in, otherwise OK. Leaving it idling in neutral he switched on the lights, full beam, with the fog light and hazard warning lights. He sounded the horn, switched the radio on and off, tried the wipers, shut the engine down and got out of the car.

OK, he said. Can we take it out for a run?

Fffff! said the guy. A run, eh? He put his hands on his hips and looked down at the floor, shaking his head and grinning. It's a run you're after. You've never been to a safe house before, have you? Certain people would be very happy to see me go out on a run. Certain people with masks and . . . he made a shaking mime with his two hands held out. Get me?

Babies? said Alan.

Heh! The guy looked round and performed the action again.

Drills? Machine guns?

Hey. Keep your voice down. People round here think I'm a salesman at Dixon's.

So this run, then.

Ever been on an anti-kidnap driving course? I'm not supposed to say anything but one time we were training these guys in the town of Hamburg. Abso-fucking-lutely crazy. One week, one week, they wrote off twelve brand-new BMWs. We were fucking weeping.

They got into the car and the guy started off. He stalled three times.

Engine problem? said Alan.

Nah! Bit of kit that checks for certain things underneath the car that shouldn't be there, know what I mean?

I won't be needing that, said Alan.

Heh! Not unless you've got half a million to spare, said the guy.

They drove once around the block in second gear, at 15 miles an hour. The guy kept his hands firmly in the ten to two position on the wheel. They stopped in front of the house. The guy's hand closed round the handbrake and tugged it. It was already on.

You OK? said the guy to Alan. Sorry about that, thought I was on the Falls Road for a minute.

Yeah, said Alan. OK, I'll take it.

I lost some good mates in this motor. Even without the electronics it's worth twenty thousand, but the sergeant at the compound made me promise to dump it for 700.

In the advert it said 600 or nearest offer.

Heh! The guy shook his head and leaned his forehead on the wheel. You remind me of a young lad I used to know. Didn't like loud bangs.

I'll take it for 600.

I'll tell you something for nothing, said the guy seriously, putting his hand on Alan's thigh. You're not as stupid as you look.

I am, said Alan.

The car was taxed and MOT'd for six months. The

matter of insurance arose. Alan had counted on cheap student insurance. But he wasn't a student any more. The next lowest he found in the shops was 400. In monthly instalments, OK, but petrol, food.

He found the piece of paper where McStrachan's number was written. The paper was about four inches square, thick, cream-coloured, hard to fold. Held up to the light you could see a watermark in it, a man in three-quarter face, either Napoleon Bonaparte or Elvis Presley. Alan had a .5 coin left in change. He put it in the slot and dialled. Someone picked up straight away. By the vibration of the receiver when the person spoke, like an electric shaver against his cheek, it was McStrachan. The LCD indicator on the phone went from .5 to .4.

Yes.

It's Alan. Alan Allen. We met at a party. You made an offer about an egg.

Yes.

I've thought more about it, I'd like to accept.

You weren't up to the mark on the moon, and place names.

Yes.

You said you didn't need my work or my money.

.3. That was the drink talking, said Alan. The egg sounded interesting. I'd enjoy delivering it.

I thought you were taking the northern route.

.23. Northern, shmorthern.

It's a very beautiful piece, this egg, and the only things that matter in life are money, beauty and a landscape garden free from the slightest trace of methane. Do you agree?

.18. Absolutely, said Alan.

So you do need my work.

.11. Yeah!

And my money.

Yes.

I'll call you back and get your bank details.

Three hours later Alan parked the car outside his lodgings. He had the registration chit in his pocket. It was just after four on a Saturday afternoon. A strong wind made the lampposts creak and an empty cherry yoghurt carton went bongoing down the gutter. The ball hit the crossbar at the Hibernian ground a few streets away and there was a blast of noise from the home fans like interstation static on an FM scanner. Alan beat a fast drumbreak on his thighs with the palms of his hands.

The machine was dark blue, a hatchback with three doors. The body was steel and the interior was black plastic. It had four wheels and a radio. The speedometer went up to 110 miles an hour. The clock went up to 12 hours a day. The parcel shelf was missing and one of the mudflaps was torn. In the glove compartment were some papers with the Dixons logo. The ashtrays contained a Mars wrapper and a piece of gum chewed and rewrapped in a silver ball. There were two tiny rugs on the floor in the back, two perished rubber mats on the floor in the front. The engine appeared a swamp of corrosion. Green powder infested one of the battery terminals, bolts had merged in rust with the components they bolted together and there was a dunt in the radiator like someone had taken an axe to it.

Alan loaded his belongings into the back. He covered everything with a sleeping bag, went back to his room, sat on the bed and opened the road atlas. He checked the index. There was a place called Little Screvving. Someone knocked on the door. It was Deirdre, with a rucksack.

Hi, come in, said Alan. Deirdre was looking rougher, she wasn't wearing any makeup and she was paler than ever. Alan wondered why he'd ever fancied her.

Deirdre took off the rucksack and sat on the bed. I'm sorry, she said.

What? What? Why are you always sorry? Alan sat down a couple of feet away.

I should've called beforehand.

That's OK. I was just about to head off.

Can I come with you? The rucksack was bulging, every pocket stuffed. I'm sorry. If it's a problem, just say so, I don't mind.

Fuck it. No problem, said Alan. Please. There's plenty of room. Where is it you're wanting to go?

The west. My family's there.

I'm not going straight to Glasgow. I've got to pick something up first. He looked at the atlas. Near the town of Northampton.

That's OK.

Shit. Great! It'll be nice to have some company.

If she'd been fey, serious, silent, golden, his true love, out of the mists, gazing dark-eyed from the red fields at sunset, and him trotting her way on goathooves, big hairy houghs.

You don't want me to come. I can tell.

What makes you say that?

You're not happy. You take time to answer. What are you thinking about?

I was thinking if I had the hooves of a goat, they'd slip on the pedals and I wouldn't be able to drive.

Deirdre smiled and leaned back on her hands. She was wearing jeans and a white teeshirt. So was Alan.

He moved closer to Deirdre, put one arm round her waist and placed his free hand between her legs. He began to massage the point just below the zip of her jeans. She didn't look at him, nor did she move away.

I spoke to my sister on the phone, said Deirdre. She's more mature than I was at her age. She says I should do whatever I want. I can't stand it when she starts handing out advice to me. Especially when it's advice I gave her myself a couple of years ago. And she took it, and she benefits from it, and I still don't do what I want. She's got three men on the go, she's having a great time, but I find it hard enough with more than one.

Yeah? said Alan, still rubbing, trying to concentrate on what she was saying.

We were brought up really strictly. If my father knew what we were doing he'd bludgeon us to death with the crucifix he brought back from the town of Lourdes. I don't know why he went, there was nothing wrong with him. He said he needed a check-up. My mother should have gone, she's the one with the migraines. My dad said if she wanted to make a pilgrimage she could go to Boots the chemist.

Deirdre's voice caught on the last words and she toppled onto Alan, who lay back on the bed with his arms round her.

You think you can pull me on top of you whenever you want, she said into his chest after a while.

Alan opened his mouth for a denial. He couldn't find anything that wasn't either brutal, or a lie.

I don't know why you do this, said Deirdre. You don't even like me.

Alan knew certain truths as colours, shapes and smells: he couldn't put words to them.

No wonder they chucked you out of college, said Deirdre. You can't even speak, never mind write.

I said I was an idiot! said Alan. You should've believed me. That wasn't why they chucked me out. That's why they should have chucked me out.

Why don't you want to take me to Glasgow?

I do! I do! I said I would.

There were thirty seconds of silence, Alan breathing hard, dizzy with rage and guilt. He cleared his throat. There were another five seconds of silence.

Deirdre lifted her head, put her fist to her mouth and, staring steadily at Alan, issued a long, careful, theatrical throat clearing, with ten stops and a reprise. She slowly lowered her fist and started to laugh.

Christ, you sound like my car, said Alan, and laughed.

After a graceless manoeuvre they were lying side by side. Alan moved to kiss Deirdre, she turned her face away. He kissed her neck, inserted his hand under her teeshirt and plucked gratefully at one of her hard nipples.

I haven't got my diaphragm with me, said Deirdre. Have you got something?

No, lied Alan.

They unfastened each other's jeans and squirmed out of them, an awkward emergence from the stiff denim. The cool air against their bare legs impelled them closer, their wrists crossed, one hand grasping, one hand reaching in. Deirdre turned her face to Alan's once and kissed him on the lips, then turned away again. Alan came partly on himself, partly on the sheet, partly on Deirdre.

I'm so glad it's warm, said Deirdre. It would be terrible if it was cold when it came out. Have you got some tissues? Was that it, then, your conversation for the day?

Yes.

Next morning at six o'clock the two of them left Alan's lodgings for the last time. The sun was up behind the tenements and there was no wind. On the main street a grocer released a catch and the steel shutters over his window went rolling and rattling into silence. A cylindrical dog with its mouth open trotted past noiselessly. A man stood on the corner, jaw and belly stuck out, a crumpled white hat over his eyes, arrested by the newspaper he was holding.

They laid Deirdre's rucksack on the back seat and got in.

Let's go, said Alan.

How long before we get there? said Deirdre.

I don't know, said Alan. If we keep on going long enough, we run out of road, or we get back where we started.

But they keep on building new roads, so you can never run out. And they keep rebuilding the old ones, so you never get back to exactly the same place.

In that case we'd better hurry, said Alan. He pulled out the choke a little way, turned the key and jiggled the throttle. The engine caught. They moved away from the kerb and out onto the infinite road.

PART TWO

PART TWO

It was still early when they hit the road off the bypass and entered the hills.

Seems like we're the first car out, said Alan.

Pheasants and peewits daundered between the hedgerows ahead of them. He had to brake to avoid hitting a deer.

It's like a supermarket, he said. Venison, shrink-wrapped, ready to cook. 1.99! Reduced to clear.

I was thinking like Bambi, said Deirdre.

A sea of rabbits parted before them. No, said Alan, if this was Walt Disney, you'd have six strong healthy rabbits and then the comedy one, the runt of the litter. The runt is crucial. It's ideology: Hopsy, Flopsy, Topsy, Tipsy, Gipsy, Dripsy and Myxomatosis.

They came to a straight stretch between fields of corn and barley. Alan looked at Deirdre. She was looking ahead. They'd begun the night together, naked, chest to chest, and steadily, stealthily withdrawn their limbs one by one, their flesh too hot, and woken in the morning back to back and a foot apart.

Why won't you kiss me? said Alan.

Deirdre opened and shut the glove compartment several times. Tt, God. Is it so important? I told you, it turns me on. You don't care as long as you get the rest.

I do care.

Are we going to stop in the town of Biggar?

We've got petrol.

D'you not think I might like some breakfast? Deirdre laughed with herself. You're a romantic. You think I can kiss but don't need to eat.

Alan burned. He accelerated in anger. On the next bend he swung the car out and then took it in too close, bumping over the verge. He slowed down, gripped the wheel and breathed in deeply, staring ahead through an avenue of beech trees. The sun flashed between the trunks as they passed.

He felt Deirdre's fingertips cool on his ear. He waited for her to stop. She kept on stroking. He looked at her. She looked at him, smiled slightly and looked away, still stroking.

You're angry, she said.

Maybe, said Alan. Deirdre looked good in the morning light. The real thing came without additives, preservatives or artificial colouring, with stones, buckshot and mould, the taste would come through better. She cared enough to fight him.

Deirdre let go his ear as they approached the town of Biggar. Alan rested his hand on her thigh. Was your dad more healthy when he came back from Lourdes? he said.

No. He almost missed the flight back. The stewardess said it was a miracle they let him on the plane. He felt that was justification for the trip.

Does it count as a pilgrimage if you fly?

Uhuh. It costs more than going by coach.

I think you should go by road, said Alan. Or at least walk up and down the aisle of the plane on your knees.

Stop! shouted Deirdre. Alan plunged the clutch and brake into the floor and a loose cassette ricocheted off the dashboard.

What? he said.

You missed that petrol station.

Yeah, right, the only one in Biggar. There's probably a caff open on the high street.

I want a packet of crisps.

Alan did a U-turn and parked in the station fore-court. He took off his seatbelt and opened the door.

Wait, said Deirdre.

What?

Wait, OK, I'll be back in a second. Deirdre got out and went into the shop.

Alan picked up the cassette and slotted it into the machine. It was a Noël Coward–George Formby–Maurice Chevalier compilation someone had made up for him.

They've certainly got a great deal more to offer than Papa, sang Noël.

Deirdre came out of the shop briskly, looking down

at the ground, though at one point in her progress towards the car Alan noted that she glanced at him. Behind her with his sports bag came the tall student. Deirdre opened the passenger door and lifted the seat. The student put the sports bag on top of the rucksack, climbed into the back and sat down.

Hi, he said.

This is Mike, said Deirdre. He said he knew you.

Yeah, said Mike.

Kind of, said Alan. He got out of the car, put his hands in his pockets and started walking off the forecourt. After a minute Deirdre caught up with him.

How come the birds make such a racket? said Alan. Have you ever noticed that? It wouldn't be so bad if I knew which was which.

Where are you going? said Deirdre. I hope you don't think I'm going to apologise.

Another thing I've noticed for the first time is how elegant lampposts are. I might stay in the town of Biggar for a few days making a study of them. Maybe some sketches or watercolours. Would you say they were elegant, Deirdre? I'd say they were elegant.

Don't be a git. Mike's in trouble. He got into a fight with a teacher. It's bad stuff, Alan, broken ribs.

Broken ribs? In a spicy bean sauce?

You're wasting your time being an obnoxious shitebag.

How am I an obnoxious shitebag? Because I'm not going to be a taxi service for your lovers with a barbecue en route for you and your broken ribs in a spicy bean sauce?

It's not good getting sent to prison, Alan. I know you don't like me. We just want a lift with you and then we'll be out of your life.

Could you not have mentioned this earlier?

You were unhappy enough about taking me along.

I was getting used to you, said Alan. You slept with me.

You wanted to. I told you there was someone else.

Why did he get into a fight?

The teacher thought he was too stupid to get on.

The same thing happened to me and I didn't try to turn the guy into steak mince.

Deirdre frowned and chewed her thumbnail. She looked down at the ground. That's because Mike takes the learning seriously and you don't, she said. She walked away back to the car.

Alan sat down on the pavement, leaned back against a creosoted fence and looked into the sky. After a while he remembered that there was nothing in it. He got up and went back to the car.

I don't give a hoot, give my cares the boot, sang Maurice Chevalier. All the world is in rhyme.

We've got a long way to go, said Alan, and started the engine.

Living in the sunlight, loving in the moonlight, sang Maurice. Having a wonderful time.

Deirdre sat in the front still but she turned herself round, away from Alan, and talked quietly with Mike for a long while. Alan tried to hear what they were saying. It was hard over the noise of the car and the cassette. It got on his tits that Mike was talking to her with his one on one briefing on his problems, and Alan the driver was not to be in on it. That was how he wanted to put it to Mike: you're getting on my tits. But for one thing he was scared of Mike. For another you didn't say that kind of thing when someone with tits was sitting next to you. It'd sound daft.

Mike and Deirdre didn't disengage till after they were on the motorway. Mike sat back and Deirdre turned round to face the front. They were chewing cinnamon-flavoured gum.

Where are we? said Deirdre.

You smell like the spice worms of Arrakis, said Alan. We're on the motorway.

Deirdre smiled, braced her arm against the dash-board and reached down into her bag for more gum for Alan.

Alan looked in the mirror and saw a pair of green eyes.

How's it going, Mike? he said, like the passenger hadn't been in the car for two fucking hours already.

Where are we going? said Mike.

The town of Northampton.

Why?

That's where we're driving to.

You said he was going to the town of Glasgow, said Mike to Deirdre.

He is, she said. This is a way there.

How much did the car cost?

400, said Alan.

You spent 400 on a car?

I thought I'd start a taxi business. Then I thought no: a charity.

You shouldn't have spent 400 on a car if you wanted to become a student again.

What should I have done? Gone tutor-clubbing? Do you actually play baseball or d'you just keep it to beat people with?

If you're too sensible to hit a teacher you could've bribed him.

What does that mean, sensible? said Alan.

400 wouldn't have been enough, said Deirdre.

Forty tenners counted into a professor's hand is enough to convince him you're serious, said Mike. It's the best thing after sleeping with him or being related.

They don't take bribes, said Deirdre.

They don't get the chance often enough, said Mike. They don't know they want it, but they do. They take their own people for nothing and if others come to them cash in hand they wouldn't notice anything strange. They'd just take it: OK, that'll be fine, go and stand over there, I'll be with you in due course. What did you do before I came in, Alan? You didn't give him money and you didn't threaten him, what did you do? Ask him for mercy?

Yes.

For fuck's sake.

Were you there when Mike was piling in? said Deirdre, looking at Alan with wide open eyes.

He didn't hang around afterwards, said Mike. A sensible man.

What are you saying with that sensible? said Alan.

I mean it's sensible not to hit a professor with a baseball bat.

You're saying you do the right thing and we don't.

No, I did the right thing and you did the sensible thing.

I did the good thing.

When the good thing is the easy thing, that's the sensible thing.

Christ, I didn't do anything! I ran away!

Mike's eyes were green in the mirror and Deirdre watched the road ahead. Her fingers played with the strip of gum she'd fetched for Alan, bending it in two.

Mike stayed quiet for the next couple of hours, gazing at the motorway verges. Deirdre let her head loll to one side and closed her eyes. Alan switched off the cassette player and turned on the radio. A programme about Hildegard of Bingen came on as the motorway rose into the Pennine Hills and they hit rain. Alan overtook to the sound of monkish chants. With the windscreen wipers going at double speed, he dived in fear at 70 miles an hour into the spray of trucks. He was blinded for a second before coming out relieved and careless on the other side. The clouds were thick. It was half dark. Traffic began to bunch as they approached roadworks.

Alan crested a summit. He could see a queue of cars ahead, leading onto a bridge. The far end of the bridge was lost in mist and rain. At the edge of visibility the line of red tail lights flowed around two immense white boxes, cargo trailers hauled by juggernauts. The thin metal flanks of the boxes quivered, gleaming with the rain. The procession crawled forward, escorting the boxes into the murky curtain of vapour. The speakers vibrated with Latin invocations of the pain of the world.

Alan looked at Deirdre's white sleeping face. Her lips were slightly parted. Her head had slipped and was rocking against the side window. She would have a stiff neck when she woke up. If she woke up. There was Mike asleep in the back too. How far would you go before you realised they weren't going to wake up? And you would just have to deliver them to the appropriate place. Here. Two more for you. They never woke up, I'm sorry. That's OK. Don't blame yourself. Leave them with us. Sign here.

Alan leaned over and prodded Deirdre in the side. She inhaled sharply, groaned and shifted position. Alan switched off the radio and was left with the sound of the engine and the wipers and the rain battering off the roof. What he would most have liked to be at that moment was an angel who would stop the car and fly out of it, leaving the lovers sleeping alone together with the key in the ignition and all they needed for a new start in life. An angel who could fly straight off to a warm sunny heaven was hardly an angel. A real angel would walk out of the car into the rain with his collar turned up, he would be soaked and freezing, and still have a grin and a joke for the first person to give him a lift, and think about Deirdre and Mike and the car no more. Alan was therefore not an angel. They were running out of petrol.

Alan pulled in at the next service station. They had come through the rain. It was noon, grey and muggy. He parked as close to the shops and restaurants as he could and switched off the engine. Through the ringing in his ears he could hear the whine of the fan cooling the engine down. Deirdre moved and opened her eyes.

Where are we? she said.

A service station south of the town of Preston, said Alan. We need food and petrol.

The three of them got out of the car and strolled into the station lobby. There was a beeping and clatter of tills from the shop, sirens and percussion and explosions from the games near the toilets. A sampled voice croaked: Wizard, your life force is low.

They stopped, beset by choice.

Warrior, your life force is low, said the machine.

I'm going to get a paper, said Mike, and went to the shop. Deirdre led Alan to the restaurant. It'd been done up to give it a high-tech germ-free country kitchen look. It was in fake oak veneer, chrome and mottled grey melamine. The menus were chalked onto blackboards preprinted with the motif of a bountiful harvest offering spilling out of a wicker basket. The staff wore green check gingham aprons and huge chef's hats. It was dazzlingly bright and then blindingly clean. Alan and Deirdre hesitated between the serve-yourself island of cold things, which had pitchers of fruit juices, baskets of rolls, jams and butters in individual foil packs, Danish pastries in Cellophane and sandwiches in clear plastic boxes; and the bar of hot things, where the chef women stood swaying from side to side, swinging ladles, hand on hip, in front of steaming steel bins of baked beans, boiled and roast potatoes, steamed baby carrots and peas, mashed turnip; and trays of chips, wrinkle-skinned chicken legs, taut sausage, crusty black pudding slices and limp wavy bacon.

Alan fancied sausage and chips but took his tray to the cold counter thinking a packet of sandwiches would be cheaper, healthier and more tasty. He was wrong. Deirdre's sausage, chips, beans and cup of tea came to 5 altogether; Alan's bacon, lettuce and tomato sandwich pack and a can of Appletise came to 5.50. In the course of its journey from farm to Alan's mouth, the crispness of the lettuce had decreased in inverse proportion to its cost, so that a single leaf, now worth about as much as two whole lettuces in the shop, had been transformed into a sheet of slimy parchment marbled with dark sludge.

He paid with a tenner. The woman at the till frowned at it for a moment, turned over her shoulder, said Check 10, love, and gave Alan a handful of heavy gold-coloured coins in exchange.

He sat down opposite Deirdre, who was already tearing into the chips. They smelled fragrant.

They don't make crinkle-cut chips in these places any more, she said. They always used to be crinkle-cut. Look at that. She held up a hardened edge-bit chip before putting it in her mouth.

It's closer to the original potato, said Alan.

It tastes like shit anyway. If chips taste like shit they might as well have an interesting shape.

Alan bit into a sandwich. The hard bacon slid against the lettuce like a boot losing its footing on a muddy bank.

What's the sandwich like?

Fine, said Alan.

Why is it we're going to the town of Northampton again?

I have to pick up this egg for that guy. You were talking to him. McStrachan.

McStrachan? Deirdre stared. You're working for him?

I don't work for him, I'm just –

Doing something for him in exchange for money?

It's a one-off.

No, whatever you like, it's up to you. He seemed, I don't know. Too confident to be trusted.

Oh Jesus, said Alan, putting the sandwich down and putting his head in his hands.

What?

Nothing. Christ, I'm just picking up his fucking egg and then we're on to Glasgow. I won't keep you.

It's OK! said Deirdre, head bent over her plate, following the path of the last chip as she drove it on the end of her fork through swirls of brown sauce and sausage fat. She put it in her mouth and lifted her head, tossing her hair back. Are you still angry? she said.

No.

You knew about Mike. I told you.

Do you love him?

Don't ask such stupid questions.

And me?

It doesn't matter to you what I feel about you.

Mike arrived with breaded fish and chips and peas, tea and a copy of the weekly newspaper *The Wigan Observer*.

Alan took the newspaper and looked through it while Mike was eating. There was a picture on the front page of a row of burned-out shops and a close-up of a sign saying Business As Usual. The headline said RIOTS WERE ORGANISED – CHIEF CONSTABLE. Underneath was a smaller headline saying Rioters acted 'like wild beasts'.

It seemed there'd been a small riot in the town of Wigan where nobody'd been killed but many policemen had been injured, more than the number of rioters. Since the rioters didn't have a press spokesman the figure for their wounded was given as an estimate, based on the number of people who'd presented themselves at the local hospital with the words: I have just been rioting, please treat my wounds. The police said the riots had been planned and initiated by a small minority determined to cause trouble in a normally law-abiding neighbourhood. Outsiders had been involved. Community leaders blamed heavy-handed policing of the area. They said the police had stepped up patrols and arrests following the incident in which a defenceless mother had been brutally attacked by a member of the town council. The councillor involved, Gregor Ferguson, again denied the accusation. The mayor appealed for restraint.

Alan folded the paper so the back page was showing and slid it across the table to Mike.

D'you know a guy called Gregor Ferguson? he said. He's a councillor. He's a mature student.

What does that make you two? said Deirdre.

What does he study? said Alan.

Geology.

How do you know?

It's in the papers. He's a dilettante. He can't concentrate on learning or politics so he tries to do both.

He's in trouble.

Is he?

They say he attacked this old woman. There were riots. There wasn't anything in the papers about you and the professor. Maybe he never went to the police.

He doesn't need to. He couldn't. He is the police. Did you never realise that? You're more in their shadow than I thought. He fashioned them in his own image. Builders of barriers, drawers of lines. Keeping us out from knowledge and holding us back. Control, you see?

No.

Mike frowned, opened his mouth slightly and shut it. He rolled his lips over each other and began to breathe heavily, shaking his head. He put his knife and fork down and flexed the fingers of his hands, clenching them into fists and stretching them out. He stood up, took his paper and walked away.

Deirdre looked at Alan with pity.

You shouldn't let him get away with talking to you like that, she said.

Fuck off, said Alan.

Sorry, he said a few moments later, after Deirdre had left.

They split the petrol bill three ways. The rest of the journey to Northampton passed in silence, apart from bursts of country and western music.

When they reached the town they came off the motorway and descended by roundabouts and dual carriageways into the one-way system. Alan's intention was to drive through without stopping. They passed a lager factory, hoardings, a gap site and a red brick building like a government cathedral without a steeple. Then they spotted the lager factory again.

We're going round in circles, said Alan. We're trapped. They have us right where they want us.

Stop talking rubbish, said Deirdre, let's get this egg and get on.

They drove into the centre. Mike and Deirdre would wander around there for a bit while Alan went and got the egg. Alan dropped them off at a pedestrian precinct. All the pubs and shops were shut.

It's kind of dead, said Deirdre.

It's Sunday, said Alan.

They agreed to meet after two hours. Alan drove off. It was 1.30 pm.

He stopped at the first callbox he saw. It was in a side street, a terrace of old, two-storey, red brick houses. A few householders had covered their walls in fake stone cladding. The false stone bulged palely from the terrace like the first twitches of madness. The street was parked out. Alan double-parked, took one of the gold coins from his pocket and went to the phone. He thought he might catch his parents before they took the sheets off the compound but there was no answer.

Little Screvving had a post office with shop, three pubs, no school, a third of a policeman and half a priest who had long since forgotten that when someone hammers a nail through your hand, it hurts. It was the kind of place where evil was so unexpected that people no longer knew how to recognise it, and was, therefore, being constantly practised.

It was 2.10 pm when Alan arrived. He asked two boys where The Elms was. They told him down a certain lane. He went down: it petered out in a muddy track. He drove back. No, that's the way, you must have missed it, they said.

I don't think so, said Alan.

Listen mate, your wheels are going round, said one of the boys as Alan drove away.

He got true directions from a woman buying a frozen vegetarian lasagne in the post office with shop. He said he didn't know what elm trees looked like.

They died, she said. The disease.

The house was near the top of a steep, narrow lane between stone walls too high to see over. Beside a sign saying The Elms was a locked gate with an intercom. Alan squeezed the car over to one side of the road, got out and pressed the intercom button. The birds were singing too loudly.

Who is it? said a man on the intercom.

Alan Allen. I've come for the egg.

Are you the student?

Not now.

With some people it lasts a lifetime, said the intercom. You've had a wasted journey. Come in.

Alan pushed the gate open when he heard the buzzing and walked across gravel to the house. It was more of a cottage. It had roses growing around the door, and very small windows close to the ground. When the door opened there was a smell of new things from inside. The guy was wearing an immaculate red lambswool sweater, white slacks and brown moccasins. He was shorter than Alan, stooped slightly and had sadness pouches on either side of his mouth. His name was Tribler. Alan never found out whether it was his first, second or only name. He took Alan into a lounge and sank him in a sighing, creaking leather settee. Everything in the room appeared so clean and in its place as never to have been used, including the antiques, which rested on glass without dust.

The egg's gone, said Tribler.

How's it gone?

McStrachan hadn't paid for it. He had first refusal. He rang today, said you were coming, the money was on its way. But I'd already loaned it to an astronomy exhibition in the region of Campania. They came and took it away.

There was a distant crash of metal and glass from the village below.

Another accident on the high street, said Tribler. Let's hope no-one was hurt.

Yeah, Mr Concern-For-The-Sick.

I drove a long way, said Alan.

Yes, it really is too bad. McStrachan asked me to tell you to call him.

Can I call from here?

Of course.

Thanks.

As long as you pay for the call.

Alan folded his hands and placed them between his knees. He said: What is this egg?

It was painted by an astronomer-artist in the town of Delft in 1650. It's thought he used a telescope and a primitive camera to project the image onto a curved surface. The visible side of the moon is rendered in exact detail.

The moon isn't egg-shaped.

The ends are painted black.

What about the other side?

It has imaginary seas, mountains and craters, but arranged so as to form the image of a woman's face. Probably his wife. He killed her. Tribler started to smile.

Doesn't sound funny, said Alan.

Tribler giggled. It was, he said. They were very poor and there was no food in the house except the egg. And he refused to blow it before he started work. She was hungry. He caught her in his workshop with a pin and a frying pan, about to put a hole in the egg. The pan was the murder weapon.

What was she going to cook?

How would I know?

How do you know any of this?

I read about it.

How do you know it's true? Were you there? You'll be telling me next they really dropped an atom bomb on the town of Hiroshima.

They did. Look. Tribler pointed to a framed photograph showing a younger him in army fatigues with his hands on his hips, standing grinning over a charred body, one burned arm outstretched towards the sky. A hand-painted sign nearby said Hiroshima. In the background were the razed lots of a city.

Why are you smiling? said Alan.

Tribler shrugged. Why not? he said. People always smile in photographs.

There's a dead person in front of you.

It was no-one I knew. Tribler shrugged again. There are dead people around all the time, it doesn't stop you smiling, does it? It's living people that are sad, not dead ones.

Can I make that call now?

Sure. The phone's in the workshop. Alan followed Tribler into the hallway and down to a brightly lit basement devoted to the production of designs for commemorative plates, sold by mail order. Tribler's latest effort portrayed a steam train crossing a bridge over a canal. A barge was just coming under the bridge, and in the foreground the guy in charge of the big-hooved horse looked as if he was about to start a fight with an individual sitting watching the proceedings. The laws of perspective had not been obeyed and the locomotive was heading not for the safety of the embankment but to a fiery crumpling in the trees below.

What's it called? said Alan.

The Viaduct, said Tribler, handing him a brochure. It said: When the puff and chug of steam echoed along the byways. As the locomotive pulls across the bridge we can almost sense the grimy intoxicating smell of freshly burned coal. Below, by the calm canal, a bargee stops his horse and chats with a local farmer. The Golden Age of Steam. This is an era when the branch-lines of the railways were a welcome sight, blending in with the local community, and working in harmony with the traditions of country life.

The brochure urged buyers to act immediately, because market analysts had selected the plate as a bright investment prospect, worthy of immediate attention. Of course, it warned, not all plates go up in value; some go down.

Tribler had to plug the phone in. He went under a table. Alan looked around. The clutter was neat. The paint-mixing was confined to the palette and all the paint tubes had been squeezed from the bottom and rolled up. Over to one side was a row of small, empty animal cages with straw on the bottom and little tread-mills. There were four. There was a photo lying nearby. Alan picked it up. It was a Polaroid close-up of a pair of staring, bloodshot human eyes. He put the picture down.

McStrachan answered the phone on the first ring.

It's Alan Allen in Little Screvving.

That non-existent village, said McStrachan. It's too bad about the egg. Now you'll have to go to the region of Campania to get it.

No, said Alan. I'm going to Glasgow. One detour is enough. Transfer the money and we'll call it quits.

The region of Campania's on your way, said McStrachan.

No it isn't.

Haven't you learned not to trust maps by now? You'll never get to Glasgow the way you're going. There's more to it than driving, you know. Why do you want to go there?

People there are hard, cool and warm. I want to be like them.

McStrachan's voice became quieter, caring. But you aren't, Alan. You're soft, awkward and cold. You can't drive straight there. You have to go the long way round.

I'm not going your way, said Alan through his teeth. I'm driving to Glasgow.

I'll give you 5,000, said McStrachan.

Alan didn't answer.

Yes or no? said McStrachan.

OK, said Alan.

The phone call cost 1. It was 2.30 pm when Alan left the house. He had an hour to get back to the town of Northampton. While he had been talking to Tribler his car had crashed.

Owing to a faulty handbrake the car had crept from its moorings and run down the hill, gathering speed, shot out onto the high street and crashed into a lamppost. The only witness, the buyer of lasagne, had been shocked more by the machine's silence than by the collision.

Alan walked down the hill with his hair clenched in his fists. No, he said several times. The rear of the car was unharmed but he could see the ragged edges of a shattered front windscreen. He hesitated as he reached the vehicle, took deep breaths and walked forward.

The bodywork was hardly damaged. Only a slight dunt to the bonnet, and one of the headlights broken. The bumper had taken most of the impact. Outwardly it seemed OK, just the windscreen. Most of the glass had fallen out of the car and glinted in the grass growing around the lamppost. There were a few fragments on the seats. Alan opened the driver's door, picked the pieces of glass off them, cutting himself in the process, and got in. He switched on the engine. It started. Shite! A deeper, rougher, sicker sound. No, because he could hear it better without the windscreen. He sucked the blood from his left index finger and with his right hand played to the gambling god: he switched on the windscreen wipers. A black rubber strip came up and smacked him hard in the face. Enraged, he grabbed it and wrestled with the wiper motor for a few seconds. There was a whine and a smell of burning electrics before the bolt came loose and the wiper flopped twitching onto the bonnet. Alan switched the wipers off and gripped the wheel. Guilty! A molester and abuser of innocent machinery! Yeah, and who was innocent in this corrupt gravitational world, where everything was falling before you were born, and would go on falling after you were dead? It was all a fix, a setup against which handbrakes were useless. The engine cut out. He restarted it. It ran long enough for Alan to pull the car out onto the road, then stopped again.

From the small crowd which had gathered came a voice: His radiator's bust. The boy who had earlier observed the rotation of wheels pointed to a wet patch spreading on the tarmac under the engine.

Is he all right? said the shop customer, standing a short distance from the front of the car and staring at Alan, the lasagne tucked into her folded hands like a bible.

I cut my hand, said Alan.

He must be in shock. Somebody should give him some hot tea.

He wasn't wearing his seatbelt, said an old man with grey sideburns and a silk cravat tucked into a striped shirt.

I wasn't in the car, said Alan.

How come it crashed, then? said a tall biker-jacketed man with bleached cropped hair, wee black studdy eyes and a tiny thin mouth.

Somebody should give him some tea all the same. Where are the police?

If he'd been wearing his seatbelt, it wouldn't have happened.

Yes it would, said Alan.

D'you know who you're talking to? said the old man in fury. Where's your licence? I don't know what it's like in your part of the world, but we have laws here.

It's terrible, said the customer, stepping towards her cottage door a few yards away. He should have something hot to drink and there's no sign of the emergency services. She went inside and closed the door.

There was a garage on the edge of the village. The car was towed there and an estimate was made. 300, parts and labour. Alan's insurance wouldn't cover it. He shrugged and nodded and was led to the bus stop by the guy in the biker jacket. They just caught the only bus to the town of Northampton, at 5.30 pm. Another 2 for the ticket.

You seem shaken up, said the guy.

I was on my way to the town of Glasgow, said Alan. The route needs rethinking.

They sat together on the bus. The guy's name was Sim. He was from Little Screvving. He was 38 and lived with his parents. He was a systems analyst. He was dying of an incurable disease.

Does it hurt? said Alan.

Not yet, said Sim.

How long have you got?

No idea. Sim flounced in his seat and folded his hands on his white-jeaned lap. He looked out of the coach window for a second and turned back to gaze at Alan with his bright studdy wee eyes. I'm thinking about having a big wake with all my friends. Everybody'll have to wear black and there'll be lots of dancing and we'll all get drunk. Or maybe everyone'll wear white, what d'you think? I'll have this room made out with all black and white crepe on the ceiling, and one of my friends said he'd get this video system in and show all Busby Berkeley musicals. Oh God, d'you think it sounds really crazy and extravagant?

No, no, sounds fine.

Oh God, I don't know. God, my friend June – he giggled – she's so funny, I told her about the wake and she said – he put on a serious face – Oh yes. Oh yes. We'll all come wearing basques and stockings and suspenders and we'll dance like in the Rocky Horror Show. He laughed. I can just imagine her in stockings and suspenders, she'd look horrible, that big white arse. You don't know her, she's really funny. He put on his serious June face again. Yes, these wakes should get proper funding, because it's very important that dying people are able to express their feelings. We'll see if we can get a grant. He laughed again. She's great. Listen, what are you doing tonight?

I don't know, said Alan. Hunting round the town of Northampton for two pissed-off people.

How late are you?

Three hours.

Oh, they'll be gone by now. You should come to Kaiser Bill's later. Kaiser Bill's. It's this gay club, it stays open till three.

I'm not gay.

I know, I can see that, but straight people go there cause the pubs close at eleven and the straight clubs are so vile. They're all women dancing round their handbags and neds with knives and white socks.

I don't think I'll bother, thanks.

Come on, it'll be fun. They've got strippers on tonight.

The main thing is to get somewhere to stay the night, said Alan. I need to find a bed and breakfast.

I can put you up with one of my friends, said Sim.

The bus groaned into the bungaloid outskirts of the town of Northampton. Sim looked out through the window like a xenophobic voyager who wanted to go home. But he was home, wasn't he?

I wish I was going to the town of Glasgow, he said. This place is a tip. There's no soul. All there is is shopping, fucking, fighting, drinking and dancing.

What about the countryside?

What, the fields? I can't stand fields. I hate them. They're full of insects and crops. I tried to sit under a tree once. But the grass doesn't grow up to the vertical bit, what d'you call it, the bit that comes out of the ground –

The trunk?

Yeah, the trunk, the grass doesn't grow right up to the trunk, does it? I imagined this meadow full of scented flowers with soft green grass like a rug. And you'd sit on it with your back on the tree as a kind of armchair arrangement and it'd be really comfy. Sim wriggled in his seat and took spongy handfuls of imaginary sward in his hands. But it wasn't like that. The grass stopped just here, and underneath the tree it was all roots and mouldy leaves and dirt and shit and insects. It was horrible. We didn't stay long. This friend of mine had a thing about sex in the open air. I mean we did it but I didn't enjoy it. It was terribly unhygienic.

Alan laughed. Why don't you go to Glasgow, he said, if you're going to . . . or anywhere? You might as well.

Oh I know, I know, said Sim, frowning and looking around as if he'd lost something. His wee black eyes fixed on Alan again. I should, shouldn't I? I have this fantasy about a beach in a warm place, where it's warm all night long, where the sand on the beach is soft and warm and white, where the water's clean and warm and blue, or turquoise I suppose, and all the boys are dressed in white teeshirts and white canvas shorts, and you just hang out under the sun or the stars drinking chilled wine and eating seafood and having sex.

That's not Glasgow, said Alan. That sounds like decadence.

Oh yes. Of course. I love decadence. I'm dying.

The bus veered sharply towards the side of the road and stopped. A police car and a minibus with a metal grille over the windscreen went whooping past, blue lights flashing. Alan thought he glimpsed helmeted figures inside. The bus proceeded.

Trouble, said Alan. He cleared his throat, swallowed, and bit on his thumbnail. Probably, eh, probably after that incident with the councillor hitting that mother who was complaining about housing conditions, he said.

Probably, said Sim.

Is that what happened?

You just said that's what happened.

Maybe I made it up!

Why?

I don't know. People should be more careful what they say. What about the local papers?

I don't know. I don't read papers. I don't read anything except a few magazines and figures for my work. It's pointless and there's no time. Even before I knew I was dying it was the same. I get bored after a few words. I just can't concentrate. I like films. And stories. When I was at school I got my friends to tell me what happened in the books we were supposed to read. I got top marks. There's no time! You can't read when you're drunk. You can't read and dance at the same time, or read and drive at the same time, or read and talk at the same time. Why should you read about people talking instead of talking? Why should you read about love instead of being in love? Why should you read about a beautiful man when you can rent a video of a Rupert Everett film?

You should read, said Alan.

Why? Tell me why, I want to know, because even in the town of Northampton you sometimes see people doing it. Maybe I'm missing something.

The bus was pulling into the bus station, the brick cathedral Alan had driven past earlier.

I don't know, said Alan.

They got off the bus. Sim looked at Alan, ready to part. Alan could see he really had wanted to know and was disappointed.

Sorry, said Alan.

Come to Kaiser Bill's, said Sim. He went.

It took Alan half an hour of wandering to find the place where he'd left Deirdre and Mike. They weren't there. The centre had been quiet before but now it was like the bad guys had ridden into town and the streets had emptied. Perhaps the funsters would emerge later. Alan found a cash machine and took out 50, which after buying the car put his account on minus 406.23, not counting the 100 he was due from McStrachan.

Alan entered a deserted restaurant. Taped sitar music was playing quietly and the tables were covered in heavy white linen and bright silver cutlery. A slim waiter from the town of Chittagong seated him and took his order. He had mixed pakora, and lamb pasanda with pilau rice and a nan bread. It was good. He drank a pint of lager, and a cup of coffee, which came with an After Eight mint lain on the saucer, a patch melted from contact with the hot coffee cup. The cost was 11.90. He wrote out a cheque and put a pound coin on the table as a tip.

The waiter came up and asked him if he'd enjoyed his meal. Alan said he had, was it always this quiet on a Sunday evening?

Sometimes it's busy, said the waiter patiently, with his hands behind his back. They all come in here for their takeaways later on.

D'you ever get trouble? said Alan.

Trouble?

People coming in and breaking things. Shouting.

Shouting? The waiter smiled. There's always shouting. People like to shout when they're happy. It's normal.

Shouting in here?

Not in here. They can do their shouting outside. Sometimes they come in and we have to throw them out.

I can imagine, said Alan. In a quiet place like this. All this nice furniture and the quiet music, someone starts shouting, it could upset people.

We try to make it nice, said the waiter.

And sometimes people can't pay.

Yes, that happens.

That makes them shout, I suppose.

Yes, the ones who can't pay are the ones who always shout the loudest. Then we call the police.

But that doesn't make them pay.

No. They can't pay. They haven't enough money. But we can't go giving free meals, can we? That would be bad business. If they want to eat they have to know the price. The waiter unclasped his hands and gripped the back of the chair opposite Alan.

Alan left the restaurant and stood on the pavement, unsure which way to go. Night had fallen. He'd already lost orientation. On the street there was a coming and going from fast food shops, off-licences and video rental stores. Single men with stooped shoulders and leather jackets would emerge with steaming packaging. Sometimes a child trotted in tow and the men guided them into cars with tired, bored care. Groups of women swept laughing towards pubs, wearing ill-fitting off the peg skirts.

Alan walked towards what he imagined to be the town

centre. He looked into people's faces as they passed, trying to catch the eyes of good-looking women; when he did he looked away. After fifteen minutes' walking along the straight, low street of shops with empty flats above them, he asked someone and found he'd been going in the wrong direction.

Is there a bus? he said.

The guy he'd asked manufactured a bitter laugh. At this time of night boy, you can lie down on the road outside the bus station and sleep right through till morning without being disturbed by a bus, he said.

Alan turned and headed back the way he'd come. It began to rain. The precinct glistened when he found it and his hair was flattened down wet on his head. He went into five pubs around the area and poked his moist nose into each bar, lounge and snug without finding Deirdre and Mike. There was a strong damp smell coming off his jacket and in each pub he sensed he was watched by drinkers keen to help him in his quest and stone him to death with empty pint glasses. In the fifth pub he ordered a drink.

He took a pint of the dark beer drunk in the town of Northampton by intellectuals and the older genera-tion. It cost 1.50. He sat on a stool at the bar. The pub was sparsely attended. It was at the tail end of the brewery's renovation cycle. The red carpet was worn away to threads in places and stuffing was starting to leak from the darkening, shiny, once plush crimson fabric of the seats around the walls. The lighting had been well arranged to begin with and the decay was not too

obvious. There were ornamental mirrors on the walls
and reproductions of hunting and racing scenes, horses
with all four legs off the ground, rear and hind legs
stretching in opposite directions. If you'd been there
with your pals you could have called it cosy. There was
a briefcase-sized jukebox which wasn't working and a
U2 cassette playing instead. Part of the place was set
aside for skittles. Men were tossing flat, round wooden
blocks like cheeses onto an object like a small grand
piano where skittles were arranged. Sometimes all ten
skittles were demolished with a single cheese and there
was a cheer.

Alan swallowed a few throatfuls of beer. He wanted
to close his eyes, lay his forearm on the varnished wood
of the bartop, rest his head on it and sleep. His eyes
began to shut of their own accord and his head lolled
forward. He began to dream of grey mountains patched
with scoops of snow and a black tarmac road slithering
through them. An inner shock of unknown origin woke
him after a couple of seconds. Through half-closed eyes
he noticed the barman watching him. He got off the
stool and stood to stay awake.

The music was switched off and the skittle game
ended. There was an amplified kerfuffle from another
part of the pub and a twinge of feedback. Somebody
was going to play. Alan went through with his beer to
the other room where a horseshoe-shaped crowd had
gathered around a boom microphone, a chair and an
amplifier. On the chair, guitar on lap, in a black suit
and tie and white shirt, was Malcolm.

He struck a chord and began to sing. He introduced himself as Don Raids. He sang funny songs about life in the city, about being young and poor and unlucky in love. He sang about being dumped on by lovers and landlords, and fast food, and supermarkets, and cars that didn't work, and cheap holidays. Everyone loved the rhymes and recognised the stories, or believed they did. In between songs the patter was sharp. He did a seven-number set ending with a song called Alice Threw The Looking Glass And I Have The Scars To Prove It. At the end he stood up and bowed to fierce applause and Bronx cheers.

Alan had listened to the songs with pride, joy and envy. He got to Malcolm as his friend was unclipping the guitar mike.

Hi, he said. Great gig.

Alan! said Malcolm, grinning. I thought you were going to the town of Glasgow.

I am, said Alan. What are you doing in the town of Northampton?

What d'you mean? said Malcolm. I'm not planning to leave.

Eh?

A slim young girl in a black dress came up to Malcolm, fingering a string of azure beads hung round her neck.

That was fantastic, she said.

Thanks, said Malcolm. Christ, what a heat in here. He was wet with sweat.

How d'you get the ideas for the songs? said the girl.

Oh, it's just life, you know, said Malcolm, making a

gesture with his free hand. Ordinary suffering! The three of them laughed. The girl looked intensely at Malcolm. We're over there if you'd like a drink, she said nervously, and darted away.

I'll buy you a drink, said Alan, unless you want to go and see that girl.

I'll join you in a second, said Malcolm. Can you get us a pint of lager?

Alan went over to the bar and got the drinks. Malcolm was about ten minutes, he had to clear up the cables and put the guitar away and accept folk's congratulations and queries. The two of them found a free space at one of the tables.

Malcolm downed half the pint in one parched upending, then put the glass down and gazed into space, still on a high from the performance.

How did you get here? said Alan.

Taxi, said Malcolm. I know. Expensive, eh? But this is not bad. I get 50 for the gig.

Taxi from where?

The flat.

In Northampton?

Where else? said Malcolm, laughing. What're you on about? Someone been telling you I was going away? I couldn't move even if I wanted to with my dad in the state he is.

What about Paula?

She's staying in tonight. She's got a cold.

Alan took a drink and looked at Malcolm, who was still distracted, reviewing the mistakes only he'd noticed.

Malcolm, said Alan. It seems to me I saw you the night before last. You told me there was no point going to the town of Glasgow.

Well, you're still here, so it looks like you took my advice.

I'm not still here. I mean I'm not still there. I've moved. I've travelled. So have you.

Well, time has been travelled, certainly, said Malcolm, frowning and rolling his glass between the palms of his hands. Everything else seems much the same. It's streets, shops and pubs, people on top and people on the bottom. You find a few friends and the rest you don't know.

I'm going on to Glasgow tomorrow, said Alan.

You put too much into riding the road and you miss out on riding the years, said Malcolm. Space travellers are spectators. Time travellers are players.

That's bollocks, said Alan, leaning forward.

Just then the rugby team arrived. Twenty men in their twenties with grey flannel trousers, navy blue V-neck sweaters and white shirts strode into the pub, singing. They were solid as frozen beeves and their skin was pink and smooth. They were flushed and their short hair was messed up. They had a desire to stomp, and they stomped as they sang. As a pack they rucked up against the bar and obtained pints in a twinkling. The pub seemed to fill with steam. As if it had been arranged beforehand one of them had his clothes removed by three others, his shoes were wrenched off, his socks removed, his sweater plucked from his fleshy shoulders, his shirt peeled, his trousers whisked from his legs and his briefs pulled away. He was hoisted onto the table where Alan and Malcolm sat and rugby men pressed around them, barking the song to the naked man on the table, who stood with his hands by his side, too drunk to sense anything but the future story of the evening. The song ended, the naked man seemed to fall off the table back into his clothes and the rugby team swept out again.

Alan looked round the silent, embarrassed pub. Malcolm had gone. Alan got up to hunt for him and heard a woman calling Alan! behind his back. He turned and saw Deirdre and Mike.

Come on! shouted Mike, beckoning him.

What? said Alan.

Come on! said Deirdre.

Alan walked towards them. Deirdre grabbed his arm and pulled him out of the pub. They began running down the street.

The car's bust. It won't be fixed till tomorrow, Alan panted. Mike was too far ahead to hear. Deirdre took no notice.

What? What is it? said Alan.

Come on, said Deirdre weakly.

They went clattering down the pedestrian precinct and darted off into a cobbled alley. Red light reflected off the wet cobbles from a big neon moustache and spiked helmet on a building up ahead. A sign picked out in yellow bulbs said Kaiser Bill's. The entrance was a tiny unmarked door off at the side. Inside was a cramped red-lit lobby, with a cashier behind a desk and a couple of guys in white teeshirts hanging around.

Are you gay? said one of the guys.

The three of them answered together. Alan said yes. Mike said no. Deirdre said they'd been there before. There was a moment's consideration.

OK, said the checker.

The cashier looked at his watch. 10.59, he said. Made it with seconds to spare. Half price: 2.50 each. They paid and went through into the club.

We thought we'd find you in some dive, said Deirdre.

Let's get a drink, eh? said Alan.

I'm wondering what's the best bar, said Mike, questing around. The place had three bars and two dancefloors on different levels. On the way up they passed a poster for the performance group Chelsea Lovenest, but there was nothing going on on the dancefloors except crowds of men and a few women, body-proud, bopping furiously in a magic forest of ultraviolet light, spinning spokes of plain light, lasers and waves of dry ice.

They found a table in the top floor bar, a large half-empty place away from the music with awkwardly sited clumps of greenery, too-soft settees and a coming and going of lost souls looking for love, or a quick suck at least. They got a bottle of Beck's beer each. Mike paid. 2.50 a throw. Alan was glad to see Deirdre. They didn't say much while Mike was getting the drinks in. Deirdre looked at Alan and smiled, not just with her mouth but with her eyes, looking right into his own and looking away, then looking back to see if he was still looking, and he was, and she laughed.

Alan told them about the crash and how the egg

hadn't been there. Mike asked when he reckoned they'd get to the town of Glasgow.

Few days, said Alan.

Thought you said the car'd be fixed tomorrow, said Mike too steadily.

Yes. I've been thinking in terms of a different route. If we cut through that way it means I can pick up the egg from the region of Campania. It's a detour, I know, it's a detour.

I thought you were going to Glasgow. You offered us a lift to Glasgow, said Mike.

I am going to Glasgow! What d'you think I bought the car for? Who trusts maps? If you looked at a map I know it might seem not the quickest route, but when you're on the road it's different, it's tricky. Sometimes you have to go south to go north or east to go west.

If you're going around the world for fuck's sake.

I didn't offer you a lift to Glasgow. I offered your girlfriend a lift to Glasgow.

Hello, said Deirdre, I am here and my name is Deirdre. Sorry.

I don't see a problem, said Deirdre to Mike. If it's a few days. You were wanting to lie low anyway.

Mike looked at Deirdre smiling at Alan smiling at Deirdre. He tore a piece of silver foil off the top of a bottle, rolled it into a ball between his thumb and index finger and flicked the ball into the air.

He says he wants to go to Glasgow, that's what he wants to do, that's his aim, and he's chasing off in search of an antique. For money.

Everyone needs money, said Alan.

Are you getting more for this Campania trip?

A bit.

How much?

Couple of thousand. It's a job.

Couple of thousand! What do you want to go to Glasgow for?

It's better. People there are hard and cool and warm. I want to be like them.

Who's going to believe you if you spend your time chasing round on rich men's errands? What did you do at university?

You know.

Are you embarrassed?

You know what he did, he did the same as you, said Deirdre calmly.

Alan took a big drink of lager. I'm fine, he said, I'm tired, I was driving all day. You know what I did. Literature.

The question has to be why. Aren't we to be proud? Are we ashamed to read so well and to know so much? I'm not. I'm proud. I'm fucking proud to know better than the teacher. Better than the writer. No intermediaries, or barriers. We needed time to see it all and that was too much. They tried to make us blind, make us to be keeking through their fucking pinholes when all along we were better than them.

That's shit. They kicked us out cause we weren't good enough, said Alan.

They kicked us out because they're a bunch of effete

bigots. They'd listen smilingly to some eloquent cunt reciting what he'd processed about the poet John Donne, knowing the guy was going to dump the books as soon as he got his degree and spend the rest of his life chairing committees and reading about wine, cheese and interior decoration. I couldn't even raise my voice in there without getting funny looks. Christ you're trying to tell them, you're trying to shout in their faces how fucking you've seen beyond John Donne to the shape shining through him, you want to tell them how it needs a week thinking about one sonnet and the old poet starts to peel away from the poem underneath like last century's wallpaper when the water's soaked it, and they're already trying to cut you off.

Deirdre was squeezing Mike's hand. Alan said: They chucked me out cause I read the wrong books and never wrote what they asked me to write.

No, said Mike, shaking his head and raising the Becks bottle to his mouth. That's not what was going on. He drank and jabbed bottle and finger at Alan. There wasn't one other student, not one other student, who cared about literature enough to attack a professor for it. Tell me if I'm wrong.

No, said Alan. You're not wrong. Me, I still can't say what the point was.

Mike stood up, hit himself on the forehead with the butt-end of the bottle, shook his head violently and sat down. Reading is how you inherit the wisdom of the centuries without having to be a fucking Methuselah. Knowledge! D'you think it comes from beer and the evening news? Don't say that to me again, Alan. That's what they'd like you to think. I'm telling you that kind of talk's no good.

That's what the wisdom of the centuries comes to, said Alan. Full contact baseball. Come on you Dodgers.

Sim arrived with a pinched, frowning, mop-headed boy in a poloneck. They sat down next to Alan, who did the introductions. The boy was called Tigger.

Someone just gave me some heroin, said Sim. I had a snort. It was good. I thought I might as well try it, I always wanted to be one of those sweating boys on the heroin ads on TV, they were cool and vulnerable. I suppose I'm too old now. What d'you think? Have you ever tried it? I wouldn't fancy injecting it. It's not the needle, it's the veins, I can't stand veins that stick out, d'you know what I mean? I'm always thinking the veins on the back of my hand are sticking out too much at work and I lift them up to make the blood run back down my arms and everyone thinks I'm praying to Allah, the Merciful. But my desk doesn't face east to the town of Mecca. It faces north to the town of Leicester. I checked.

Are you the driver? said Tigger, looking up from the floor and focusing on Alan's nose with a gently swaying head. On one of Tigger's sharp cheekbones a flash of drying semen glinted silver.

Yeah, said Alan. Why are you called Tigger?

Bouncy bouncy bouncy bouncy . . . eh . . . bouncy bouncy.

I'm embarrassed, said Sim.

What's it like, being a driver? said Tigger, ratcheting his head over to one side.

Tigger's taking driving lessons, said Sim.

Oh really? said Alan. In which dimension?

Alan felt a small, warm, moist hand on his. He snatched it away then realised it was Deirdre.

Sorry, he said.

Let's dance, she said.

They went through to one of the dancefloors, merged with flat-stomached lovelies and balding pelvic thrusters and danced for two songs. There were a couple of policemen in uniform, hatless, in the thick of the action: they were tanned, with strawblond hair. They danced superbly, like professionals.

Alan and Deirdre went to another bar and sat on barstools.

There's something I've got to tell you, said Alan. I can't keep it a secret any longer. I'm not gay.

Mother will be devastated, said Deirdre.

I want –

What?

Alan waited so long to say You that he didn't say it.

Deirdre twisted her hair into a ring with one finger. I don't know what you're feeling, she said. You don't talk about it.

Is Mike OK?

Deirdre looked like she was going to cry. I don't know, she said. She picked up a beer mat and held it in front of Alan's face. If you're insane and I'm not, which side of the beer mat are the mad people on?

This is one of those trick questions. But I'm an idiot. Handy for you.

Better to be a genius acting like a twat than an idiot pretending to be smart.

You're not a genius either. I always thought you had a whale-sized ego tucked away in there.

Bigger, said Alan. Whales lack self-confidence. They're burdened with mammalian guilt.

I'm going to dance, said Deirdre, getting up. She left the bar. Alan bought a bottle of Pils. There was a film showing on TV behind the bar. It was night in the desert. A young guy in a teeshirt was driving a long, finned, 1950s car into a parking lot outside some kind of jazz venue. He got out of the car and they showed him standing there, lit by red neon, hesitating. He looked like the young Henry Fonda in the film of *The Grapes of Wrath* – hard and cool, but warm. He went into the place and looked surprised to see the band playing and the woman singing. She looked like Neneh Cherry. She finished her song and he intercepted her as she came down from the stage. Hi, he said.

Frank! she said. The film cut to the desert outside, Frank and the woman walking side by side past parked cars.

So how d'you like touring? said Frank.

It's like the good old days, Frank. We rehearse on the bus, every night a new bunch of people comes and sees us.

You must have seen a heck of a lot of new places.

You know I was never one for travelling. All these

towns, they kind of look the same to me. We must have travelled thousands of miles but it don't seem like we went anywhere, it just seems like all these people, all these strangers, are coming to hear me sing.

You sure have picked up some pretty big ideas about yourself, Meonie, said Frank.

What's the matter with you? You didn't ever talk that way before.

You didn't think you were so special before.

I don't know what your problem is, Frank. Maybe you liked thinking you were far away from home and you're mad cause home has come to you and found out that things aren't going so well. Where are you working, anyway?

In a used car lot, said Frank.

What's this film that's on? said Alan to the man behind the bar.

I'm not watching it, said the man. It's crap. Here. He handed Alan a copy of the *Northampton Chronicle & Echo*. Alan found the TV listings. The film was called *Bandicoot Bebop*. Mediocre adaptation of a Robert Bewick novel, it said. Alan turned to the front page. The town was at peace: Teenagers Die In Horror Blaze, Death Jump Girl In Coma, Pensioner Conned By Child Trickster.

D'you often get policemen coming in here? said Alan.

Never. Why? said the barman, looking around.

There's a couple on the dancefloor. They're dancing.

That's Chelsea Lovenest. They'll be getting their kex off in a minute. There's never any trouble here. The pigs've got enough to do dealing with all the haircuts and shirts spilling out of the straight pubs down the road. There might be a riot tonight.

How come?

Some councillor beat up an old woman in the street when she asked about getting rehoused.

Who told you? There's nothing about it in the paper, said Alan.

The barman shrugged. That's the story I heard, he said.

From who? Who told you?

The man couldn't remember. Alan went out towards the dancefloor with his drink. He sat down on a padded bench in a kind of alcove. The music changed. The policemen separated from the dancers, moved onto a part of the floor raised a fraction from the rest and began taking off each other's clothes, still dancing. The buttons on their jackets were not buttons but press studs. They were quickly naked. Their skin was yellowish and lightly powdered. They started a chaste, fluid-free simulation of sex. Alan's eyes closed. He saw millions of sperm writhing and dying on the vast, barren plain of a man's cheek, twitching their tails and raising their heads in search of that which was their destiny but which was not to be found there.

He fell asleep listening to the Pet Shop Boys' version of Always On My Mind.

He dreamed of a bed of nails tacked to the red crepe skirts of a menopausal flamenco dancer, and within the dancing folds of crepe Neil Tennant riding an electric bucking bronco, battering the edges of a hydraulic massage couch with rubber-headed polo mallets, and around him thousands of sweating West African lobsters stripped to the waist, fighting duels with scaffolding and girders so sparks flew and steel rang. And Neil swung the mallets into a juicy lobster and looked it in the eyes.

He apologised for careless advance preparation and the poor sauces he'd cooked it in, without the proper herbs and cream; how in times of lovemaking his soul cried out for lobster but had been denied. He mourned the pressures that had kept him from side dishes and anointing the shellfish with tender, tasty, time-consuming dressings; and Neil's head was a lobster crown with a garland of marinaded mussels, steaming through his uncurling curls.

Young Sean Connery held a chubby pink prawn up to the Montego Bay moonlight on an empty kingsize bed. Sean smiled cruelly, put the prawn in his mouth and lay back on the silk sheets in silent sucking ecstasy, ignoring the second course lobster which lay steaming in congealing juices beneath his hungry, angry, unseeing eyes, and on the skin behind Sean's ear a tattooed crayfish jerked and jived with the moves of his jaw.

Sean and Neil were together on their knees, weeping as they poured warm chocolate over a mortally ageing lobster; they sharpened their knives and took the lid off a boiling saucepan, smiling through bouillon tears, licking their lips. The lobster screamed before it hit the water, it plunged in and was falling, then rising, shooting upwards through a gleaming copper column, accelerating through the clear, scorching stock past herbs and bubbles to the sky and mouths.

Alan woke up with a pain in his neck and waves of nauseating force crossing the interior of his head at a rate of one every two seconds. He knew exactly where he was. It was necessary to make a fresh start, drink tap water and march into the cool night. He stood up. The waves rippled madly from forehead to hindhead. The music had stopped: Kaiser Bill's was lit by plain lightbulbs. It looked worn, empty and sticky. On the dancefloor were the strippers from Chelsea Lovenest, reclothed, standing talking to each other with their hands in their pockets.

Alan began to walk towards the exit. He heard one of the strippers say: Hey, there's another of them.

Here you, said the stripper.

What? said Alan.

Come here.

Why?

Cause I'm telling you to, my man.

I'm too tired, said Alan. Great show. What's that stuff you put on your skin?

I'm going to have this cunt, said one of the strippers quietly. The other one put a hand on his partner's chest and moved towards Alan. Alan backed away a few paces and stopped. The stripper approached close. A marvel how he had danced in those heavy boots. There was a frying of static from the radio on the stripper's jacket and a woman's voice said: Do what you can to keep them from doing any damage outside the area, over.

What, said Alan.

Where've you come from? said the stripper.

I was asleep.

Come on my man. Let's take a look at you over here. The stripper took Alan's arm. Alan pulled himself free and ran towards the exit. The strippers came tanking after him, shouting: One coming down!

Alan ran into the arms of two more strippers waiting at the door. These ones had hats with their uniforms. He realised there were too many of them and didn't resist when they put him into the back of a police car. Inside it was more comfortable than his own car. The same woman's voice came on the radio: You're not out there to help them, you're there to hold them back.

It was a couple of minutes' ride to the police station. The man sitting next to Alan in the back of the car shook his head when Alan mentioned Chelsea Lovenest.

I thought those guys upstairs were strippers, said Alan. That was why I ran.

Strippers? said the policeman.

Yes, said Alan. Everywhere I go for a drink in this town there are men taking off their clothes.

That's because you're a homosexual, explained the policeman in an orderly manner.

I'm not.

What were you doing in that place?

They parked opposite the police station and Alan was led inside to a waiting area. There was a smell of disinfectant. A man was arguing with a whiteshirted policeman over a book on a counter. It's the buses, the man said, it's the fucking buses, man, you just can't get anywhere.

You should have left the house at the proper time, said the policeman.

Come on man, you've got to let me sign, it's not my fucking fault.

You're four hours late, said the policeman, closing the book. The new day's started already.

Let's go, said Alan's policeman, who had opened a door marked No Entry.

Why? said Alan.

There's someone wants a chat with you.

About what? I haven't done anything.

What was all that shouting and running away about, then? We had a warrant. We can show you. We want to ask some questions over a cup of tea. Do you have a problem with that? Nothing bad's going to happen. You're a student, aren't you?

Yes.

Nothing to worry about.

I want to sign the fucking BOOK! shouted the man at the counter, banging on it with his fist.

It's a waste of time putting little wankers like you on bail, said the policeman calmly.

The man grabbed the book and ran towards the door. The two policemen went after him. A whole fresh load of people came in at that point, blocking the escape of the man with the bail book. There were three stomping policemen in blue denim overalls and armoured vests, black nightsticks swinging from their belts, one of them with a blue crash helmet on his head and a transparent visor covering his face. They were breathing hard. They were driving three stumbling handcuffed men before them, all wearing denim shorts and gorgeous polyester shirts. One shirt was printed with a reproduction of Breughel's painting of the Tower of Babel. It had D-D inside it.

The bail book was retrieved and a fourth member of the public was fitted with shiny handcuffs.

What did you come in this way for? said Alan's policeman to the riot gear threesome.

The laundry van's backed up to the other door and we can't get the villains in, said one of the riot policemen.

Yeah, they've got to clean the fucking blood off your uniforms, said one of the arrested, whose shirt glowed red and yellow like lava. I want to see a lawyer. I was beaten up.

You shouldn't be out bowling pints of unleaded if you've got delicate skin, said a riot policeman. They started driving the arrested in through the No Entry door.

As they passed Alan D-D looked at him and made a lunge. His teeth were pressed together and his mouth was compressed into a ring. One of the policemen caught him round the throat in an armlock. D-D still almost managed to connect the toe of his Reebok with Alan's face. The prisoner had launched his attack silently but as soon as he started to move the policeman and the other prisoners had begun to shout incoherently, like hounds and huntsmen around the kill. Afterwards the seven of them shuffled rapidly through No Entry. Alan's policeman closed the door behind them.

D'you know those people? said Alan.

Their numbers are displayed on their helmets, said the policeman uneasily.

The guys in the handcuffs, I meant.

I didn't notice their faces.

I thought I recognised –

Eh?

No.

The boy that went for you. You know him?

He's got asthma. He lives in the dark.

They thieve from each other where they live. They smash their own windows and board them up and live there waiting for the council to rehouse them. It's his mother started all the trouble.

What trouble?

Nothing that doesn't happen every Saturday night somewhere in town.

This is Sunday.

A few lads had a bit too much to drink, that's all. They hear some rumours and before you know it heads are getting knocked together, there's a couple of cars afire, the council's got some rehousing to do, someone's got a lot of glass to sweep up.

Where?

I didn't say that's what happened tonight, did I?

There was a shuddering, battering sound from the other side of No Entry, like part of someone's body was coming into repeated, violent contact with a firm but yielding fixture. At the same time a man's voice could be heard screaming: Bastard! Bastard! Bastard!

Alan and his policeman found each other's eyes.

He's doing it himself, said the policeman. I know their little ways. Nobody's touching him.

Why?

Maybe he thinks someone can hear him.

Can I go now? said Alan.

No, said the policeman, and led him through the door.

On the other side it had turned quiet. A grey carpet-tiled corridor led off past small offices with glass partitions. Half of them were empty and unlit. Alan's watch said it was approaching 3 am. A few policemen and women were drinking tea and filling in forms. Alan heard a clicking of computer keyboards, the whine of printers and some words: backshift, time and a half, poof patrol, Hieronymus Bosch, possession, just one Cornetto, always one good apple, what's the point, the whole fucking dump down.

Did you take everyone down here? said Alan.

You don't need to know that.

Did you charge anyone?

With what?

Where are we going?

To see the cruelty woman.

They went through a plain wooden door with a number on it into a room with a table and chairs. A wider than average policewoman was seated at the table, writing on plain paper with a fountain pen. A half-eaten sandwich was on a plate in front of her. She looked up.

Just when I put the surgical gloves away, she said.

I haven't been making trouble, said Alan. I'm not from these parts. I didn't know there was rioting going on.

Rioting? said the policeman. I didn't hear anything.

The policewoman put down her pen. Where did you find this one? she said.

In the club.

Were you in that place?

Yes, said Alan. I was having a drink. I fell asleep.

You know why you're here.

No.

The policewoman lifted a card and read from it: In connection with reports of unnatural practices, the police and inspectors from the Society for the Prevention of Animal Cruelty have been jointly empowered to enter these premises and conduct searches and external medical examinations of those present. Your co-operation is requested.

What unnatural practices? said Alan.

The policewoman produced a large, foggy negative and showed it to Alan. This is an X-ray of a man's tracts, she said. Look.

I'm not a doctor, said Alan.

Look! That tiny skeleton!

I can't see anything.

Everyone denies it.

Denies what?

The woman stood up. Alan saw she had the letters SPAC in silver metal on her shoulders. There are no sexual perverts in the animal kingdom apart from man, she said.

Come on, empty your pockets, said the policeman.

Alan did as he was told. The policeman went through his wallet. He lifted out the condom.

What flavour's this, then? he said.

Ready salted.

You're too young to be using these things.

What do you mean?

Heh. The policeman didn't know what he meant. He grinned on silently, shaking his head. He came to a crumpled piece of yellow paper and unfolded it. He stopped grinning, straightened up and handed the paper to the woman, looking at Alan in a new way: yes, that's the one.

Hamsters, said the woman, reading the paper. Freezer bags. You're a disgrace to the species.

Loosen your trousers, said the policeman.

What are you going to do? said Alan.

It's an examination.

Alan stood with his hands on the table, his legs spread and his trousers round his knees while the policeman and the cruelty woman murmured behind him. He could smell the cruelty woman's perfume, the policeman's aftershave and sweat in the too hot room. For a moment when they touched him he felt a draught and cold metal against his sphincter.

You can pull them up now, said the policeman. Sit down.

Alan sat down on a hard seat. He sat opposite the cruelty woman, who picked up the sandwich and bit into it. It was brown crusty bread, ready sliced, full of chewy particles. The filling was something pink and meaty. The woman's face was broad and sagging off the bone, like a circus tent with the poles half-down. Her eyes were shallow, dark and staring.

Why do you do it? she said with her mouth full. Why use innocent living creatures? Can't you buy machines?

For what?

The woman put the sandwich down and wiped her mouth with a yellow-trimmed handkerchief she pulled from her sleeve.

Do you hate animals? she said.

You must like them, said Alan. You're eating one.

The woman lifted up the sandwich and peeled the slices of bread apart with a sticky butter sound. It was ham, with yellow mustard, a thick slice. Ham, she said. Home-made. D'you know what ham is? You homo-sexuals are all vegetarians, aren't you? When it suits you. That's what sickens me the most. You're breaking into chicken farms one moment and turfing the birds out into the cold, the next thing you're blinding horses and sending them off to be eaten, organising dogfights and using hamsters to satisfy your sexual cravings. I know for a fact this pig was killed painlessly, according to the rules. It's natural for people to eat pigs. Pigs are good meat. It's their life: to feed, die and be eaten. What's wrong with that? They feed on the fresh grass of our pastures. They're part of our landscape and our heritage. Eating them is natural and wholesome. We're humans, at the top of God's evolutionary tree. We're responsible. For caring for pigs, and killing them. You can't have a pig dying of old age. There aren't any homes for elderly pigs. They have to be killed. But they shouldn't be tortured. They have to be treated until slaughter according to the rules and the traditions. Be good to them. Let them feed in our heritage, and then be traditionally killed and made into fine ham. Horses and dogs are not to be eaten. They are glossy, loving animals to be fed and stroked and be part of families. That's the heritage, and they mustn't be eaten. Would you eat a dog?

If I was hungry enough, said Alan.

That's because you're a pervert. You've lived too far away from the heritage. Drugs and television have affected your twisted mind. You can't see the difference between a dog and a pig. A pig is meat. Meat! Understand? Good, fine meat. It should be well treated and killed. It's obvious, damn you! The sheep and cows graze on our pastures, the pigs roam, the chickens lay their eggs, little children give milk to orphan lambs and the shops are full of healthy red meat. The huntsman rides by on his stallion and the dog lies by the family fire. The rabbits are in their burrows, the mice are in the wainscoting, the hamsters are running on their little treadmills and the monkeys are in their laboratories.

What about snakes? said Alan.

Snakes?

I've got a boa constrictor. It's a pet. They only eat living things. I had to keep going back to the pet shop and buying hamsters, week in, week out. They began to look at me strangely after the first couple of times. Especially when I asked for fat ones.

A snake? said the cruelty woman.

I felt sorry for the hamsters, of course, but as you say: natural. I tried carving a joint of pork to look like a mouse and jiggling it around on the end of a piece of string but the boa wasn't deceived.

The woman picked up her pen and fidgeted with it, crossing and uncrossing her ankles under the table. I want to take your details, she said. Where are you from?

Alan told her, up to Little Screvving.

Tribler! she said. I never knew he lived so close. I bought some of his plates a few years ago. They're gorgeous. Kings of the Woodland, they were called. Incredibly lifelike. There was Brock the badger, Reynard the fox, some owl, and another one.

Michelin the hedgehog, said Alan.

No, there wasn't a hedgehog. They were amazing, it was like being there, in the moonlit woodland.

Here, said the policeman, are we going to book this one, or what?

We'll send one of our people round to check up on this snake, said the cruelty woman. Snakes . . . also have their place. Let him go.

Supposing he does a runner? said the policeman.

People who are moving through space are easy to catch, said the cruelty woman. You just put out your hand.

The policeman wouldn't release Alan immediately. He made him wait in another room, one of the glass-partitioned sections, on the promise of tea. Every so often a police officer would walk past, right to left, sometimes in riot gear, sometimes with a prisoner, or left to right, in civilian clothes. The civilian ones never failed to shout something down the muffling corridor as they went past. They sounded like fragments of jokes, although no-one smiled, even when they laughed. The tea never came. After a time no-one went past any more.

Alan walked out of the police station just after 4 am. It was nearly dawn. The empty streets and unlit buildings were the bright grey of undefined things. A cool wind moved over the town and a piece of lit cloud showed where the sun was approaching.

Alan had to wait two hours for the first bus to Little Screvving. Afraid to miss it by falling asleep he made himself patrol the windscoured busbays. Gathered on the benches when the bus pulled up were a tired, bowed woman in a chocolate-brown overcoat, a teenage policeman in camouflage uniform with a kitbag as big as he was, and one of the Little Screvving anarchists with a jet-black plume of hair, black jumper, black wool jacket and black jeans laminated onto his stick legs. He had the anarchist symbol painted in white on the back of the jacket.

The bus moved out into the sunlit town. The red brick of the houses seemed to glow hot in the horizontal light. In Horror Blaze. There was no smoke and nothing blackened on the main road. That didn't prove anything. Main roads were constantly swept clean, like hospital corridors. Perhaps they had machines for clearing the blood off the road after an accident, or a riot. You could hardly rely on the rain. Or maybe it was out with the mops and buckets for the women in the chocolate-brown overcoats. Night duty. Roads. Special detail. You, you and you – blood and bits, on the double. And the broken glass, bucket after bucket. Stored as a crystal mountain. You'd need a good pair of gloves to save your hands being cut to ribbons climbing that mountain.

Alan was woken by the policeman when they got to Little Screvving. He thought he remembered asking the anarchist to do it. Most likely they'd exchanged clothes while he was asleep. Getting off the bus he came across the boy mechanic and asked where Sim's house was.

What's it worth? said the boy.

It's worth nothing to you, but a lot to me, said Alan.

Bottom bandit, said the boy, and cycled away.

Alan sat down on someone's doorstep and cupped his chin in his hands. Tribler came walking by, carrying a small animal cage.

Morning, said Alan.

Morning, said Tribler, not stopping.

Are hamsters native to the woodlands around these parts? said Alan, nodding at the cage.

No, said Tribler, walking on past.

D'you know where Sim lives?

Five Briarwood, called Tribler without turning round. Alan got up and went to find the place. It was a fair walk in the warmth of the morning to Briarwood, a curly street of new houses on the edge of the village.

Sim answered the door wearing maroon pyjamas with thin gold stripes and a maroon woollen dressing gown with gold braiding. He looked at Alan without saying anything for a few seconds, then led him to a darkened spare room with a single bed made up and left him there.

The houses on Briarwood had been sold as a group: executive homes. They were two-storey, timberframed brick buildings. They had red-tiled roofs, conservatories, double garages and gardens front and back. They had been marketed as spacious, exclusive, handsome and secure, advertised with line drawings featuring a young couple with children and a labrador puppy and a Ford car, bumper on in exaggerated perspective, in front of the garage. Ten years previously a farmer had harvested a last crop of turnips from the land, singing Cole Porter songs as he did so, drowned out as they always were by the sound of the tractor and audible only to him.

Sim's father presided over meetings, dictated and signed letters and gathered up the ideas of younger staff members at the credit card centre in the town of Northampton, for which he was paid 60,000 a year, got free use of a company car and received other material privileges. Among the accessories he'd acquired to go with the house was the phrase: I just fell in love with the place. He used it when people asked why he lived in Little Screvving. He was glad he'd picked it up.

Sim's mother drove into town once a week to shop. She could trot certain horses round a paddock, hit a tennis ball forehand and backhand, play Für Elise, distinguish between a painting by Pablo Picasso and a painting by Jan Vermeer, swill a red wine from the region of Aquitaine around her mouth without dribbling, eat a ripe cheese from the region of Lombardy without gagging, list examples of the use of coincidence in the works of Charles Dickens, dab the leaves onto a birch tree with the point of a paintbrush and make braised duck with turnips.

They did not know how often they thought of Sim at the same time, suddenly and for a short while. The previous Friday, for instance, at 3.45 pm, Sim's father had been approving a promotional poster showing the fields of the region of Northamptonshire yielding a crop of credit cards to the far horizon when he thought: once Sim dies, there won't be a homosexual in the house, which is fitting for an executive. At exactly the same moment, Sim's mother, cutting the shrinkwrap plastic off a hand of salami slices, thought: once Sim dies, that'll be one less place setting in the evenings. Would she and his father have to sit opposite each other? They were fond of Sim. They loved him as a guest. His forthcoming death made them anxious. It was easy to be serious, but was that enough? Shouldn't they be sending away for something?

Alan woke up in darkness on a strangely firm mattress under a strangely bulky quilt, which he'd pushed down off his chest in the morning heat while he was asleep. He was dressed in his underpants and could hear birds singing. He felt clear-headed, strengthened and healthy.

He lay there for fifteen minutes thinking of nothing at all and went back to sleep.

He woke up again a couple of hours later. His head was spinning, he felt nauseous and exhausted and had a single line from Cole Porter's Every Time We Say Goodbye creaking round his brain. He was still wearing his watch. It said two o'clock. He swung out of bed and stood on the floor.

How strange the change from major to minor.

He got dressed and left the room. Someone was playing Für Elise on the piano and stopping at the fifth bar every time. There was a smell of coffee. He followed the smell and found the kitchen, and Sim, sitting in the same dressing gown at a pine trestle table, talking on the phone. In front of him was a glass and stainless steel cafetière with half a pint of coffee in it, resting on a cork coaster, and a mug with the Visa logo. When Sim saw Alan he finished and put the phone down.

God, you look dreadful, he said. D'you want some paracetamol? I've had three already. I had so much to drink last night. D'you want some coffee? D'you want some croissants? They're really good. I can put them in the microwave for you. My mother puts them in with the wrapping still on. She says you're supposed to do it that way otherwise they explode. It's not true. She knows it's not true, she's trying to minimise the risk of crumbs falling off them when they're being transferred from the microwave to your plate. Or you can have some yoghurt if you want. Fruits of the Forest. It's not true, is it? There aren't any fruits in the forest. There's juice.

Coffee, said Alan.

Or there's some bacon. You could make a bacon sandwich. And there's eggs. Bacon and eggs. There's some blueberry muffins. They're delicious. I don't know what they are. They look like cakes to me but it says on the pack, blueberry muffins. They look like cakes with raisins in. They're really good heated up with butter. I had one this morning with the paracetamol. It'd be much easier if they baked these things with the paracetamol already in them, wouldn't it, then you wouldn't have to swallow the tablets.

Just coffee, thanks.

D'you mind if I come to the region of Campania with you? I'll help pay for the petrol and everything. Oh God, you hate me now, don't you? Sim pressed his hands against the side of his face, looked away and looked back at Alan. He hates me. He hates me! He giggled. Would you mind? If there's room. There is room, isn't there?

Yes, said Alan. There is room. What happened to Deirdre and Mike?

They're out in the garden, said Sim. Sunning themselves. I should be out there as well but I can't be bothered getting dressed so I can get undressed. What happened to you?

Alan told him.

Come on, they actually took you to the police station? Never.

They did.

And you let them poke around with your trousers down? Why?

What choice did I have? Didn't everyone else at the club go through the same thing?

Don't be stupid, they searched everyone at the door going out and asked a lot of questions. It was horrible. There's going to be a protest tomorrow. God, if they'd tried taking anyone down to the station there'd have been a riot. How could you be so passive? They've got no right to treat you like that. You've got to resist, Alan. Come along to the protest tomorrow, it'll be fun, there'll be a band and costumes. Didn't you ask to call a lawyer?

I don't know any lawyers.

You could have called your family.

And told them I was in a police station in the town of Northampton under suspicion of sticking small furry animals up my arse for the purposes of sexual gratification?

Poor Alan. Never mind. Have some coffee. What was the policeman like, was he good-looking? I still can't believe you let them lead you into the station without trying to get away. You shouldn't always do what you're told, it's too dangerous. What could they have done if you'd said no? If that's what reading does for you I'm not interested, thank you very much.

Reading, said Alan. I've got the answer. Reading is how you inherit the wisdom of centuries without having to be a fucking Methuselah.

That sounds boring as hell, said Sim. I don't need the wisdom of centuries. I want to be entertained. I want stories about lovers who would kill for each other and die for each other. Even though they like to screw around.

That's what half the books in the world are about.

Are they? Sim wrinkled his nose. Is there one set by the seaside, under very bright light in the daytime, and warm at night?

Probably.

With strong young men dressed in white cotton? And one very tall woman with masses of black, piled-up hair, in a red ankle-length crushed velvet dress with a gold-braid hussar bodice, who walks along the promenade alone every evening?

I'm not sure about that.

Take me with you to the region of Campania.

Sure, why not.

Alan poured some coffee and went into the garden. It was about the size of a tennis court, a lawn with an empty greenhouse in one corner. Mike was sitting in a deckchair facing the sun, stripped to the waist, shading his eyes with one hand and holding open a copy of John Milton's *Paradise Lost* with the other. He was not as strong as Alan had imagined, more meaty than muscular, with a slight belly-bulge over his jeans. He was browning nicely though. Deirdre was lying face-up on the grass a few yards away, tanning in her under-wear. She'd taken off her bra. Her skin was still very pale. Her eyes were closed but as if she'd sensed him watching her she lazily raised one knee and scratched her flesh. She opened her eyes and looked at Mike. It seemed a long time to Alan, a minute maybe. Then she noticed Alan, propped herself up on her elbows, stared at him for a few seconds, sat up and picked up her bra.

Where the fuck did you get to? she said, trying to put the bra on too quickly and getting it tangled. Eh? If you're trying to lose us could you not just say so? Shit!

Mike glanced up from his book and went back to it. Alan came over and tried to help fasten the bra behind Deirdre's back. He couldn't make the two parts intersect.

Mike! shouted Deirdre.

Mike put the book down, came over beside Alan, took the bra parts from him and fastened them together. He walked back to his deckchair and picked up the book.

Thank you, darling, said Deirdre. She got up, went behind Mike, put her arms around his shoulders and kissed him upside down. She nuzzled, her hair falling over his face. He put the book down on his leg, open at the place, and stroked her head, then lowered his hands and let them rest on the book. Deirdre came round, lifted the book carefully off his leg, put it on the ground and sat on Mike's lap, looking at Alan. Mike's fingers strayed towards the spine of the book and stroked it. His eyes seemed to come into focus more, he put both arms round Deirdre and squeezed.

Why do you keep running away from us? he said to Alan.

Deirdre looked away when Mike said this as if she'd just seen an interesting thing, ninety degrees away.

I fell asleep, said Alan, sitting down on the grass. His

story took a while because he was watching Deirdre's thighs in Mike's lap and every time she moved he thought about sex with her and forgot what he was saying. When he got to the bit about the policeman and the condom Deirdre interrupted.

You told me you didn't have any, she said. She turned to Mike. He told me he didn't have any, Mike, when we had sex. The two of us. Me and Alan. Wonder why he did that? Not very safe, is it? Deirdre looked at Mike's face and stabbed her thumbnail between her teeth. They heard the sound as she bit it. Sorry, she said.

Mike put his hands on Deirdre's waist, lifted her off him and picked up the book. She stood with her thumbnail still in her mouth, her body bent slightly towards him.

It was just the once, said Deirdre.

Alan stood up.

Don't be angry, said Deirdre. It's true I wasn't fighting him off. I felt like it. He was there. I told him about you. Tell him, Alan.

Why not say you were drunk? Why not say I raped you?

Give us a break, Alan, eh, stop trying to be clever. You'll make it worse. Let's forget about it, eh? Let's all forget it. It happened once and it won't happen again. How about that, eh, Mike? Please don't be angry, Mike. Please don't be angry. Deirdre put her arms round him and kissed his face. Please don't be angry. Mike waited, still stroking the spine of *Paradise Lost* with one hand. Deirdre lowered her voice. Just because I let another man put it inside me, don't be angry. Mm? Just because another man is in bed with me, it doesn't mean I don't love you, does it? Come on. Don't be angry.

He isn't angry, said Alan. Deirdre flung her head round and hissed at him. Sh! You don't know him. Want your head broken?

I am angry, said Mike. It's what keeps me going. He stood up and Deirdre stepped back. I don't like you, he said to Alan. You're not a serious person. You like to play. Light entertainment. Deirdre and the car and this antique hunting, it's light entertainment for you. You've given up looking for knowledge. You're beaten. I'm not beaten.

He picked up the book. I'm going into the house to read. It's too bright out here. There's a glare coming off the page. He went inside.

Mike! said Deirdre. I said not to get angry! I said not to get angry with me! She raised her voice to a shout as he moved further away, her face went red, her eyes wrinkled up and tears came out. I'm not his light entertainment and I'm not your fucking light entertainment, you fucking bastard! She went running into the house after him.

Alan took off his shirt and sat in the deckchair. He leaned back and closed his eyes. A cloud moved across the sun and the warmth was closed off. Alan got up and went into the kitchen. Sim was dropping tablets down the shaft of a throbbing food processor. The colour of the processed food was pink. There was a smell of guava fruit.

Where's Deirdre? he said.

Upstairs, straight ahead, said Sim.

Alan went upstairs to the door and opened it. Deirdre and Mike were naked on a bed, fucking away, Deirdre on top, her back to the door. Mike's eyes were open. He looked at Alan. Alan closed the door and went back downstairs.

He walked through the village to the garage. The car was ready. The new windscreen shone clear and bright. Alan put his palm on the bonnet. The painted metal was warm from the sun.

The car doctor wiped his hands on a rag and looked at the machine with regret. Returning it to the wild.

OK? said Alan.

You should be all right, said the car doctor sadly. You could go round the clock a couple of times in that. He gave Alan the bill. Alan lanced it with the credit card.

Where are you going? said the car doctor.

The town of Glasgow.

The car doctor inhaled between clenched teeth, exhaled with puffed cheeks and shook his head. You wouldn't rather sell it? he said.

I need it.

The car doctor looked for a moment as if he was about to weep. Then he frowned and looked into Alan's eyes.

Don't try and muck around with the engine yourself, he said. You're not capable.

What are you saying? said Alan.

Something's bound to go wrong with your motor

between here and the town of Glasgow. There's one thing you've got to learn that's difficult for you.

What's that?

Letting yourself be helped by strangers who don't expect a reward.

OK, said Alan, getting into the car.

It's harder than you think! shouted the car doctor over the noise of the engine. Alan drove back to Briarwood.

Sim was packing in his room. He had changed into white knee-length denim shorts, a blue and white striped teeshirt and white plimsolls. Two suitcases were open on his bed. It was a double bed. They covered it. In one he was laying clothes, precisely folded: silk and polyester shirts, teeshirts, some nice light jackets, some white cotton button-down shirts with ready-matched ties, white cotton ankle socks, white boxer shorts, blue jeans, cream-coloured canvas trousers. Everything looked new. The shirts still had plastic wrappers on. The other suitcase was filling up with prescription drugs and CDs.

I don't have a CD player in the car, said Alan.

That's all right, I've got one, said Sim.

This is too much stuff.

Oh, do you think? How long are we going to be away for? Is it not like, for ever? There's plenty of room in your car, isn't there? There's loads of space in the back. I always take too much, I know. Someone else always has to help me carry it. I don't know how long it'll be before we get to the next tumble dryer and the next iron. If I spill wine on my trousers or my tie I've got to change straight away. It's too demoralising otherwise. That red stain on your thigh. It's like carrying a wound. I feel less ill when my clothes are perfectly clean.

But there's my stuff in the back, and two rucksacks, and four people in the car.

Alan, don't be upset. Cars are strong. They're made of metal. They don't break.

It's not that, it's the volume. Too much stuff. You stop feeling like a traveller. More like a refugee.

What's wrong with refugees?

I don't want to be one.

It's not good, is it? There's always mattresses and furniture lashed to the roof and you spend too much time in tents with children and goats. But these are suitcases. I'm not taking a mattress. Everything'll be inside the car. There'll be no lashing. Your car won't look poor and ugly. That's what you're worried about, isn't it? God, we don't want some nasty big conglomeration of sticks and vinyl swaying on top of the car, everyone looking. Everything'll be inside the car, and it'll be all streamlined and everything and look like rich tourists. Let's leave tonight. After dinner. We can get a long way on a summer evening, can't we? It'll be warm and fine and the roads'll be quiet. What d'you think? We'll find some nice café somewhere later. It'll be warm and we can drink under the stars. God, am I getting on your nerves already?

Is your mum going to give us a meal? said Alan.

Of course. Served in the kitchen. Not the dining room. On plain plates. In case you foul the good ones.

Sim's mother served up lasagne with lettuce salad and a side dish of turnips, with a choice of mineral water or Coca-Cola. It was 6 pm. The car was loaded.

I'll have a lager, said Sim's father. He had taken off his executive jacket and tie and sat at the top of the rectangular pine trestle table with his eggshell blue button-down shirt open at the collar.

Sim's mother looked at Mike, who was drinking Coke. Anyone else want a lager? she said to him. The formula he craved to unleash the beast in him.

No, I'm fine, he said.

Sim's mother handed a small green can of Heineken and a tall glass to her husband. He popped and poured it with great attention to minimising the head.

Alan was trying to catch Deirdre's eye. She was avoiding his face. Her chair was moved up right against Mike's. She was so into his space he could hardly move his arm. He wasn't paying her any attention. He was staring into the layers of lasagne, watching it congeal. Every once in a while his eyes would flick up and he would scan the faces in front of him, Sim's father, Sim, Alan, like he was wondering what truths they were finding in the pasta in front of them. When he saw they weren't studying their food he went back to his.

Nice lasagne, said Alan.

Reminds me of something, said Mike. These leaves, these rectangular leaves, stacked on top of each other, what does it remind you of?

He wasn't looking at anyone, he was looking at his plate.

I know what it is, it's a book, said Mike.

Books don't have cheese sauce between the pages, said Alan. Deirdre gave him a quick look with her eyes narrowed.

Why aren't there any books in this house? said Mike. Eh? This lasagne's the nearest thing I've seen to a book since I got here.

I've got some books, said Sim's mother. I bought two the day before yesterday. I buy books all the time.

Where are they, then? said Mike, looking at her and tapping the prongs of his fork irregularly with a loud, lazy action on the china plate. Where are the old ones?

I threw them away.

She threw them away, said Mike.

Are you leaving us tonight, then? said Sim's father to Sim.

Yes, father, said Sim. I'm away down south where the nights are warm. That'll suit you, won't it? You'll have more room for your 78s. You'll be able to have a little rumpus room.

You're coming back, aren't you? said his mother.

I'll come back with a tan, a flat stomach and a drop of gold in my belly button, and my eyes'll have gone distant from watching sunsets over a turquoise sea. I'll bring you little bulls and dried starfish and a thing saying somebody went to somewhere and all I got was this lousy something, and you'll welcome me back with a big hug, won't you? Big hugs?

I'm going to Glasgow, said Alan.

He'll drop me off, said Sim to his parents.

He's not well, said Sim's mother to Alan. I hope you know what you're taking on with him in your car.

I don't understand it, said Mike, gripping the haft of the fork and striking the end of it on the plate with a steady rhythm. It's not right, is it? For people in positions of power to be so fucking ignorant as not to have books in the house. There I was thinking power was knowledge and knowledge was getting stuck into John Milton. I was so into *Paradise Lost* I was there, a fallen angel with the others, running backwards through the waters of hell, trying not to fall over or get crushed when Satan came rising up and not able to take my eyes off him. And the strange thing is it turns out that means fuck all, it means no respect to feel that way, you've either got all the books and you're doling out the points to the folk who go through the motions or you've finished with reading for life and you don't need to bother with books at all, and the nearest you've got to a book in the house is this. Mike stuck his fork in the lasagne and raised it off his plate. It held together.

If I'd known you were leaving tonight we could have organised something, said Sim's father.

Oh, that would have been nice, said Sim. Something expensive. A carousel in the garden with bonfires and barrels of wine and fireworks. A festival for us. You'd have all the women in the village dressing up in your suits and ties and all the men wearing mum's dresses, and they'd parade through the garden in front of me offering me symbolic gifts of electronic consumer goods which I'd symbolically buy with a golden credit card, and we'd commute from house to house in the village, and in each one I'd be offered a cold beer and a bowl of salted peanuts by a girl roughly daubed with cosmetics and I'd kneel in front of a television set and I'd say Where's Sim? And everyone'd chant Where's Sim! Is he in the garden? Is he in the garden! Is he in his room? Is he in his room! He must be out again. He must be out again! Shall we get a video? Shall we get a video!

We left you alone, said Sim's father.

I wish you'd punished me more.

Mike got up. His chair fell backwards. He held out the lasagne on the end of the fork towards Sim's mother.

Read it, he said. Go on. If you're so fucking rich, read it.

Sim's mother screamed, not loudly, three on a scale of one to ten.

Sim's father stood up and took Mike by the wrist. Hey, he said.

D'you know what Goethe was thinking when he wrote *Young Werther*? said Mike, turning to him. I do. But you're the one ends up with the house and garden.

Let's go, said Deirdre, getting up and pulling at Mike's shirt.

Read it! shouted Mike, taking the lasagne off the end of the fork and thumbing through it in Sim's father's face. Chapter one: my intellectual struggle. How I was boiled, baked, eaten and excreted.

Deirdre was hauling him away. Sim watched. He was smiling.

The doorbell rang.

Alan left the kitchen and pulled the door open. It was the wrong door. Turnip jackpot. Turnips cascaded out, bouncing on the shag pile, bowling down the hall. Whoever was at the front door was battering on it now.

What are you doing? said Deirdre, dragging Mike past him. Mike stumbled through the turnips with his face frozen in the form of a man about to tell his best friend about the stupidest thing he'd ever seen in his life. Sim's father appeared at the door of the kitchen, wide-eyed, lipless, holding a stainless steel Sabatier meat cleaver. He watched but came no closer. Sim pushed gently past him and opened the front door. The cruelty woman stood there holding a dead boa constrictor in her arms.

Sim closed the door in her face. He led the way back through another door to the garage and out towards Alan's car. The four of them got in. The cruelty woman put the snake down and tottered towards them.

It starved to death! she shrieked.

Alan drove off.

Did you have a snake? said Sim.

I gave them a false address, said Alan.

PART THREE

Deirdre was in the back, murmuring incantations into Mike's ear and stroking his head. Sim was plugged into the CD player. Alan had Frank Sinatra on cassette.

They cruised onto the M25 motorway at a steady 85 and swung around the town of London. It was dark. The town burned like a flare. Its size tugged at them till they flew off its orbit and the lights thinned out. They entered a region of low hills. Alan occupied the centre lane.

The other cars and trucks slowed down and became fewer. Alan let his left foot rest on the floor and kept his right foot down on the throttle. Every few miles he avoided a vehicle in front with a long parabola. Only afterwards did he realise he'd done it. The tarmac was like suede and the curves and gradients gradual. The roar of the air flying over the car was unchanging. Alan watched the tenths of a mile turning in the green instrument light. The car was travelling at 1½ miles a minute. How fast would those plastic cylinders need to roll along a sandy path to move at the same rate? He would need to be lying down to watch them, but there was dew on the grass, and nowhere to wash his clothes.

He jerked the wheel to stop the drift of the car halfway into the slow lane. The dry ache in his eyes cleared and his body released a dose of wakeup chemicals. He sat up and gripped the wheel. He looked round. No-one had noticed. Sinatra thanked the audience at the Sands and moved on through the agenda of the tape god.

Alan overtook a truck with twelve glittering chrome wheel hubs and a silver cab, studded with scarlet and emerald lights flashing and picking out the words If You're Feeling Sad and Lonely. It was a truck made to carry death in, lean and alligator-eyed in a dinner suit made from the ripped black skin of totalled limousines. Alan was suspicious and afraid of pain. Death swore he would be warm and tender. Death beckoned with his arm, his head and his shattered-windscreen smile. He wiped broken glass from his mouth and said he was always available, at night, in the regions of speed, Alan just had to tell him and he'd be around. Alan was looking for Deirdre, but death was ready to play them off against each other. Death took Alan up on stage and the audience was astounded by their skills together; they folded steel and juggled fireballs and cut people in half, spectators were amazed by the glory and violence of it all. Call me, said Death. We've got an act.

Alan woke up. Crash barriers filled the windscreen, dirty in the headlights. Something mainlined into Alan's heart and his pores needled with sweat. While he was asleep the car had drifted into the slow lane at 90 and the motorway had gone into a sharp curve. The car was going too fast. Alan clutched the wheel into the curve, not daring to brake. He felt the tyres about to lose their grip and slide across the tarmac, slamming them into the barriers and from then on an exercise in two-dimensional collisions.

They slowed down. The road straightened out. Alan massaged the slimy black plastic of the wheel and took deep breaths.

Sorry, he said.

For what? said Sim.

I drifted off.

God, did you? I thought that was deliberate. It was a good feeling. Like a ride. Mind you, I don't want to die before my time, even if it is soon. If it was an artistic arrangement of young corpses in the wreck of a car that'd be romantic, but you wouldn't be there to see it, would you? And who's to say you'd be a corpse and not still twitching, a vegetable. You shouldn't drive if you're tired. Let's stop and have a coffee.

They pulled off into the town of Gent and found a bar on the outskirts. The bar had six bar stools painted white, standing on single metal spars fixed to the ground, spaced in front of the bar at yard intervals. The stools had spongy seats covered with floral fabric and on each seat was a man in a dark suit, drinking a tall, brightly coloured drink through a straw. There was a fish tank behind the bar. A neon Budweiser sign flashed through it. How could they sleep? It was said that fish had a memory span of ten seconds. Perfect for the brewers. A novelty every time.

There was a free table near the door. It was round and painted blue, the same shade as Sim's father's shirt. Deirdre had left Mike in the car. Mike wasn't asleep. As soon as the car stopped he'd pulled away from Deirdre and rested his folded arms on the seat in front, looking out of the window, saying nothing, ignoring questions.

Three of the men in suits kept looking round at them. The other three were personal friends of the woman behind the bar. They were making statements at her. She moved along the bar, gathering the statements up and handing them out to the others as she poured drinks and washed glasses.

A waitress came. They ordered coffees. Sim asked for a cognac.

I'm going to begin my indulgence now, he said. Everything's going to be in combinations. Nothing plain. Something with everything. Coffee with cognac. Lobster with truffles. Men with a boy on the side. D'you think that's disgusting? I went through an ascetic phase once. I cleared everything out of my room, I threw out all the music and all the clothes except plain white ones, I took all the pictures off the wall, I got rid of the bed and the carpet so there was nothing left except a mattress on wooden floorboards and plain white walls, and a wooden chest for my clothes. It was a nice wooden chest, though, varnished pine, that was the trouble. And I sat on the floor with my legs crossed and meditated.

Meditated about what? said Deirdre.

I couldn't think where to start, so I started with a tree. But I didn't know any trees except Christmas trees, so I started thinking about this Christmas tree, and it had presents hanging from it wrapped in red crepe paper, and I started wondering what was inside, and I meditated about opening them, and they were full of chocolates and aftershave and psychedelic spinning tops, and I meditated about whether to keep them or give them away, and I meditated about giving them to my friends, especially Frieda who's got a thing about aftershave, she puts it on her legs . . . so I couldn't get down to meditating. So I stood up and looked at the room and thought how pretty it looked all bare and ascetic, and the best thing was the chest, and what a brilliant piece of furniture it was, and how it looked much better without all the other crap I'd been storing, on its own. And I thought I wonder if some of my other stuff would look nice in an ascetic setting, so I put one of the pictures back up, and sure enough it looked excellent. So I started bringing everything back, and it was amazing what a difference it made. Now it's all where it was before, only ascetic.

He glanced over at one of the men in suits.

How do I look? he said. He was wearing black jeans and a baggy black silk shirt with maroon embroidered details on the pockets and a small silver star on each shoulder.

Good, said Deirdre.

Healthy, said Alan.

Sluts, said Sim, I bet you say that to all the queers.

What is it that's wrong with you? said Alan.

Sim smiled and leaned closer to them. I'm getting old, he said. He laughed and stood up. I'm getting old! I gave my teacher the kiss of life.

He walked away towards the bar.

Can you see something wrong with him? said Alan to Deirdre.

He's all right.

Physically, I meant.

How should I know?

You're a nurse.

I'm a mental nurse.

Oh.

I quit my job just before we met. I thought I quit my job. I don't know now. There's a lot of care involved with you, did you know that?

With me? What about Mike? Alan laughed. What care do I need?

You need to know I love you so you can concentrate on more important things, like driving, money. Eggs that look like the moon.

There's no way I need the services of a mental nurse. No way.

That's the problem. You don't admit it. You've got it the wrong way round. You think I'm miserable cause you don't love me and cause Mike didn't kick shit out of you when he found out we'd slept together. I'm not miserable. I'm disappointed. I wanted it to be casual with both of you. I wanted to be seeing two different men at the same time. Why shouldn't I? Everyone does it. Like Sim. He's not bad, he's not guilty, he's not being punished.

He's dying.

That's not much of a punishment. And it's me ends up with a total case like Mike, and you, always watching me, always on edge, waiting for signs from me.

Mental is right for you.

The waitress came with the drinks. She'd already given Sim his. The coffees were .30 each. Their money had changed colour. Alan paid.

Mike's a case, he said.

Yeah, said Deirdre.

Is he dangerous?

Don't be daft.

You know what I keep wanting to ask?

What?

Whether he's still got that baseball bat.

I don't know.

Let's go for a walk, said Alan.

Sure, said Deirdre.

Alan swallowed some coffee. He looked towards Sim, who was leaning on the bar and laughing with his head thrown back at something the guy in the suit was saying. There was a newspaper sticking out of the guy's jacket pocket.

Are we somewhere else from where we were? said Alan.

Are you asking me? said Deirdre.

Wait a minute. Alan got up and went to the bar, the other end from Sim. The woman behind the bar, her eyes were black and bright, of the hardest substance known to man.

Yes? she said.

Did you have trouble in town over the weekend?

Like what?

Fighting.

Always.

But about a councillor who attacked an old woman.

Maybe. It was in another part of town. A rough area. A theatre was burned down. There's always a lot of troubles there. The police were there, I think.

Do you know a boy whose name begins with D and ends with D?

No.

D'you know where Malcolm is?

Who?

A philosophy student who sings songs in bars.

Be more specific.

It's OK. Thanks.

Alan went back to Deirdre. They left 10 on the table and went out.

They walked past the car. Deirdre didn't look. Alan tried to see what Mike was doing but it was too dark inside.

They walked down beside the highway under bright streetlights as high as building cranes. They were out beyond shopping streets. A fast coach moaned past, lit within by blueish fleshtones from *Rocky IV*. Alan took Deirdre's hand. It was warm and dry. A high embankment rose up on their right, thick with tall grass. They began to climb the embankment. Near the top they stopped and sat down in the grass. Alan put his arm round Deirdre's waist. She rested her head on his shoulder. On the other side of the road, in the distance, were apartment blocks, crowded with lights. The air stirred. There was a smell of hay.

Alan watched a group of three figures walking along at the foot of the embankment. There were two boys in shellsuits and a man wearing dark glasses, black trousers and a white bandage covering his upper torso. His arms and stomach were bare. He was angry. It was Gregor Ferguson.

I'm not saying you weren't justified within the framework of the injuries received but you could have fucking spaced it right, he said as they walked past below.

It wasn't planned, said one of the boys. We thought you were wider.

The councillor stopped. Nem! he said. Three letters out of four! He lifted the bandage to show the letters NEM cut into the flesh of his chest. My wife's a teacher for Christ's sake.

The three walked on.

So what d'you reckon, then, said one of the boys. He says to say he's sorry and that.

He's got no business being sorry, said the councillor. He's got every right to defend his mother and the community. Better to carve me up than fucking let it drop. It was a provocation, that's all. They've been wanting a chance to fucking insert the toecap ever since . . . ever since.

Ever since when? said a boy.

Since the dawn of fucking time, said Gregor Ferguson.

Alan and Deirdre walked back to the car. It was midnight. Mike was lying across the bonnet on his back, with his hands folded on his stomach and one knee raised up. His eyes were pointed towards the sky.

I'll go and find Sim, said Alan.

No, I'll go, said Deirdre. She went into the bar. Alan moved towards Mike.

Mike, he said.

Uhuh, said Mike.

Have you still got the bat?

Uhuh.

Why?

To get through things.

First base?

Mike laughed.

Get through what things?

Things that block out the light.

Maybe there are other ways for you to get to Glasgow.

No, I like it fine the way it is. Are you afraid of me? Mike's head lolled over and his eyes pointed at Alan. Are we going?

Yeah, said Alan. Get in.

Deirdre came out with Sim, who was moving slowly.

Something happen to your legs? said Alan.

They're still serviceable. They may be getting old but I bet they're nicer than yours. You can see the lines dividing the muscles. It's good, isn't it? I could do part modelling for shoes.

They drove on for two or three hours. Just before the town of Trier Alan turned off the motorway to a road that climbed up to a high ridge. He drove into a parking place and switched off the engine and the lights. In the starless moonless darkness he heard Sim, Mike and Deirdre breathing steadily in their sleep, and the first bird before sunrise.

It happened that Alan had parked the car facing west, and the sun woke them more by heat than by light. Alan was the first to open his eyes and get out. The others were still sleeping. He opened the door quietly and left it half open to let some cool air inside. There were no other vehicles in the car park. He walked to the edge of the tarmac away from the road. The ground fell steeply and he could see far across the hilly green land around the town of Trier, to lines of vines, woods and expanses of pasture. Twists of soapy grey mist lay in the low scoops. There were no animals to be seen and no people. There was the sound of a machine from somewhere below, clanking in the still airspace.

He heard the car door creak behind him. It was Sim.

What are you looking at? said Sim, coming up and peering into the valley. His voice was hoarse. The view? Is it nice?

Yeah, it is nice, said Alan.

It is nice. But look how small the farms are now. I remember, when I was down there, they were this big. He stretched his arms out. They used to be taller than I was, two, four times. Now look at them! I can cover them with my pinkie nail! Sim closed one eye and sighted up on a farm with his little finger. Yeah, that was when I was down there. Now I'm up here. You see more from here, don't you, and everything seems smaller and not so real. I hate the country. You're always being pushed up into high places so you can look down on low places. I just like places. If I was a god . . . he twisted his little finger in the light. I could squash the farm like a spider. But I never squash spiders with my bare finger, the mess and the feeling of a body bursting under you, it's horrible, isn't it? It'd be the same with a farm, just a squeeze and a collapse and a spurt of sticky blood and insides from the farmer's family. If I was a god I wouldn't ever stand in the high places looking down. I'd visit the low places one by one. Why did we come up here? How did we get here so fast?

It was dark. You were asleep, said Alan.

Are we near town? said Sim.

The town of Trier.

Let's go there.

There's no hurry.

I don't like the views from these high places, Alan. You're one of these people that likes views, aren't you? You like to watch from a distance because you see a bigger picture that way. I wish I was like that except I get scared when I can't talk to the people I'm watching. I'm scared I won't be able to get down among them again. How do I look?

Alan looked him in the face.

Is it bad? said Sim.

Depends what you mean by bad, said Alan. Sim's flesh had shrunk around his cheekbones, an item like a freckle half an inch across had appeared on his right cheek, the lines in his forehead had deepened and wrinkles forked out from the corners of his eyes. The eyes themselves were redder than before, a sticky red around them. The flesh of his neck had begun to sag.

Look at my hands, said Sim, holding them up, palms downwards. They were blotched with dark brown marks and the veins bulged out across white tendons. The joints of his fingers were swollen.

You've looked better, said Alan.

I have, haven't I? And it's going to be a great day. Hot. Let's go into the town of Trier and find a café and get rolls and coffee. I'll wear something loose and white and no-one'll notice. It'll have to be trousers. I should have a hat. Why didn't I bring a hat? A Panama. I've got a cap, a blue cap. And a linen suit. It's on the beige side. That's terrible, beige, isn't it? If I wore it with the dark rose teeshirt I'd get away with it. God, I was really looking forward to wearing those shorts but I can't, can I, my legs'll be all blotched blue and brown and I can feel some kind of vein wriggling up the outside of my shin, like a worm. Sim lifted his nose, bared his teeth and made a fake shudder. You've no idea how it hurts, Alan, all the joints, it's like they've been taken apart and put back together with all the lubrication wiped off them. I won't look too bad, will I, sitting there in a café, not having to run about. Is my face OK? I don't want it just to collapse. I don't want it to fall, I don't want a soft leering dribbling face. I want to look experienced. Even ravaged. Not tired. Not bitter. Definitely not bitter. Hard and cool and warm. And old. I can't believe I kissed him. What a fool. Born yesterday and die tomorrow.

Where did you hear that? said Alan.

I don't know. Was it somebody's song?

Alan went to the car and opened the back. He took out a bag of clothes, the red towel and his washing stuff and went into the toilet block. It was clean and smelled of air freshener. The fittings were stainless steel. The tap didn't have a knob. He ran his hand over it, searching for a mechanism. When he passed his hand under the nozzle a stream of cold water gushed from it automatically. He took off his shirt, soaked a flannel in the water and began washing himself. Sim came in.

Sorry, he said, and went out again.

It's all right, said Alan. He smiled. He cleaned his teeth and stroked his stubble. He didn't shave. He took the clothes bag into a toilet cubicle, bolted the door, had a piss and changed, putting on white Y-fronts, black jeans and a dark blue teeshirt and black tennis shoes without socks. He put his dirty clothes in the bag with the clean ones and went out of the toilet block. Sim was waiting outside with his two suitcases.

D'you want a hand? said Alan.

If you wouldn't mind.

Alan carried the suitcases inside. Sim followed him slowly.

Anything else? said Alan.

No thanks. Have you got shaving stuff?

The water's cold.

That's no excuse. You've got to keep up appearances. I think you look better without the stubble.

Thanks. Alan went out.

Mike was sitting on the edge of the slope with his back to the car park, looking out across the big green land. Deirdre was sitting in the car still. She smiled when Alan came up to her.

How d'you feel? said Alan.

OK, she said.

How's Mike?

Mike? Deirdre looked over towards him, still smiling. She shrugged. I don't know. I don't care. She looked at Alan and laughed. What? Is one case not enough?

Me?

Oh, I don't know, she said, putting her hands on her hips and rocking her head from side to side with the words. She scrambled out of the car and started running across the car park. Alan ran after her. Deirdre shrieked a couple of times. She reached the grass first and sat down on it.

Beat you, she said, taking big gasping breaths.

No, you didn't, said Alan. I was about to lap you. He put his hands on her waist. The warm cotton of her teeshirt rubbed against her skin. She was wearing a long black fringed skirt. Alan put his hand on her bare ankle and moved it up her leg, feeling a prickling of hairs. Deirdre took his wrist and moved his hand away. Later, she said. Maybe.

Maybe! said Alan. Deirdre's eyes were grey-blue. Alan put his hand over one of them.

If the pupil of the eye is dilated, it means you're attracted to me, he said. Your pupils are too narrow.

I'll make a bigger hole.

If I put a hand over one eye, it fools your brain into thinking it's getting dark and both pupils get wider. It works. See?

You think my brain is so stupid? I've got a better idea. You walk around with your hands over both your eyes. Then you won't care whether I'm attractive or not and you won't know whether my pupils are big or small.

OK, said Alan, putting his hands over his eyes.

How's it looking?

Good.

What do you think of me now?

I like you. My pupils are . . . immense. Like music on black vinyl.

Alan took his hands away from his eyes. Deirdre was walking towards the view. Alan looked at the car. Mike was at the back, reaching in. He pulled out the baseball bat and swung it a few times, it was hard to tell whether as if the ball was flying towards him or as if smiting the enemy. Mike put the bat back, closed the door, climbed into the car and waited.

They drove down a steep road into the town of Trier and found a row of bars and restaurants along the bank of the river Moselle. They sat at a round white table near the water under a Martini umbrella and had coffee and rolls with butter and cherry jam. It came to 25 with tip. They split it. Their money had changed colour again. Mike was beginning to lobster up on the forehead and forearms but otherwise looked brightly healthy, alert and silent, turning his gaze from face to face as if waiting to be asked to explain their problems to them, but not being, so not telling. He was wearing long blue denim shorts and a pale blue polo shirt. Sim was in his linen suit with cap, the peak pulled way down over his face. He was wearing dark glasses. It was hard to see anything of him except his hands when he reached for food and drink. The rest of the time he kept them on his lap under the table. They were thinner, the veins stood out more, and they shook. Deirdre in a black dress, freckles coming out in a band across her nose and cheeks, talked about the hospital where she used to work.

It used to be an aristocrat's house, she said. You came in through a stone gatehouse like a castle by itself, between statues of unicorns on pillars. On either side there was this wall, a grey stone wall with nothing growing on it. The wall ran along the road in both directions. You couldn't see the end of it, even from the top floor of the hospital. The wall must have gone all the way round but from the other side of the hospital you couldn't see it at all. It just looked like the country-side going on and on.

God, how awful, said Sim.

Didn't you go walking in the grounds? said Alan.

Once I walked across the park, away from the house and the wall, when the patients had been taken back inside. It'd clouded over. The park ran out and I was walking through a wood. I came to an artificial lake and walked round it. By that time I couldn't see the house any more, or the wall. It wasn't late but the clouds were very dark. I heard thunder. I went back. I was scared.

Of the storm? said Alan.

Uhuh. I was scared I wouldn't find a wall as well. I was scared the wall was only on one side and I'd keep on walking and just walk into town, and . . .

What town? said Alan.

Town.

What town?

What's the matter?

What town would you walk into?

Deirdre looked at Sim, and back at Alan. Why are you shouting at me? she said.

I was asking what town you would walk into.

Deirdre shrugged. You walk into town, you walk into town, she said.

Alan got up. Let's go, he said.

Sim and Deirdre moaned together.

What's the hurry? said Deirdre.

I've got a job to do.

Let the egg wait. It's not going to hatch now, said Sim. This is perfect, a café in the sunshine by the river. It's ten o'clock. We can start on some chilled white wine.

I can't afford it, said Alan.

I'll pay.

I can't drink and drive.

Oh, Alan, let the rest of us drink, why won't you? We love you for your driving. You can drink juice and watch us disintegrate. We'll be all the quieter for it later on. It's an act of mercy, isn't it?

We know you're dying.

Alan, said Deirdre.

Everyone's dying, aren't they? said Sim. It's just that I'm going to die first. D'you think I'm going to get sentimental? I don't think so. I don't look enough like Dirk Bogarde to get away with it. I'd much rather this place was full of people and I wasn't noticed among them. Except they might think I was nice-looking. Or not that any more, OK, just interesting. And they'd dance around me, pretending not to look, trying to get a peek under my hat. That would be good, wouldn't it? Is it too late to organise the wake? We could have fireworks here tonight, rockets going up all along the riverbank. That'd be brilliant. Or would it be corny? What d'you think? You'd get two explosions for the price of one, one in the air and the other reflected in the river. This would be a place for a carnival, though. I wonder where Tigger is.

The waitress brought two bottles of chilled white wine and a Coke. She brought four wineglasses. Sim poured some for Alan and proposed a toast to the driver. Sim, Deirdre and Mike clinked glasses and the four of them drank. The wine was cold and sweet.

What about this kiss? said Alan.

God, what an embarrassment, said Sim. He covered his mouth with the wineglass and giggled into it hoarsely. The metalwork teacher caught me pulling a boy off. It was in the toilets. He didn't say anything. He just looked for a few seconds and walked away. Maybe he felt it wasn't his territory because I hadn't done metalwork for three years. I was fifteen. When I was twelve I made a brass shoehorn in his class, and a cement trowel. He liked the cement trowel, I remember. Sim's done a perfect rivet, he said. Gather round, boys, that's what I call a perfect rivet. Maybe that was it. He didn't want it remembered he'd praised the rivet of a boy who liked the feel of another boy's penis in his fist. So he didn't tell anyone. It might rebound on him somehow. All those tools and implements in his workshop, and those boys' fists around them, and him the instructor, you can just imagine him getting the shudders, can't you? He retired a few months after that and I didn't see him again until about ten years later when I was working in the library.

Library? said Mike.

I had a part-time job in the public library before I started college. You didn't have to read the books, just stamp them and put them back on the shelves. They're all numbered. And this teacher used to come in every week for a western novel. I don't know who wrote them. The only difference I could see was the cowboy on the front. I was twenty-five and the teacher must have been seventy-five by then. He had a metal walking stick and usually wore a raincoat the colour of those horrible mushrooms you see in the countryside, in fields. Or whatever they are. Someone once told me it was cow shit but it couldn't have been, they're so dry, aren't they, you'd see them flying around a field of cows like Frisbees.

He might have been good-looking once I suppose,

but he looked terrible to me when he came into the library. He walked in short steps like he was afraid of falling down. He was very intent on looking ahead, the way he was going. The stick in one hand and the book in the other. He had thick square glasses with black frames and red filaments running down through his face. His lips were really thin, they were slightly open and a bit wet.

I was changed too but he recognised me. He smiled and laughed when he handed the book in the first time. The cowboy looked like Dean Martin with no hat and an embroidered black shirt and blue jeans. I don't know if the teacher had forgotten what he'd seen. What d'you think? Maybe he thought because my hair was short and I'd got a job I was cured of my disposition for boys. We had conversations. It was hard to find common ground. He wasn't much interested in what the cowboys were wearing and I couldn't get excited about the metal-work issues involved. He said I'm making my own branding irons. I said who're you going to brand here, your wife? He said she's been dead five years. No, you can brand wood, he said, soft wood like pine. It creates a nice effect. This went on for a few months and then he had a heart attack right there in fiction.

The ambulance was taking its time and I'd done some first aid in the Scouts so I knew he was going to die without the kiss of life. God, what a sight he was, lying there on his back with his wet old lips open, gagging for it. He'd been good about my rivet, hadn't he, and didn't tell the head about my indiscretion, and I'd get my picture in the paper. So I did it, I put his head back and took a big breath and put my lips over his. It's not easy, is it, giving someone the kiss of life, you have to blow really hard to inflate the lungs. Have you ever done it? It's like blowing up a balloon, the hard bit at the beginning before the rubber begins to stretch. After a couple of blows I could feel him coming back. He was starting to breathe of his own accord. God, I should have left it there. I had my mouth over his and even though everyone was standing over us and watching they couldn't see what was going on inside. It was like something you'd do on your own behind a closed door, an experiment that makes no sense. I put my tongue into his mouth and gave his tongue a quick lick. It was nothing, I just wanted to see what an old man's tongue tasted like.

What did it taste like? said Deirdre.

Like anyone else's. Warm and wet. For a second I thought he was responding. I suppose he did in a way. But badly. He came to life, pinched my nose with one hand and gripped my shoulder with the other. Our mouths were still together and he sucked my air. I'd been blowing all the air out of my lungs into his and it was basically the same backwards but you can't imagine what it was like to feel the air sucked out of your chest by this old teacher. Don't ever let anyone suck the air out of you. It's horrible. Your breathing is out of step for the rest of your life. I blacked out. The ambulance that was coming for him picked me up instead, and he got his book stamped and walked home.

What happened to him? said Deirdre.

He's still around, said Sim. I saw him in the shopping centre a few weeks ago. He looked good. He had on a denim shirt and jeans and hand-stitched cowboy boots. He was with a woman dressed the same way, only she had a red silk scarf on. They were holding hands. I was sickened. She was much younger than he was, she couldn't have been more than sixty.

Did you catch something? said Alan.

I lost something. My breathing was terrible after that, I was always thinking now don't forget to breathe, what if you forget to breathe, Sim? You must get the rhythm right. But I didn't know what the right rhythm was, whether it was supposed to be fast or slow. And I thought no Sim don't worry, just be natural, let your motor functions take care of it, so I'd carry on with whatever I was doing and pretend I wasn't watching. My lungs. And after five minutes I'd suddenly check to try and catch my motor functions by surprise and I thought I'd caught them out and they hadn't been breathing at all and I'd missed five minutes of air so I'd start gulping it down as fast as I could and all the oxygen'd go to my head. It was awful. I went to the doctor and he said Very strange. I said What, am I going to die? And he said Die? Of course you're going to die. And I said Oh God, of what? And he said Of old age, I think. And I said Is there anything you can give me? And he said No. And I said What should I do? And he said Well I should enjoy yourself while you can. That was it. I've been to all the chemists but they don't have anything for it, do they? I never read anything, of course. What do the books say about old age, Mike?

In the books they don't live to die like that, he said.

Sim paid the bill. He could hardly grip the money. His hands were shaking violently and the fingers had become almost fixed in a claw-like gesture. The solidity of his neck had shrivelled leaving twin wattles hanging down and his jowls drooped below his jaw. Mike and Deirdre took an arm each to help him to the car.

I suppose I should take some drugs, said Sim. If I took one of each it might be interesting, what do you think? I might discover something miraculous.

They sat him down in the front passenger seat and fetched drugs from his bag, one of each. There were seventeen different tablets and capsules.

You should write it down, said Sim, popping the first. In the right order. And watch me for changes.

We'll remember, said Alan.

Yes, I always think I'll remember, but then I can't even remember which order of drinks doesn't give me a hangover. If I turn into a young god in front of your eyes and you haven't got the order right you're going to regret it, aren't you? I could do it in alphabetical order. That was Adalat, that first one.

Adalat, said Deirdre. She fetched out a notebook from her bag and wrote it down.

Allopurinol, Anti-TNF, Aspirin, Capoten, Cardizem, Colchicine, Enalapril, Indomethacin, Lopid, Methotrexate.

Wait. You're going too fast.

What does it taste like? said Alan.

Torture, said Sim. It tastes like experiments and billions worth of research going down my throat. It'll be lost down there. There's nothing to be done, is there? They're supposed to build defences but there's nothing to build with any more. The bloodstream's dry.

Away, said Alan. Your heart's still beating.

That's true, it is, isn't it? Maybe I do feel better. Better isn't good enough, though, I want something miraculous. Wings to sprout. Or horns. Mevacor, Naprosyn. They sound like the names of princes, don't they?

Angels falling by me, said Mike.

Penicillamine, Sulphasalazine, Vasotec, Voltaren. That's it.

OK, said Deirdre.

How do I look? said Sim.

Fine, said Alan. Sim looked terrible.

Not worse, said Deirdre.

Nothing miraculous?

Give it time.

You forgot something, said Alan. Sim leaned out of the open car door and vomited onto the pavement. Pastel-coloured shapes dotted the sick soup.

What did I forget? said Sim.

Wine comes last.

Old fool, said Mike.

Less of the old, if you don't mind, said Sim. They drove back onto the motorway.

The road went through hills covered with forests of larch and fir. It crossed gorges on slender white concrete bridges. After an hour they crossed the river Rhine and the road straightened out. It ran along flat country beside the river. They could see the water shining through the trees on their right.

The motorway was two lanes in each direction. It was early afternoon. They were driving into a high, hot sun. Alan was doing around 85. Mercedeses hammered past in the fast lane at 110, all that was chrome in them burning with a brightness that left marks on the vision for minutes afterwards.

Inside the car it was warm, even with the windows open, the slipstream roaring in their ears and the fan blowing. The trees by the side of the road looked dusty and parched. The traffic began to clog up. A stream of crawling steel glittered in the haze ahead. They were being cooked in their skins. Through the windscreen the sun heated the black plastic dashboard and the steering wheel. Sim leaned against the door with his arms folded and his mouth open.

At 2 pm they pulled into a service station set in trees between the road and the river. They left the car and moved very slowly with Sim towards the cafeteria. It was air-conditioned. Galleries of hot food waited along one side, trays of sectioned lasagne, crisp-skinned shed-raised chicken and scalloped potatoes with onions. The dishes were illustrated with lit pictures above the servers, where everything was a shade of yellow. It smelled good. In the cooled enclosure they chose from the hot menu.

This all looks very tasty, said Sim, trying to pick up a tray and dropping it on the floor. Alan, I can't manage the tray on my own. How embarrassing. You wouldn't mind carrying it for me, would you, while I choose? I'm completely helpless. If only someone nice'd take pity on me in this state it'd be worth it. The love of a good boy'd see me through. God, I've got a completely new pain in my back. Why do they call it the nervous system? Nervous of what? Being hurt? It should be called the pain system. I'll have some of that schnitzel with the sauce. At least I've still got my own teeth. I can't hear a word you're saying.

I'm not saying anything, said Alan.

I said I can't hear a word you're saying, shouted Sim. It's brilliant being old, isn't it? Apart from the physical torture. Everyone looks after you and you don't have to talk to them. My eyes are OK. I'll have some chips and wine.

They sat down with plates of schnitzel and chips. Sim had a bottle of white wine to himself. Mike and Deirdre had beers. Alan had orange juice. It was 36 altogether. Deirdre stopped Sim from paying and took money from Alan and Mike.

This is brilliant, said Sim. Can someone cut up this meat for me? Eating and drinking and sleeping all day. If only there could be sex as well, and things didn't hurt, it'd be heaven. What more would you want? Let's go to the river afterwards. D'you mind, Alan? Maybe there'll be a beach.

You don't like the country, said Alan.

I can't hear you. There's a rushing in my ears.

Alan shouted it.

The river isn't the country. The river is different. I can cope with the river. It's more like a road, only it moves and you sit still. I want to paddle. That'd be good, wouldn't it? That'd be perfect. I want to have cool river water running round my feet. Then I'll be happy. I'm selfish, aren't I? I talk all the time about what I want and you have to listen. I can't help it. You all look so worried. You shouldn't, should you? I don't worry enough. I don't worry like I don't read, they're both something you can't do at the same time as doing something good. You should dress better, drink and talk more and have sex more often. Even when things start to hurt.

I read and I don't worry, said Mike.

Oh! Babe Ruth speaks, said Alan.

Let's go to the river, said Deirdre.

Alan and Deirdre got up and helped Sim to his feet. Mike stayed where he was, staring ahead.

Are you coming? said Alan.

Mike said nothing.

You don't talk a lot for someone who knows so much, said Alan. If there's something on your mind, say it.

He gets like this, said Deirdre.

He can get like this in another person's car. I feel he's about to pronounce something and it never comes. It's like travelling with a hung jury in the back.

Let's go to the river, said Deirdre.

Mike opened his mouth, still looking ahead. I've been falling for a long time, he said. The whole day. Before I began to fall I said a lot of things to people who didn't listen.

OK, let's go, said Alan. Deirdre and he walked with Sim to the door. Mike was saying something else but they didn't hear.

Behind the restaurant and the car park there was a broad path of yellow dirt leading through the trees to the river Rhine. It took them quarter of an hour to reach the water's edge. At the beginning Alan found a branch of hard wood in the undergrowth and offered it to Sim as a walking stick. Sim's right hand was no longer capable of grasping it. He put his arms around Alan and Deirdre's shoulders on either side and they walked to the river that way. He was still taller than Alan but only by half an inch now, and was light. Together they could have carried him bodily more quickly, but he wanted to put each foot on the ground. His head was trembling and his wattles shook with every step. He stopped twice to cough his throat clear of phlegm.

I like this heat, he said. I like days that are hot enough not to worry whether it'll start to get cold. What do you think? Should I take my trousers off or roll them up? I want to look good. If I rolled them up I might look like a philosopher. Wise. That'd be good. If I took them off I could look like Mahatma Gandhi in the river Ganges. He had thin legs. But he had a good tan. The tan's everything, really, isn't it? Thin white legs aren't right for wise men in rivers. Especially when they've got veins wriggling up the outside of them.

They reached the river. There wasn't a beach. The track led down to rocks and pebbles and the broad stream, two hundred yards across. The water was a dark olive colour, shot with yellow and flashing where the sun caught the current. Deirdre and Alan helped the old man take off his shoes and socks and roll up his trousers. They bared their legs and waded out with him into the cold water. Their feet felt for holds on the smooth, flat, slimy stones, warmed by the sun in the shallows. Sim leaned his head back and smiled, cracking his wrinkles.

Let me sit down, he said.

You'll catch your death! shouted Deirdre.

It's all right, he said. Let me sit down.

What about your trousers? shouted Alan.

It's all right.

They were about five yards away from the river bank. The water came up to their knees. They lowered Sim into the water until he came to rest on the bottom. He gasped a little as his arse hit the water, then smiled again and sat there. They were afraid to let go.

OK? shouted Deirdre.

Fine.

They stepped a few feet away and looked at him. He sat on the stones, the water up to his chest, his hands and lower arms trailing. He faced into the current. They could see his legs, yellow and stunted by refraction, rippling below the surface. Alan watched the stream break around him. It looked as if Sim was powering through still water in a submarine canoe.

How do I look? said Sim.

Great! shouted Alan.

Like an old fool! shouted Deirdre.

Sim giggled. I am an old fool, he said. I never learned anything. I never wanted anything except to be happy at the moment. I don't have a single memory. Isn't that useless? As soon as something happens I tell somebody about it and then forget it. I wish Tigger was here. I'd love to have sex in the stream. It'd be hard though. If he tried to give me a blow job he'd drown, wouldn't he? I don't think the river's very clean, either, is it? Where's Mike? He's a very rigorous boy. I like rigorous boys. He's looking forward to something very much, isn't he, something in the future. I think my parents were always looking forward to something very much when they were young. They still are. They'll always be looking forward to something until one day they suddenly start looking backwards to the times when they were looking forwards. Maybe I should try looking backward, what do you think? Except I've got nothing to remember. I've got nothing to remember at all. Mind you I've got nothing to forget either. Poor Tigger. Poor Mike. Listen, I bet I could still get it up.

He stopped talking.

His voice sounds just the same, said Deirdre.

What are we going to do with him? said Alan.

We should have brought towels, said Deirdre.

They stood still in the river for a few moments more. It didn't make much of a sound, big as it was, and fast. Children were playing on the far bank, upstream. You could hear them shrieking and splashing.

There's a teaspoon down there, said Deirdre, looking into the water.

The magic teaspoon of the Rhine, said Alan. Be careful. You might start an opera cycle.

Deirdre stepped forward, lost her grip and fell into the water. Alan helped her up and they walked back to dry land. Her skirt and part of her teeshirt were soaked.

We'll need to get you out of those wet things, said Alan, grinning. The kindly uncle.

Oh really, said Deirdre. She went and leaned against a tree with her hands behind her back. Come on then.

Alan became nervous. He looked around. There was no-one. The trees were thick between the river and the car park and they were out of sight of where Sim was sitting. He went close to Deirdre and put his hand around her waist. She looked up at him and smiled. He leaned down and they kissed. He pulled her teeshirt out of her skirt and slid his hand under it, over her cold wet breast.

What about the wet things? said Deirdre.

Sit down, then.

Deirdre sat down. Alan fumbled behind her back, undid the skirt and peeled it off. Deirdre leaned back on her elbows and flicked her wet hair out of her eyes.

My knickers are wet as well, she said.

Alan lay down beside Deirdre. They kissed as he moved his hand inside her knickers and began to gently rub a spot.

Alan felt footsteps behind them and heard leaves pushed aside. He looked round and saw Mike standing a few yards away, watching them. His left hand was in the pocket of his shorts and his right hand held the handle of the baseball bat resting on his shoulder.

Hi, said Alan.

Hi, said Mike.

Leave us alone, said Deirdre.

It's hot, said Mike. Burning hot. He squatted down a few yards from them. Deirdre got up, took her clothes and went into the trees.

Alan turned and sat cross-legged, facing Mike. What's your problem? he said.

I don't have any problems, said Mike. Everything's resolved.

Good, said Alan. He got up. Mike lunged forward and held Alan's wrist.

Sit down, said Mike. I didn't say it was good. That's one of the things I don't like about you. You get used to a bad state too easily. You think it's good.

Alan pulled his wrist away, not as hard as he could have. Mike held fast. Alan sat down. Mike let go.

What bad state? said Alan.

This bad state, said Mike. Where we are. This heat and darkness. Where we've been sent.

It doesn't seem dark to me, said Alan.

What did you say? Why are you speaking so quietly? Are you scared?

I said it doesn't seem dark. The sun is shining.

You see the sun because you've given up, said Mike. He looked up into the sun with his eyes wide for a few seconds, then turned back to Alan, blinking in spite of himself. You've surrendered to him. He conquered you. You wanted to be loved by him more than you wanted the knowledge he should have stood aside to let you take. You're weak. You don't understand that teachers are barriers. They have to be knocked out of the way.

I thought you wanted to be a teacher, said Alan.

That was when I was weaker. I'm not weak now.

Don't, Mike, said Alan. You need help.

You're weak. You pretended to be a student but you never were, you were a teacher-lover. They frightened you away and now you're lying here in the heat and the darkness, crawling around, looking for antiques. You're not strong enough to travel with me.

That's fine, said Alan, getting up. The university's a long way away now. It doesn't matter any more.

Mike stood and unshouldered his bat. Long is the way, he said, and hard, that out of hell leads up to light.

Alan wrapped his arms across his face and moved to try to run away. The bat thudded into his guts and folded him in half. He collapsed onto the ground, scared to groan in case slippery red stuff came out of his mouth. Pain over an infinite space, everlasting. The next one square on the head, please.

Oh God, he said, squirming in the dirt and leaves, moving his arms down to clutch his stomach, moving them back to protect his skull, up and down, the feet treading earth. Oh God.

He heard Deirdre shouting Mike's name, and someone running. Then only the faint sound of the motorway and the children shrieking and splashing in the river.

After a time Alan rolled onto his left side, brought his right hand up to his mouth and spat into it. He examined the saliva. It was clear. He wiped his hand on his jeans and sat up. He lifted his teeshirt and examined his stomach. There was a faint bruise. Three strikes and you're out.

He got up and started to walk towards the river. He stopped for a dry retch. Nothing came out. It renewed the pain and he sat down again.

OK, he said.

He looked around and saw Deirdre coming through the trees towards him.

He's gone, she said. Are you all right?

Seem to be.

He ran off somewhere. I couldn't catch him.

What, you tried?

Deirdre knelt down and felt Alan's stomach with her fingertips.

Does it hurt? she said.

Of course it fucking hurts.

Doesn't seem too bad.

Was he always this way?

What way?

Criminally insane.

He's gone, Alan. You're OK. Let's forget it.

Alan looked at her pale, serious face. She stared steadily into his eyes. I'm ready to forget about him if you are, he said.

They stood up and remembered about Sim. They went back to where they'd left him. He was still there, in the same position, smiling, head inclined towards the sky, the dark river flowing over him. They shouted at him from the bank. He didn't respond. They waded out to where he was.

How're you doing? shouted Alan.

Very nice, said Sim.

Time to go, shouted Deirdre.

Very nice, said Sim.

They hoisted him up out of the water and took him back to shore.

We'll need to dry those trousers! shouted Deirdre.

Very nice, said Sim.

They led him painfully back to the car and sat him on the back bumper. The return journey took twenty minutes. Very nice.

It's not funny any more! shouted Alan.

Very nice.

Deirdre took off Sim's dark glasses.

D'you recognise me? she shouted.

Very nice.

Who are these people you're with now?

Very nice.

Is there something wrong with him? said Alan.

I think he's in with Dr Alzheimer.

They sat down on either side of Sim and watched the Mercedeses come and go. The parents were seared red or brown in their bright light clothes and moved slowly in the quivering heat, fetching ice creams and drinks like heavy burdens. Their tiny pink children ran around them and in between them. Deirdre took off Sim's trousers and laid them on the car roof to dry. Sim's legs were white and blue, crooked, thin with a round bulging joint like a heron's. Alan took Mike's rucksack out of the car and set it down on the tarmac. He went to fetch three cans of Coca-Cola. Very nice.

We'll have to find somewhere to leave him, said Deirdre.

How did he get old so quickly? said Alan.

People do.

Do they?

Of course. Look at you. You were a baby. Now you're a man.

It took me twenty years!

Years, minutes, they're all the same once they're over.

But I remember.

Do you? Are you sure? If you don't have it any more it's nothing. The rest is imagination.

Bollocks.

Well, you've got a good imagination. You're lucky.

Alan frowned and finished the can of Coca-Cola. Let's go, he said.

They put a fresh pair of trousers on Sim and laid him down on the back seat. It was 3.30 in the afternoon. Mike's rucksack was beginning to cast a shadow. Alan asked Deirdre if she minded. She shrugged. Why should I?

He was your . . .

My what?

I was never sure, said Alan.

Forget it.

They drove back onto the motorway. They crossed the river Rhine and searched in the town of Mulhouse for an institution which would take Sim. After asking several people in the town centre they found a three-storey white building with a red-tile roof and steel mesh on the windows, behind a row of poplars. They took Sim to the entrance and showed him to a man in a white coat. The man asked Sim some questions, to which Sim answered Very nice. The man went through Sim's pockets. He found 10,000 in cash. He asked if there was anything else. They fetched Sim's luggage from the car. The man rummaged through the clothes. When he found the bag with the drugs he began to smile. He invited Deirdre and Alan into his office and sent for coffee. He told them about the institution, how it had been founded, how the patients were cared for, the outings they were taken on and the food they were given. With the coffee came a number of forms. Alan and Deirdre drank the coffee and signed the forms. When they came out of the office, Sim had disappeared. They shook hands again with the man in the white coat. He said Sim would be fine. Alan said he wouldn't. The man in the white coat said I didn't say he'd get better, I just said he'd be fine. Alan and Deirdre left, got into the car, drove back across the river and headed on south.

It began to get cooler. The motorway became more perfect, a harder, smoother grey, like a pigeon's back. Roadworks were tiny, clinical incisions on a moment of tarmac. They passed broad blue lakes flaked with white sails, and the Alp mountains began. They ascended and descended through galleries and tunnels lit by orange light, cut through the rock so precisely that the hands of their creators were not to be remembered. Their lungs were half-filled with car exhaust when they came out of the mountains.

In the flatlands the motorway straightened out, it became thinner and rougher, and you had to pay to use it with the new colour of money: 40,000. Yellow figures were painted on the road surface so you knew how thick the fog was. There was no fog, no clouds. There was a low sun in a gold sky in the west, by pylons painted red and white and fields of maize and sunflowers. They stopped for coffee, bought bread, cheese, sausage and water, and drove on.

The road rose into hills again. Instead of tunnels, there were bends, one after the other, swinging them back and forward over the contours. It was still two lanes in each direction. The only speed restriction was how fast you could take the bends without coming off the road or puking your guts. Alan took the curves as hard and tight as he could but the tiny Fiats beat him every time, the smallest ones, the size of vacuum cleaners with the vents at the back. He could hear the little engines roaring as they took him, on the inside or the outside, it didn't matter. If they couldn't get past they hung onto his bumper, inches away, flashing their lights.

When they passed the town of Genoa and the motorway turned down the coast it started getting dark. There was black in the blue of the Tyrrhenian Sea under the warm, dirty, yellow dusk sky. The road was far above the sea. Tunnels were cut through cliff-spurs of pale rock falling sheer to the water, and between them they looked down from steel and concrete causeways at the light-clusters of coastal towns and deep folds of thick forest. In under the trees were the single lights of villas, spread and dimmed by the screen of leaves.

It looks good down there, said Alan.

Let's go down, said Deirdre. It's late.

I'm tired.

We'll find a place to sleep there.

They turned off the motorway and went winding down a spiral road to the town of Rapallo. In the town centre there were many bars and cafés. They couldn't recognise cheap hotels among them. The citizens of Rapallo moved slowly through the warm darkness and stood to talk at the edge of the pavement, smoking and watching. Horns sounded from cars invisible in side-streets and mopeds croaked diagonally from streetcorner to streetcorner, swaying as they moved.

I don't see a sign that says hotel, said Alan.

It's warm, said Deirdre. Maybe just in the car.

I want a room, with running water.

They found another road upwards out of the town centre. All the roads coiled out of town, like the springs on a broken cartoon clock. The road went past villas with lamps shining at their doors, behind dark glossy leaves. One had an illuminated sign saying pensione. Alan stopped and got out of the car. There was a locked metal gate in front of a driveway and a bell. He rang the bell and heard it ringing inside the villa. He rang three times. No-one answered.

Wouu! he shouted. A man's voice came from the villa: What do you want?

A room for the night, said Alan.

We only work when the sign is lit, said the voice.

It's lit! said Alan.

I'm sorry. So it is. Just a moment.

The sign went out.

Goodnight, said the voice.

Alan kicked the gate and rang the bell again.

What? said the voice.

We want a room!

I told you we only work when the sign is lit.

It was lit until you switched it off. Switch it on again.

We can't.

Why not?

Because then we'd have to give you a room.

That's what we want!

But it's not what we want. We've got weapons. We don't want to have to use them.

You don't have to use weapons. You're a hotel. Just give us a room.

We can't give you a room when the sign's off.

I understand that.

But you still want a room.

Yes, very much.

Then you leave us no choice. A window opened beside the sign and a figure holding a shotgun leaned out. With the butt of the shotgun he staved in the plastic of the sign and smashed the bulb.

The window closed.

Alan got back in the car.

What was that about? said Deirdre.

No good, said Alan.

Why?

They didn't have teamaking facilities in every room.

They drove on. The villas thinned out and dis-appeared as they climbed into the woods. Alan drove slowly, in third and second gear, squinting to the boundary of the beams thrown by the headlights. Cars overtook them, flying into the bends at impossible speeds. After a time Alan parked in a scoop of extra space between the road and the steep slope. He switched off the engine and the lights and got out. There was no moon. He could still see faintly, maybe by the stars, maybe by the glow of the town a long way below them now. The parking place was not level; it sloped back sharply. Alan probed with his foot in the old leaves and found a half brick. He wedged it under one of the back tyres.

They sat in the front seats and ate and drank. In the blackness beyond the windscreen they saw a pattern of tiny flashes, like they were on stage, at a silent moment in a concert, looking down at an arena-sized audience spitting with cameras.

What's that? said Alan.

Fireflies, said Deirdre.

One of the insects sailed in through the open window. Its arse flashed cold green fire.

Get, said Alan, trying to wave it off.

Leave it alone. It's harmless.

Harmless? With a name like firefly and a backside that flashes on and off?

They laughed. The laughs fell away into the silence of two.

We shouldn't have left him, said Deirdre.

I know. It was the right thing and it was the wrong thing.

It was the wrong thing.

Yeah, it was the wrong thing.

He might've come back from where he was.

No, said Alan. He'd gone. He was more than just old. He was gone. He was such a good man.

Who, Sim? said Deirdre.

Yeah.

Oh right.

He was good at being happy, wasn't he? He was an expert. He made it look easy. But it isn't, is it?

No.

Are you OK?

Yes.

Later Alan had what he thought was a good rhythm going with Deirdre on the back seat. The condom was in use. He was inside her, she was around him and they were perfectly shaped for each other.

First he heard her silence, then he heard her sniff, then he felt her tears on his cheek. He stopped moving and felt his cock shrink into the rubber. Guilt was a nasty drink: it was the smell of sex in your nostrils and the taste of someone else's tears on your tongue.

What is it? he said.

I'm sorry.

What is it?

Nothing.

I'll keep on asking.

Deirdre threw her arms back and sniffed a big long sniff. I'm not right for you, she said.

Translated as I'm not right for you.

I'm not right for him, said Deirdre. The bastard. She rubbed her nose with the back of her hand. How can he read so much poetry about love without loving anyone?

He's insane, said Alan.

Yeah, he is. He likes you more than me.

Don't be stupid.

He cares about you enough to hit you with his fucking bat because you didn't go mental about being kicked out of college. He wanted you to be like him. He only hit you once, didn't he? And where was I, I was out of the picture. I was nowhere. It wasn't because of me two-timing that he went for you, was it? I wasn't worth it.

I don't understand why he matters to you.

You think I understand?

Is it because he's had a hard life?

A hard life! He hasn't had a fucking hard life, said Deirdre. What, you think he's poor? His dad's loaded. He made a mint on tenders for council work. His mum loves him. No-one's ever lifted a hand against him.

Christ, it's not my fault he's a nutter.

It's not my fault, mocked Deirdre through her nose.

That's all you care about, whether you're going to get into trouble.

Ah, fuck it, said Alan, withdrawing. He swung his legs out of the car, threw the condom out of the open door, pulled up his pants and trousers and stepped onto the ground. He leaned on the roof and looked out into the dark woods. Deirdre was saying something. He couldn't hear. There was a faint siren sound. Far below a flashing blue light appeared, traversed a space between two objects and vanished.

Harmless, said Alan.

They slept late next morning, sheltered from the sun by the hillside and the trees. They were lying on the front seats, with the seat backs horizontal, the sleeping bag unzipped into a single covering for them both. Alan woke up several times. The third time Deirdre was gone. Her door was open. The birds again. The air was cool. It was half nine.

Alan got out of the car. He heard Deirdre moving around in the bushes below the road. After a minute she came back up with a towel and the bottle of water and her washing stuff. She was wearing black leggings, a black vest and a necklace of wooden beads.

Hi, she said. It's a good morning, eh?

It's good. I feel we got away finally.

Away from what?

From where we were.

Yeah. Let's go back, though, and get a coffee.

Go back?

Into town.

What –

What?

No, not again. How much money do you have?

Deirdre had 65,000 in her purse. She didn't have an overdraft or a credit card. Alan had 48,000. His credit card bill was 25 times that much, the overdraft 17 times. He owed 42 times as much money as was in his pocket. 50 times as much if he counted what he owed his parents. About 2,500,000 altogether. But he had 10,000,000 coming to him from McStrachan once he got the egg that looked like the moon.

What if he doesn't pay you? said Deirdre, smiling.

He won't get the egg.

What if there isn't an egg?

Alan hated Deirdre for that. He hated her openly without saying anything. She knew but she was in a good mood that morning. It was as if she'd discovered something wonderful in her sleep.

Did you dream about something last night? said Alan when he'd finished hating and they were driving down the road to the town.

Nothing at all, said Deirdre. I had a lovely sleep. There are sleeps that're a quick break and sleeps that move you a thousand years from the last day you were awake.

We should get to the town of Salerno tonight, said Alan. Then on to Glasgow.

Fine.

They had coffee and cakes flavoured with cinnamon in a bar near the waterfront. It was 7,500. The sea was a quiet sea. A man was slowly sweeping areas of tarmac in the ornamental gardens. Another man, older and fatter, sat on a bench watching him.

That's a good job you've got there, said the watcher. Only you missed a bit under that bush.

Why not come and give us a hand? said the man with the broom.

It went silent for a bit after that. Then the exchange was repeated, with a few variations of words.

Alan and Deirdre got into the car and drove up out of town. To save money they went for the trunk road south instead of the motorway. It was a sweaty haul past dry fields, behind crawling old trucks, along the crooked main streets of small towns where people clung to the shade. By the time they reached the country south of the town of Siena the heat was hard to bear. The sun seemed to shine through each window of the car.

The land was parched. The cornfields on either side were bleached white. Alan drove off the road to what looked like a stream with trees. He could see the dust they were kicking up as a blankness in the rear mirror. He stopped under the bare shade of the trees. They swung the doors wide open and tried to rest. There was a stream, or had been once, it was dry now. The leaves could have been green at one time. Now they were smothered with the white dust. Everything was the same colour. It was a world of ash. There was no wind and their clothes were damp.

How is it with you? said Deirdre.

If 90 per cent of human body weight is water, 45 per cent of it's in my teeshirt, said Alan.

Poor Alan. Deirdre leaned over and kissed him. I do like you, she said.

Like?

With all my heart.

Why were you crying last night?

Last night's a long way back.

Something different again tomorrow.

Did I give you the impression I was jealous of my sister? I'm not. You have to plan a lot with more than one lover. Nobody can be really happy if there's so much planning involved in it. When she plans, she's looking way forward, to the end. That's too far for me.

You're starting to talk like Sim.

Don't brood about Sim. You'll go and visit him, won't you?

What, back there?

In town, why not? What is this thing of yours about going into town?

After an hour of sleepless siesta they drove on into greener country. The main roads went stepping down slopes between stretches of pine, poplar and cypress, and in the distance was a turquoise lake, between them and the diffused lemon-coloured light of the sun on the horizon. The light stayed with them as they wheeled around the town of Rome and started to fade as they left the ring. At around 9 pm they stopped to eat at a roadside restaurant. The restaurant was just about to close. It had metal tables set up on paving stones outside a small brick building with a bar. The metal chairs were rusting. They sat at one of the outside tables and ordered pizzas. Two men in slacks and polo shirts were the only other people there. They sat at a table over a bottle of cognac and reasoned with each other in low voices. There were long pauses in between them speaking to each other. You could see them thinking deeply, fondling their chins and scratching their armpits. The pizzas came after twenty minutes. When he lifted the first forkful to his mouth Alan stopped, wondering if the crickets would suddenly fall silent to embarrass him. They didn't. The pizza was the worst he'd ever eaten, but he finished it.

They drove on and reached the motorway within an hour. South of Rome the motorway became cheaper and more dangerous. On either side of the two lanes were high concrete walls. The lanes themselves were narrow. There was no margin for error. In one lane it was mainly cars travelling too fast, trying to get past the trucks. In the other it was mainly trucks travelling too fast, trying to get past the cars. Every truck was lit up like a carousel, the cab outlined with patterns of orange and green bulbs, sometimes the trailer starred with the same glory. The whole convoy swept endlessly south in the darkness with a roar that could rise to a scream, panting a hot bad breath of exhaust. It was submitting yourself to the collective madness, because there was no stopping, no slowing down, no turning off: to try to turn against the torrent would be instant death and destruction for you, your car, your passengers, and torn flesh, mangled steel, shredded rubber, fire, for hundreds of yards down the motorway.

At midnight they passed the town of Naples. Three quarters of an hour after that Alan pulled into a layby that looked down on the town of Salerno. The road was several hundred metres up, hacked into the side of a cliff; just ahead it went into a tunnel. Salerno port was floodlit, stark and organised on the edge of the black, trembling, humid murk of the sea. The lights of the town rumpled up the slopes from the docks. Alan and Deirdre got out and leaned against the barriers. Alan put his arm round Deirdre's waist. She moved closer to him.

Let's see each other in the town of Glasgow, said Alan.

Big plans, said Deirdre.

D'you think I'll find work?

No chance.

And you?

What d'you mean? I'm still working, said Deirdre. A field worker.

Alan laughed. Deirdre didn't. He wanted to ask her why but he didn't. He was afraid.

They drove down into town and found a cheap hotel. They got a double room for 50,000. It had a basin, a mirror, a small chest of drawers and a big bed on a worn parquet floor. There were plastic daffodils in a vase on the windowsill. From the bed they looked real enough. Deirdre sat on the bed. Alan sat beside her and they kissed.

D'you mind if we don't have sex tonight? said Deirdre. I'm tired.

No, it's OK.

Alan got up when he woke up, at eight, splashed his face in the basin and went to the window. It was closed with heavy shutters, painted a milk chocolate gloss. He opened them. The room overlooked a narrow courtyard strung with washing. The sun was coming over the roof opposite and about to hit the wall. He closed the shutters. He took the plastic daffodils, rinsed the dust off them under the tap and put them back in the glass jug. Deirdre was still sleeping. He took a towel and his washing stuff and went down the hallway for a shave, a shit and a shower. The water came weakly out of a blotched chrome showerhead. It was lukewarm and pleasant. When he got back to the room Deirdre was still asleep. He touched her shoulder. She didn't move. He shook her gently. She mooed.

Are you getting up? he said.

What time is it? said Deirdre into her pillow.

Half eight.

It's too early.

I'll go for a walk.

Can't you wait for me?

I won't be long.

Wait.

I'll be back in a few minutes. I'll leave the key here.

Wait.

Alan left the room, went down in the small slow lift and went out into the street. The car was where he'd left it, a hundred yards down the road. There was a smell of new bread. The gutters and pavements were still wet from a water-truck. The air was just starting to warm up. Shutters were coming up off shop windows. He went into a newsagent and bought a copy of the local newspaper *Il Mezzogiorno*. He walked on for a couple of blocks in the direction he imagined the sea was and stopped at a café. A guy in a white shirt and black trousers was laying heavy ashtrays on the street tables. Alan sat down and asked for a coffee. He started reading the paper.

There'd been a fire in a new council building under construction. Someone had been found shot dead in their house by the sea. Pensioner conned by child trickster. The town was at peace.

The waiter-owner brought a tiny thick-walled cup of black coffee with a skin of fragrant yellow foam and a bill for 2,000. Alan put two sugarlumps into the coffee and drank it. It was good. He turned to the inside pages.

Councillor Urges Bail For Riot Youth, said a story. Councillor Gregor Ferguson warned that anger among his constituents would explode if magistrates failed to release seventeen-year-old D-D from custody. The teenager had been among a number arrested by police during disturbances in the town of Salerno on Sunday night. The rioting had followed an assault on D-D's mother during a protest about housing conditions by a police provocateur posing as Councillor Ferguson. In the course of the disturbances a community theatre had been burnt down and Councillor Ferguson had been attacked by angry residents before he had convinced them of his innocence. Councillor Ferguson gave warning that he would stand shoulder to shoulder with his constituents in the event of D-D not being released. The rights of his deprived and oppressed community had been trampled on for too long.

Alan stood up and sat down. He looked around. He closed the paper, folded it into four, rolled it up and began tapping the edge of the table with it. The waiter-owner came out of the café and looked at him. Alan put the paper down, put his elbows on the table and covered his face with his hands. He heard someone come up to the waiter-owner. There were greetings and a murmured chat. Alan heard one of the chairs at his table being pulled out. He took his hands away from his face and saw Malcolm sitting opposite him.

Hi, said Malcolm. Never seen you here before.

I've never been here before, said Alan.

It's good at this time. The old men come and take the tables later. I usually sit inside. Malcolm was wearing a nicely cut suit of mid-blue linen, a white silk shirt and dark glasses.

How's Paula?

Fine. How's it with you? You look worried. More than usual.

I have a lot of worries. Listen, is that your new costume?

Malcolm laughed. Is it that bad? I kind of like it. You mean the Don Raids thing? That's part-time, it's occasional. I'm meeting some people today. Some business.

What business?

Just some business during the holidays.

I thought you had a dissertation to write.

Yeah, I'm writing it, I'm enjoying it. It's great. It's got a title. It's called The End Of The Road.

Philosophy?

Yes, philosophy. It's a good title, it can mean all the things I want to write about, death, insanity, dead ends of speculation.

You should write about the beginning of the road. That's the difficult thing.

The waiter brought a coffee and a glass of water for Malcolm. Malcolm sugared the coffee and stirred it for a minute, staring at the cup with his mouth slightly open. The two of them listened to the teaspoon clinking on the china.

I don't know, said Alan. I've been driving since Sunday morning. It's Thursday now and I haven't got anywhere.

Don't worry about it. You'll get there.

You warned me.

Malcolm shrugged and drank his coffee, not looking at Alan.

When I look at you it's you who looks like the travelled one, said Alan.

Malcolm put the cup down, licked his lips, folded his arms and looked out into the street. He turned back to Alan. I live, he said. Believe me. Time moves you along faster than a car. You should try it. It's better than the space travelling thing. That's fantasy. It's a distraction from doing real things.

In Alan came the words: You're right. From his mouth came: That's shit.

Malcolm shrugged and looked unhappy.

Are you saying I'm a coward? said Alan.

No!

What you're saying is I'm scared. It's easier for you. You've got a sick father.

Leave my dad out of it, eh?

It's a good excuse for you not to go anywhere. That's what it's about, isn't it? You don't like it that I'm getting away. You don't like it, do you? Ach. You can rot in this place as far as I'm concerned.

Alan got up and walked away from the café, burning blind. To go back, on his knees, right there, that was the time. On his knees. He didn't. He was half a mile away before he remembered he'd left Malcolm to pay for his coffee, and he burned again, hotter and colder.

He found a block of callboxes. They took tokens. He bought 10 for 200 each in a tobacco shop. He'd gone halves with Deirdre on the hotel. She'd paid for the pizza. He had 16,500 left. He'd need to find a bank. Maybe he could catch his parents before they began combing the woods. He dialled their number and there was no answer. He called McStrachan.

The phone rang seven or eight times before someone picked it up. It was a woman. The first token rattled through the box. He put another one in.

Hello?

Could I speak to – The second token went through. Alan fed in all eight. Hello? Could I speak to Mr McStrachan? Another token.

Are you a relative? Six left.

No, I'm doing some – five – work for him. It's Alan Allen. Four.

He's not allowed – three – to take calls from outside. Two.

Not allowed by who? One.

By the hospital.

What hospital?

They were cut off.

Alan shivered. He put the phone down and lifted his hand to see if it was shaking. It wasn't, though it felt as if it was. His head was made of polystyrene. To lie down and sleep forever and at the same time to run down the streets and dive into the sea. He took out his wallet and dropped it on the ground. He picked it up and counted the money again. The same: 16,500. He went back into the tobacco shop.

Can I have some more tokens? he said.

How many?

I don't know.

Is one enough?

No. No. I need about a hundred.

That's 20,000.

Yeah. Never mind. Have you got anything cold to drink?

We don't sell drink. Cigarettes. Stamps.

Do they calm you down?

Perhaps. If you lick enough of them.

The cigarettes.

Yes. They calm you down. Especially if you're a smoker.

Give me one. A cheap one.

A Silk Cut?

Yeah. That's fine. Thanks.

200.

There you go.

Alan walked out of the shop with the cigarette held between his thumb and index finger. After a couple of minutes he threw it into a bin fixed to a bus stop. He walked on a few yards and went back. He put his hand in and pulled the fag out from among potato peelings. Fuck's sake, the bus queue potato fiends. He licked his lips and tried to work some saliva into his mouth. He headed back to the hotel. He was wearing a black cotton teeshirt and black jeans. They soaked up the heat of the morning. After a while he moved to the shady side of the streets. It was just after 9.30 am when he got to the hotel. He went up to the door and stopped. He went over to check the car. It was fine. Someone had written in the dust on the rear windscreen: All is not lost.

Alan ran back to the hotel, inside and to the lift. He got in and it shuddered upwards. He kicked the formica lift wall hard with the toe of his shoe. It left a dark mark. Their room was on the sixth floor. The door was closed but not locked. Deirdre wasn't there. Her rucksack was gone. She wasn't in the shower room.

Alan looked around for a note. He found a piece of paper scrunched up in a ball in the bucket in the corner. He sat down on the bed and smoothed it out on his thigh. She'd written Darling Alan then crossed out Darling and written Dear. Why couldn't you wait for me? You make out that you like me but you don't. You want to have sex and be loved and then to go away on your own whenever you choose. I know you don't do it on purpose. You believe you're good. Everyone does. The difference between you and Mike is you get confused between right and wrong, and he doesn't, he's sure. He may be insane sometimes but he always knows exactly what he's doing. When I say I like you better than him I believe it, I really do, but the trouble is it's not true. You won't understand, will you? Please don't go to the police. I'll bring the car back as soon as I can. You should have waited.

Alan dropped the note and looked in the place where he'd left the car keys. They weren't there. He ran out of the room, down the stairs and into the street. He saw Mike and Deirdre getting into the car. Deirdre was on the driver's side. Alan drew a deep breath and shouted a hey, ending in a kind of scream and empty lungs and a dry mouth and sweat and a heart hammering like a real muscle not a soft beating thing. He started to sprint towards the car. He closed on it by about fifty yards before Deirdre got it in gear and glided away from the kerb. Alan kept running. Deirdre hit a red light at the first junction and stopped. Alan caught up with them, banged his fist on the side of the car and grabbed the doorhandle on Deirdre's side. She'd locked it.

What the fuck are you doing? Alan tried to shout through the window with what air he could get from his racking lungs. Deirdre had both hands on the wheel.

Quarter to three. She looked up at him. She looked afraid. Then maybe it was pity.

Get back! shouted Alan, waving his left hand at her and pulling his right arm back to hit the window as hard as he could with the side of his fist. He brought the fist swinging towards the window and pulled it back at the last moment. He did this a couple of times. Deirdre didn't get back. Her head turned forward and her hand moved to the gears. The car moved forward. Barriers dissolved, Alan's arm swung through the air from the shoulder and his fist smashed into the passenger window, puncturing and crazing the glass and scoring his flesh. Deirdre accelerated away. Alan stood on the pavement in wonder, and looked at his hand in fascination. He lifted it to his mouth and licked the blood off the cuts. He picked a crystal of glass off his tongue and flicked it away into the road.

Oh, what's he doing, said a woman wearing a red floral print dress and a white headscarf, watching him from a few feet away with her hands on her hips.

Did she leave you for him? said a man with thick brown trousers drawn up high over a big belly, almost to his armpits.

Yes, said Alan.

Oh, terrible, said the woman.

You should never hit glass, said the man. Never. I'd never hit glass.

How much was the car worth? said the woman. Was it a lot?

What's a lot?

I don't know.

You should put some spirit on that hand, said the man. And a bandage.

Why did she leave you? said the woman. You're not so bad-looking. Did you hit her?

No.

Good. That's good. Still. Maybe you should've. She was pretty.

Go and get a bandage, said the man. Go on.

Alan went back to the hotel. On the way in the owner asked if he was staying another night. Alan said he didn't know.

Out by noon if you're leaving, said the owner.

Alan washed his hand. The cuts weren't deep. He sat down and looked through the paper. There was a What's On section. It listed the astronomy exhibition, in an observatory outside the city. Bus 24. He left the hotel, in a street leading onto a sloping main road which led down through the centre towards the waterfront. In a pedestrian precinct lined with hundred-year-old buildings there was a bank. At the door there was a policeman with a machine gun. Alan went into the bank, to the cool, white money hall, took his credit card and approached a woman teller behind a glass window. She smiled at him.

Can I get some cash with my Visa card? he said, nudging it under the window.

Certainly, said the woman. How much?

100,000, said Alan. Make it 2.

The woman ran the card through a machine beside

her. The machine chugged out a printed slip. The woman hummed a tune as she assembled the card and the slip and ticked boxes.

What's that? said Alan.

Depeche Mode, said the woman. D'you like Depeche Mode?

No, said Alan.

I'll just be a moment, said the woman, getting up and heading for the back of the bank.

It sounds OK when you hum it, said Alan. She wouldn't have heard him.

Time passed. The woman didn't come back. Alan looked at his watch. The second hand went chopping through the moments. Time was like a warehouse full of cucumbers. It looked like you could never run out but every day you kept slicing away and pretty soon you noticed that big mound over by the door was gone.

He saw the woman moving through the desks at the back bearing his message. She held his card against her breast. She looked insulted. She wore purple. She spoke with a man in a suit. He took the slip and shook his head. The woman came back. Alan was ready.

It sounds OK when you hum it, he said.

I'm sorry, you're not authorised to withdraw cash. You went over your limit. Your card's been cancelled.

Eh?

The woman pushed the card back to him. He pushed it back to her. She pushed it back to him.

We can't help you, she said.

I do like Depeche Mode. Honest.

The woman shook her head and tried to see round Alan to the customer behind him.

Listen, I haven't got any money, said Alan. They can't cancel cards. It's against the law. I need money now.

We can't give you money if you haven't got any money.

I have got money.

What money have you got?

I've got a card.

That's not money.

It's the same thing! Look, it's got the name of a bank on it. You're allowed to borrow money with it. It's allowed. Everyone does it. It's called finance. I give you the card, you give me money, that's the way it works. I'm the one who's left with the problem. It's not you who has to pay it back, is it? I'm the one who has to walk around owing millions on the card. All you have to do is give me the money. I don't see the problem. I have the card, you have the money. Everything's normal. If someone went around cancelling cards then the people who had nothing in their pocket except a card wouldn't be able to buy clothes, they wouldn't be able to buy shoes, they wouldn't be able to buy food.

Don't you have a job? said the woman.

I'm an antiques collector.

Don't they pay you?

Alan chewed his thumbnail. He put the card back in his wallet and left the bank. He glanced at the policeman as he walked out. The policeman shifted the strap of the gun.

Who do you report a car theft to? said Alan.

Traffic police, said the policeman. Has your car been stolen?

No, said Alan. Borrowed.

Borrowing isn't a crime.

Oh no? Ask the fucking Depeche Mode fan in there.

Alan walked back to the hotel, packed up the holdall his stuff was in and quit the room. Most of his things were still in the back of the car. He asked his way to the bus station and bought a ticket to the observatory. It was 6,000. He had 10,300 left.

The bus was full, mainly of women wearing headscarves and carrying baskets and shopping bags. They drove up out of Salerno and along a straight road through flatlands near the coast, past stalls selling watermelons and pottery. Alan saw a mudspattered black buffalo standing still in a stockade, staring at something. The bus turned off into the hills. The grass by the roadside was dried yellow. Prickly pears grew on the verge. The villages were on summits and ridges, marked with churches and cypress and poplar trees. As they climbed the sun clouded over and people on the bus began talking about rain. The sun came out again and the talk stopped.

The observatory had a stop to itself: a car park with forty spaces, empty except for a police car and a Toyota minibus. Alan was the only one to get out. There was a light wind blowing. The cypress branches quivered and the prickly pears moved not at all. It was 3,000 feet up. When Alan climbed several score steps to the white domed observatory building he saw the blue and the green land and sea flattened out to the horizon, broader than his vision and silent. The words were down there and he was up above with the wind in the land of the idiots. There was no birdsong. The wind even seemed to have done for the insects.

The observatory's closed, said a policeman, coming up behind him.

Eh? said Alan.

The observatory's closed. There's no exhibition.

I've come to pick something up.

Oh yeah?

An egg.

Really? An egg that looks like the moon?

Yes.

This way. The policeman gestured for Alan to go ahead of him. Alan walked towards a door which had a poster pinned to it. It said MANY HEAVENS, ONE EARTH. There was a photograph of the world taken from space, surrounded by different representations of heavenly bodies, Mars with green canals, the sun as a complacent fat-cheeked man, the moon with the face of a woman. The face was serene, grey with pink highlights on the cheeks and the tiny lips pinched in a smirk, and black eyes.

Alan went through the door into a gallery, a broad sparsely filled room with white walls and a parquet floor and skylights. There were pictures on the walls, and glass cases. The policeman pushed Alan towards the case which was smashed, the one which was empty. There were two men standing beside it, one wearing a suit and tie and the other wearing jeans and a blue denim shirt. He had a beard and glasses and had his hands on his hips. He kept shifting his weight from one side to the other.

This one says he's come for the egg, said the policeman.

Who are you? said the bearded one. He was angry.

Alan Allen, said Alan.

Who sent you? said the one with the suit.

McStrachan, said Alan.

Who's he?

A collector. He bought the egg from Tribler. What happened?

Were you expecting him? the suit asked the beard.

I do remember something, said the beard reluctantly.

It's been nicked, said the suit. An eclipse of the moon. He grinned.

Don't do that any more, said the beard.

Are you the head of this place? said Alan.

Yes, said the beard. Dr Igliatti. Is this a big problem for you? I'm sure it'll turn up. It's very fragile. It was never blown properly.

Yes, said the suit. It's a full moon. He creased.

This man's from the police, said the doctor.

What happened? said Alan.

Someone walked in, smashed the glass and took the egg. Looks like they used their fist. There's blood on the floor.

Most of the exhibits aren't worth much, said the suit

seriously. His mouth twitched. But the value of the egg was astronomical. He doubled up again.

Alan and the doctor looked at the uniformed policeman, who shrugged.

Oh dear, said the suit, wiping his eyes. We'd best take a statement. Alan gave him the details without mentioning Deirdre and the car.

We'll get your egg back, doc, the suit said afterwards. Everyone knows what it looks like. The posters are all over the place.

But that's only a paper moon, said Alan.

You'd never get near a newsdesk with that line, said the suit. It takes more than a cheap pun to sell a story these days. Ah well. Off to the lunatics. He grinned and led the uniformed policeman out.

Alan looked round. The doctor was leaving by a different door. Alan followed him into the main observatory building where the telescope and reflector sat under the dome. The doctor climbed the steps to the platform at the foot of the telescope, sat down in an old armchair and stared at his feet with his chin resting on his hands. Alan went up and sat on a wooden stool nearby.

Are you all right? said Alan after several minutes had passed.

The doctor turned his head slowly towards him and focused on the unfamiliar life form. D'you want some wine? he said.

Sure, that'd be good.

The doctor went down the steps and disappeared

under the platform. He came back with a ten-litre plastic canister half full of red liquid and a couple of canteen glass tumblers. He put the tumblers down on the floor, unscrewed the canister lid and poured from the standing position. The stream of wine jerked from the mouth of the canister, spreading a thin rose-coloured pool across the platform and filling the glasses at the expense of a couple of lost litres.

Thanks, said Alan, taking one of the glasses from the doctor's hand. The spilled wine lapped around his feet. The air thickened with the smell of stale booze.

It seems like a waste.

A waste? said the doctor. He shook his head. There's nothing but wine around here. They've got more wine than they know what to do with. People bring me gallons of the stuff. God knows why. Maybe they've nowhere to keep it. Maybe they want something from me. I'm not grateful. I drink it, but I'm not grateful.

Alan drank. The wine was cool, watery and astringent.

What was that about lunatics? he said.

There's a mental hospital lower down. It's ridiculous to say one of them broke in, but the individual in the suit, the inspector, he likes visiting them. He wants to see if the schizophrenics laugh at his jokes. Listen, I'm sorry about the egg.

Was it worth it? Was it beautiful? Alan nervously filled his mouth with wine to wash out the feathery taste the last word left in his mouth.

He was an astronomer, said the doctor. The beauty

was in the accuracy of the work. The more it looked like the real moon the better it was. As for the other side, the woman's face, it wasn't his wife. That's a sentimental story. It was a scientific attempt to depict the substance of the ideal woman. One moon, unique, alone and unattainable. One woman the same. This story about his wife and the omelette, it's rubbish. He became obsessed with this idea of the one true woman as a heavenly object and one day his wife's face suddenly cut across his vision and he couldn't stand it and went crazy. He lost his temper. She wasn't perfect. She didn't matter. D'you want some more wine?

Their glasses were empty. Let me do it, said Alan, getting up. He set the glasses on the floor, hauled the canister over and kneeled down. Holding the canister with both hands, balancing the heavy end carefully, he didn't spill more than a glass's worth.

There's no need, said the astronomer.

Somebody must have taken trouble. Picking grapes. Pruning. Treading.

You're not from the country, are you? said the astronomer.

No.

I am. There's only one good thing about it: you can see the stars at night. If they want to bring me wine it's their problem. I can't be concerned with them up to their arses in grape skins. I'm dealing with cosmic measurements here.

He got up, picked up the glass and walked over to

the telescope. He tapped some rattling plastic keys. There was a sound from below like somebody striking sheet steel with a wooden mallet and a broad hum with squeaky highlights. The platform, the ten-foot telescope and the dome over their heads began to rotate. The astronomer drained his glass and sloshed himself another measure.

Last night I looked into the heart of a galaxy ten million years ago. You know what? There's a darkness there, at the very centre, swallowing worlds. A feeding darkness. You can't see it but you know it's there. A tiny space so heavy and dense with gravity that nothing can escape, not even light. It plucks suns, planets, unlit stars, it plucks them from space and they go rolling in. When the bodies are sucked towards the darkness they move faster and faster and get squeezed together into a disc, and they start to shine. They shine fit to blind an angel. The sun up there's no brighter than an old copper coin by moonlight. They shine because they're burning, they're being eaten, they're using each other for fuel. You can see the disc burning. It gets brighter and dimmer over a single day. It's a dance of destruction three hundred million miles across. Try lifting your face to that. A three hundred million mile inferno brighter than a billion suns. I can hear the noise it makes, like a mill-stone with stars for corn.

Alan poured himself some more wine. The platform was still rotating.

The astronomer punched a few more keys and the assembly came to a stop with a sound like ancient

trucks braking. Cosmic scale, he said. No-one under-
stands. I had an assistant once. I left her by herself one
night and came back when she wasn't expecting me.
She had the telescope lowered below the horizontal.
Below the horizontal! She was watching her parents
watching television in the village down the hill. She
was supposed to be hunting for comets. She said she
got scared looking into space. Said she'd expected to
see nebulae and the rings of Saturn and all she could
see was blackness interrupted by cold white dots, and
what was the point of spending your life staring at
places you could never visit? She made very detailed
notes on her parents. As far as observation was
concerned it was a model. The exact times her parents
got up, when they scratched themselves, even what
they appeared to have been saying to each other. But
her parents are not an astronomical phenomenon, and
after observing them she went down the road and had
breakfast with them.

I knew someone like that once, said Alan. He got old
all of a sudden. The day before yesterday. We left him
behind. I left him behind and went on ahead.

Where?

Here. Look, you're an astronomer. Help me.

The doctor poured more wine for the two of them.

What's the problem? he said.

It was going badly for me in the town of Edinburgh.
I want to start again in the town of Glasgow. To move.
People are different there, I'm sure of it. They're hard,
and they're cool, but they're warm. I want to be like

them. I've been driving since Sunday and I feel I haven't got anywhere. Nothing's changed. Except maybe the trees and the architecture and the colour of the money. And I saw a buffalo down the road.

The astronomer leaned back in the chair, took a long drink of wine and licked his lips. His eyes went out of focus. Astronomy doesn't reckon desire, he said, only energy, time and gravity. A soft, cold body – a satellite of frozen gas, say – is moving away from a fixed point in space to a different fixed point in space where it would become a hard, cool, warm body – something like a comet, perhaps.

I'm not a satellite of frozen gas, said Alan. The astronomer took no notice.

In a closed solar system, he said, all motion is repeated. The satellite's path relative to other bodies within the system is fixed. It can't shoot off by itself into space, to another system. But the path does change, with time, as the energy within the system wastes away without being renewed, and as a movement continues which is almost indistinguishable from time itself, the movement of the system relative to the universe. What's that on your hand?

I smashed a car window.

Oh yeah? Which car?

My car.

Right, said the astronomer, right. Sure you did. You think I spend so much time looking at the sky I don't know when I'm being had? Come here. He got up and switched on the rotation mechanism. Alan got up, swayed, did Al Jolson for a couple of seconds and lost his grip. He fell sideways into the pink wine puddle, landing on his thigh and left buttock and the palm of his window-smashing hand. The doctor was holding onto the keyboard with one hand and his wineglass with the other. He hurled his right foot towards Alan, connecting the point of his brown brogue firmly with the ridge of the bone on Alan's left shin, and followed through with his left foot, which did not connect. For a measurable period of time the astronomer enjoyed a condition of near-weightlessness, both his feet out of contact with the planet on which he lived, his right hand gripping the wineglass and his left no longer supported by the keyboard but clutching at it as the momentum of his body carried him through the air. At the end of the period he collided with the wet horizontal. Alan pushed himself into a sitting position, swung his legs out over the edge of the platform and jumped off. It was only five feet or so but the spin of the platform made him misjudge the trajectory and he landed poorly, fucking his right ankle. He got up and hobbled to the door. He heard the astronomer shouting over the noise of the platform motor, the sound of his feet hitting the floor as he jumped off the platform and a shout of pain.

Alan limped through to the gallery, taking the weight on his left leg, and on out into the open air. The heat and light of the afternoon stunned him and he stopped for a second.

Come back! shouted the astronomer from inside.

Alan looked round at the dark, open doorway, shaded his eyes with his hand and headed off down the road in the direction of the town of Salerno.

PART FOUR

The road twisted downhill and Alan tried a kind of run to begin with, grabbing a couple of feet forward with his left leg and dragging the right behind. Once he'd rounded several corners he sat down on a yellow rock by the side of the road, pulling in breaths of hot air. The insects were back, croaking like a male voice choir without the voice. The astronomer was to be heard still, faint further up. Come back!

Alan's body offered him a variety of pains. There was an ache behind his forehead, his mouth was dry, his stomach remembered the blow of a baseball bat, his left fist needled with cuts, his left shin expressed a swelling bruise and his right ankle was shot. Alan lifted the frayed hem of his jeans over the ankle and looked at the white skin sown with hairs. He moved the foot from side to side. Back and forward. That which had been woven together was hurt, not broken.

Alan stood up. The bag.

Come back!

He walked on down the road. His legs competed at sending pain signals. He supported the left. He was a dedicated fan of the left leg's efforts to hurt. There was more art in it. Sharper. The right was an ache. Any limb could ache.

Come on you ce-ells.

Alan came round another bend in the road. On the left, sloping downwards, was a turned-over field with fruit trees growing out of it. A woman with a headscarf was gathering sticks and twigs off the ground. She had a thin bundle of them under her arm. Alan stopped.

The woman would gather three or four sticks and straighten up and look around. It was thin pickings. She moved over to another part of the field and bent down again. She straightened up, turned and looked at Alan with her hands on her hips, resting. She looked at him in such a way that his eyes flicked to the ground to see if he had shed parts which could be used to make a fire.

The woman gathered more sticks, bound the bundle with a piece of string, put it down and looked at Alan again with her hands on her hips, for ten seconds. She walked over to one of the trees and shook the trunk. Fruit fell onto the dry brown earth. The woman took a plastic carrier bag, bent down and began dropping the fruit into it. After a minute she straightened up and looked at Alan again. She put the bag down, reached in and took out one of the fruits. She held it close to her face with her left hand, wrinkled her nose, showed her teeth and rubbed it with her right sleeve. She rubbed it against her thigh, staring at it frowning, and held it

up to the sky. A gust of wind lifted Alan's hair. He saw
that clouds had accumulated overhead on the mountain's seaward side. The woman lowered the fruit, held
it in front of her face for a second, scrutinising it, then
closed her eyes and bit into it.

Alan walked off the road into the field. He stopped
a few yards away from the woman. They were pear trees.
The woman was eating a small pear. It was rotten. He
could see how it was brown under the skin, through
and through. The woman watched him as she ate. She
was shorter than him and twice as broad. She ate the
whole pear except the stalk, which fell from her hand.
She bent down, reached into the bag, pulled out another
pear, cleaned it as before and offered it to Alan.

Here, she said.

Is it OK? he said.

Yes, it's good, said the woman.

It's not bad?

No.

Thanks. Alan took the pear and bit into it. It was
brown and rotten. He spat it out. The woman looked
down at the peary gob.

What's wrong? she said.

Alan held out the fruit to her. It's rotten. Look, it's
brown.

It's supposed to be brown. It's a sweet pear.

Oh yeah? Alan nibbled at the edge of the bite. The
flesh was sweet and rich like toffee. OK. Sorry. It's
supposed to be like that. It's good.

Alan ate the rest of the pear. The woman went on

picking fruit up. Alan threw the core away and helped her. The sky was a deep grey.

Give the tree another shake, then, eh? said the woman. Alan put his hands round the trunk and pulled it sharply towards him. The leaves shivered and a few pears fell. He pulled and pushed again, more slowly. The wind came up and lifted the leaves. They waved against the stone sky as fruit thumped into the earth.

It's going to rain, said Alan, bending down to get the pears nearest him.

You reckon? More likely they'll get the rain over the hill as usual. We haven't had a drop since June. Are you working up there? The woman nodded towards the observatory.

No.

From town?

From the town –

Got relatives in the village of Albari?

I don't know, said Alan. I haven't been there yet.

The woman laughed, straightened up and kneaded her spine. She picked up the bag full of pears, put it down again, picked up the sticks and looked at the sky. Maybe it will rain.

The wood'll get wet, said Alan.

Then it'll dry. She picked up the bag. Alan offered to help. The woman gave him the sticks. He stashed them under his arm. Snapped-off ends of twigs pressed through the teeshirt into his flesh. They walked up the field to the road and went on in the direction of Salerno.

Is it far? said Alan.

About half an hour.

Thunder sounded above and beyond them. They left the main road and walked towards the village of Albari, the woman in front, Alan a few paces behind. The woman moved slower than Alan would've, rocking slightly from side to side.

Is there some kind of harvest going on here? said Alan.

Are you looking for work?

Yeah. I need money. Enough for a bus fare and a couple of phone calls. Maybe I could pick grapes.

The grapes aren't ready.

Maybe I could plant grapes. Alan shifted the bundle of sticks from the left to the right side. A couple of small ones fell on the road. He looked over his shoulder. Let them lie.

Can you work in the kitchen? said the woman.

Yes.

You could help us. We've got a party the day after tomorrow. We'd give you 60,000 and you'd stay with us.

Great, said Alan. Eh . . . can you see the village from the observatory?

Of course, said the woman. But the doctor doesn't look on us.

I guess he thinks your movements have a limited effect on the expansion of the universe.

I don't know what he does up there apart from drink our wine. All I know is you can't raise a family with the moon for a wife.

Why do you give him wine?

Ask my daughter.

The woman stopped and turned round. It's Paolina, by the way, she said. She peered past Alan down the road.

Alan, said Alan.

Wait, said the woman. She put the bag of pears down and walked back the way she'd come. Alan watched. She went a hundred yards down the road, picked up the sticks he'd dropped and walked back.

Here, she said. You dropped these. Be careful.

I will, said Alan.

Paolina, her husband Massimo and their daughter Angela lived in a two-storey house in the village of Albari. Massimo was away from the village for a fixed period of time when he was younger and when he came back he built the house on land his parents had owned. He'd squeezed it into the crowded yellow stone fabric of the village by means of a bridge, spars, bricks, wine, persuasion and friends. There was a walled yard at the front and a vegetable garden at the back. A while previously the house had been divided into two lengthwise, with Massimo's brother's family in the other half. The two families hadn't spoken to each other for five years, ever since gold jewellery disappeared from Massimo's brother's house. They didn't speak even about the bit of land they had between them down the road. Massimo had the lower part and his brother had the upper part where the cistern was. It was difficult. It was most difficult when there'd been no rain.

Alan and Paolina got to the house around two. Paolina showed him where to dump the sticks, in a dim alley going down under the house from the yard through to the garden gate. The clouds had been fried off by the sun and it was hot. Alan's teeshirt was sopping. He dropped the sticks and worked his shoulders in the cool of the shade. His legs weren't so bad. Bodies were tougher than you knew till they'd been knocked about a bit.

Paolina took him into the house. It smelled of polish and old cheese. The doorway went straight into a big room, kitchen lounge, where a television with the sound turned down was showing a Lieutenant Pigeon video. Paolina introduced Alan to Angela, who was cutting circles out of rolled-flat dough on the kitchen table with a glass. Angela smiled and got up. She wiped the palms of her hands on her hips, on her blue cheesecloth dress. It stretched. She shook Alan's hand.

Let's eat, said Paolina.

Alan stood watching the women and MTV alternately while they moved around him. Angela put spoonfuls of soft white cheese onto the middle of the dough circles, covered them with another circle and pressed the edges down with a fork. Massimo came in with a bag of cement and a bucket of water.

Great, cement for lunch, said Angela.

I've got to do the floor, said Massimo, sitting down. Who's this?

Alan, said Angela. To help with the cooking.

We can't afford servants.

For the party.

Can he help me do the floor?

Ask him, said Angela.

Sure, said Alan.

Leave him alone, said Paolina. You do the floor. Give us some of that water.

Why? said Massimo.

You want raw ravioli? You're welcome. Angela, give your father a couple of those ravvies.

For God's sake, Mum, you've got a tap in front of you, said Angela.

We should save water.

It comes from the same tank!

No it doesn't, said Massimo. I got it from the shop on my way back from the land.

Oh, great, now we have to buy our water from the thief at the shop, said Angela.

He gave me it for nothing!

You see? He must be trying to poison us, said Paolina.

He's all right.

It's probably all his piss from the last week, said Angela.

Smell it!

Smell it? You want me to taste it?

Here, said Paolina, put some in this. She held out a saucepan.

Mum! Angela picked up a wooden spoon and battered the saucepan with it. Use the tap.

It went quiet for a moment. The TV trailed an old Madonna concert. Paolina filled the saucepan from the tap and put it on the cooker. Angela went on making ravioli. Massimo sat on a chair in the corner near a spiral stairway that led upstairs, staring down at the floor. Flies danced round the lampshade in the lounge.

If it was piss, said Massimo, the cement would be stronger.

Listen to you, said Paolina. I married a chemist.

D'you mind if I watch television? said Alan.

No! said the family together.

How many channels've you got?

Forty, said Angela.

Why've we got so many? said Paolina.

They just send them out, said Angela. You can't stop it.

You don't have to have a television, said Alan.

If we got rid of it his brother's family next door'd say we had to sell it to pay for drugs. They've no shame.

The boy's right, said Massimo. The TV's immoral. Too many young girls dancing naked.

Immoral! said Paolina. An archbishop in the house.

What young girls have you been watching? said Angela.

I haven't seen them. They were talking about it in the shop.

If you could spare the time between church business and your chemical research, cardinal, there's a floor needing fixed.

Alan picked up the TV remote control off a chest freezer in the lounge and rubberbuttoned through the channels. There was an interview with Madonna and an interview with Maradona. There were eight news channels, nine showing different forms of motor sports and three showing soap operas. The daughter of the matriarch in the first one played the stepmother of a wild child in the second, who was played by the matriarch, and in the third they played twins separated at birth. On one of the video channels the daughter-stepmother-twin was singing a three-handed version of The Man I Love with a computer-generated head and the voice of Billie Holiday. There was a trailer for the film version of *Bandicoot Bebop*.

Friday at 6.30 pm, *Bandicoot Bebop*. A shot of the one that looked like Neneh Cherry singing Ain't Misbehavin' with fifteen bars of free improvisation per syllable in front of a banner saying Dance Night at the Bandicoot. A shot of Frank watching. A shot of a hotel burning, the flames reflected on Frank and Meonie's faces.

When Frank and Meonie's world went up in flames, Frank knew it was time to leave town and the woman who loved him.

Meonie on the darkened jetty, waving and crying. Frank in a cap and donkey jacket with a duffel bag over his shoulder, hitching. Frank working behind the counter in a diner.

But the world Frank thought he'd left behind began to catch up with him.

Meonie's smiling face turned to Frank's in the desert. All these people, all these strangers, are coming to hear me sing. Meonie waving into the flash bulbs, grinning, one hand gripping an award trophy. A guy in the diner with his elbows on a newspaper, looking up at Frank. Say, did you hear another dance joint got burned down last night? That's the third this month. Somebody sure don't like jazz. Close-up of Frank, eyes, nose and mouth only. Closer shot of Meonie at the awards ceremony. Shot of Frank in the audience jumping up and screaming Why are you following me?

In a race between a man and his past, there can only be one winner.

Shot of an old man standing thigh-deep in a raging river in a storm at night, clutching a drenched boy above the waters, shouting at him. Two things you don't ever get away from, Frank, that's true love and your own damn fool self. The rest's scenery. You go all across the country and it don't matter, you can't cut 'em out.

Bandicoot Bebop. Friday, 6.30 pm. Tonight at 7 pm, Antarctic Odyssey.

Wow. A whole icefield covered in penguins.

What're those? said Paolina, looking over.

Penguins, Mum.

Oh. Paolina smoothed the tablecloth, frowning. Can you eat them?

Angela sighed, looked at Alan, and laughed. Alan smiled and switched off the TV. The ravioli was in the pot and the cutlery was on the table. Massimo got up, shook some cement onto a piece of hardboard lying on the floor, sloshed some water into it and folded it in.

D'you want to wash your hands? said Angela to Alan.

Sure.

Don't use too much water. Angela showed him the

bathroom. When he came back a couple of minutes later the three of them were sitting round the table, Paolina was dishing out the ravioli and there was a perfectly smooth area of fresh cement on the floor where some parquet tiles had been lifted up.

That's amazing, said Alan. He sat down. Massimo shrugged and looked away towards the door, then looked down at the bowl in front of him with the pasta steaming. He picked up his fork, dropped it and shouted out a vowel that died as he fell sideways under the table. False teeth flew out of his mouth and skittered across the floor. He was still on the chair but the upper half of his body was bent down under the table. He was shaking. Angela got up, took hold of his chest with both hands, kicked the chair away and laid him down on the floor on his side. She sat down beside him, placed one hand on his side and wiped a globe of foam off the side of his mouth with her skirt.

Dad, she said, stroking his side. There you go. You'll be all right.

The pills are upstairs, said Paolina. She looked over at Alan and down at his plate. What's the matter, don't you like ravioli? Eat!

Alan shovelled a ravioli moon into his mouth and chewed. The hot cheese juices burst out and ran over his tongue. It was good.

Delicious, he said. Is he OK?

He'll be all right, said Paolina. Massimo was still quivering but it was turning to breathing. Angela was stroking his side and whispering in his ear. He has fits.

He was in prison a while back and it wasn't good for him. D'you want some wine?

Alan drank the wine. It tasted of astronomy.

Maybe I should go, he said.

Don't, said Angela, looking up.

Stay and do your work, said Paolina. Lord, Angela, he's taken you at your word about cement for lunch.

Massimo's false teeth had landed in the cement, the front incisors embedded in it and the rest flying free like a tiny orthodontic monument. Paolina got up, plucked them out and went to rinse them. Alan shuddered.

Has anyone heard of a guy called Gregor Ferguson? he said.

No.

He's from town.

We're a long way from town here, said Paolina.

Yeah? said Alan. Are you sure?

My sister lives there. She moved about twenty years ago. It's fine if you've got money, but she's had trouble settling in. Getting a decent flat. None of her children have work. It's hard if you're from the country. I'm not saying Albari's not full of thieves and parasites but you can grow a bit of food here for yourself.

It's good to hear, said Alan. I was starting to think there weren't any different places any more.

The young folk are always getting in trouble with the police. There was a theatre burned down a few days ago.

That was a provocation, said Angela. There now, Dad.

There you go. She moved his head onto her lap. He whined like a dog in pain, and winced, but his breathing was steady. Yeah, the police started it. One of their people pretended to be a councillor and beat up some old woman, and her sons went out looking for the guy and that was how the trouble started. It was all planned.

I don't like it when you talk that way, said Paolina. Come and get your lunch. I'll take your father to bed. She came round and lifted Massimo up. He stood with his mouth slightly open and his eyes closed, feet together, swaying. They went slowly upstairs with the steps creaking.

Angela sat close to Alan and looked alternately into her plate and his eyes as she ate the ravioli lazily. Her forearm on the table was touching his.

How old are you? said Angela.

Twenty-one.

Are you married?

No.

Girlfriend?

I have a girl enemy.

What did she do?

Took my car and went off with another man.

What a bitch! Do you miss her?

I miss the car.

Right. I feel sorry for her now.

Ah, she doesn't need it. She isn't a bitch either. She did the right thing. She loved him more. Women love bastards more than nice guys, if only they believed it.

Are you nice, then?

No!

Is it an insult?

Yeah, it is.

Are you a bastard?

All I know is I'm not a satellite of frozen gas.

Eh? What are you? What do you do? Are you a cook?

I used to study literature at university.

Lucky you.

I didn't like it.

Why'd you do it then?

Cause I thought it'd be easy. I like to read but – Alan looked round and lowered his voice – I like to watch television as well.

Boring. What else d'you like?

Eating, drinking, driving. Masturbating.

Euh! Angela made a face and got up. She laughed. Not in this house, please. She stacked the dishes and took them over to the sink. Not while I'm looking, anyway. Come on, get to work. Wash your hands again first.

What've I got to make?

Sausage rolls.

Sausage rolls?

Yeah, sausage rolls, you know what they are, don't you?

Yeah but I don't know, I thought maybe something else . . .

Like what?

Pizza maybe.

Angela laughed loud and long. You make pizza? I

don't think so. She shook her head and turned her back to him, scrubbing the dishes.

To make the sausage rolls it was necessary to make flake pastry from scratch, which meant rolling out a wad of dough, putting a whole pound of butter in the middle, folding the dough over it, battering the package with a rolling pin and rolling the thing out flat. Alan had a few minutes before it began to melt and run and he had to put it back in the freezer and proceed with another block, all the while waving off the flies. After a time he didn't bother. He found they always flew away just before the rolling pin could press them into the dough. Another implausible achievement of evolution. After an hour or so he had several pounds of smooth sticky yellow pastry ready to roll.

Angela and Paolina were chopping and stoning olives. Angela looked over.

Keep your hands above the table where I can see them, she said. The sausage is in the fridge.

The sausage was long, rigid and thin, with a black skin, meaty inside with pearls of white fat.

This stuff? he said.

What's wrong with it? said Paolina. Was that a good pear or not?

It was a good pear –

Have another one.

I was expecting more like sausage meat.

Hm, said Paolina, hoisting a basin up onto the table and rolling up her sleeves. Wait. We'll get you on the cat and dog pie later. She and Angela laughed.

Yeah, and the cockroach dip, said Angela. They laughed again.

Alan took a block of pastry, rolled it flat, put a stick of sausage on it, rolled it up, cut the roll away from the pastry and sliced it up into short lengths. He went on doing this till he'd run out of sausage.

What's dip? said Paolina.

We should get the oven going, said Angela. She took Alan with his two hundred sausage rolls in layers of cloth in a baker's tray out of the house and down to where he'd been told to leave the sticks. She unlatched a door and they went into a cool, murky cellar filled with junk smelling of damp. There were a few tools and some big glass bottles. The rest was a mixture of wood, wickerwork, leather, dust, leaves, iron and plastic. On the right in from the door was the oven, a brick dome about a yard across, enclosing a stone floor on top of a brick platform.

Paolina came in with bowls of stuff, put them down on a heavy wooden counter like a pair of railway sleepers opposite the oven, and started breaking up the sticks and putting them into the oven through an opening at the front. Once there was a fair pile of sticks she poked in some kindling and set light to it. The sticks blazed up all at the same time, sending a blast of heat up to the oven dome. Alan and Angela put the sausage rolls onto baking trays. Paolina fed in more sticks, blinking and frowning as her face came close to the furnace heat from inside the oven. After ten minutes the flames had died down and the sticks were bright red embers in grey ash.

Paolina wrapped a wet cloth round the end of a thin broom, stuck it into the oven and shook it. Drops of water hissed onto the hot ash and stone. She swept the embers out to the edges of the oven, put the broom aside and fed the baking trays in with a wooden paddle.

They passed the rest of the day baking in the cellar. The sausage rolls came out OK, too much pastry and not enough sausage Alan thought, but Angela said they were good and Paolina didn't say anything against them. Then there were a couple of batches of pizza done on the floor of the oven, without trays.

Good anchovies, said Alan. Is there a fish market near here?

There's a supermarket in town, said Angela. They're thieves. There's a market too but it's not what it used to be. We saw a woman there trying to sell snake meat yesterday.

Snake meat? What kind of snake?

Boa constrictor, it was supposed to be. Is there any of that pastry left?

Uhuh. What did the woman look like?

Make some cream horns. There's a recipe upstairs. We're paying you, aren't we?

What's the party for?

My engagement.

Are you engaged?

No.

Angela! said Paolina. Her arms were working at a great lump in a basin. Give us a hand.

Alan went up to make the cream horns. He found

Massimo in his vest and trousers, sitting on the chair in the corner near the stair, looking at the floor.

Are you OK? said Alan.

Massimo waved him away with his hand, not looking at him.

Can I get you something?

Massimo shook his head.

Alan fetched the pastry out of the freezer and sprinkled some flour on the table. He was being not looked at very hard. It was a bad feeling. Something had to be said. It couldn't be conversation because he didn't have any conversation. Nice weather. Apart from it not raining for two fucking months. Nice place you've got here. Nice daughter you've got here. Not that he'd. Not that he wouldn't he meant, he certainly would given the chance. And then he'd be marrying her and'd inherit it all when Massimo died, which he soon would, and'd inherit Paolina too. A black widow, cooking, cleaning and complaining when they slept in of a morning.

Looking forward to the party? said Alan.

Massimo shook his head.

You're right, said Alan. Last time I went to a party I was lied to. Promises were made. Somebody offered me some business and I took it on. I was an idiot.

Something like a smile haunted Massimo's mouth though he didn't look up.

And I met a woman. I thought she was nice, I thought she liked me, she was good-looking –

Stop! shouted Massimo. He stood up and looked at Alan. Alan took a step back and gripped the rolling pin with both hands. Stop. Have some dignity. Have some dignity, would you not, in my house?

I'm sorry, said Alan, burning red.

I don't ask you to be sorry. I said dignity! D'you understand?

No.

Massimo went upstairs and Alan went on with the cream horns. It took him an hour to make the horn shells. He took them down into the sweating bakehouse-smelling basement and handed them over. It was the last batch of the day.

Alan went into the garden with Angela to get some cucumbers for dinner. They were small, thick and hard, a dark blackish green streaked with yellow. The garden had a few cherry and lemon trees and divisions of vegetables, row by row, tomatoes, aubergines, potatoes, lettuces and beans. Half a dozen chickens were foraging in the lee of the house. Over on the left the village curved along the ridge of a hill, red roofs among the trees and the white church spire. Up beyond the village there was a higher ridge, a few hundred feet above them, and another village. The slope rising to the other village was steep, it was a wonder the pines could stand upright on it. Further still, beyond the higher village, was the observatory, a white bump, hard to see through a smudge in the air.

Is that smoke? said Alan.

A fire, said Angela. They sent a helicopter to drop water there yesterday. The woods've been burning for months.

Too bad for the astronomer, eh? He can't see the fires in heaven for the fires on the ground.

Angela laughed, and frowned. Have you been there? she said. Did you meet him?

Yes. I meant to ask: why do you give him wine? He's not grateful.

He's supposed to marry me, said Angela. She grinned. I don't give him wine! It's my parents. Nice, eh? Like he'd bear going through with it only if he was drunk. True. There are guys like that. I know some. Not him.

The light started to go. There was the groan of a badly tuned car engine from another part of the village. Alan looked to see where the sound was coming from. He saw white houses turning blue-grey in the twilight, hiding the roads and cars between them. There was something fucking miserable about hearing a car travelling in the country when you couldn't see it and when you were standing still. There was maybe some pale anxious face behind the windscreen peering out for signs along the darkening road. He'd got used to seeing Deirdre's face lit by the headlights of approaching cars or the brightening and fading of streetlights on interchanges and ring roads. She'd lean forward in her seat as if she'd get there sooner that way.

A telephone rang inside the house.

Is that yours? said Alan.

Uhuh, said Angela.

I didn't know you had one.

Of course we do.

Can I use it?

Not for expensive calls.

Maybe in part-payment.

Maybe. After the party.

The telephone stopped ringing.

I used to work at the observatory, said Angela. It was a holiday job. I was his assistant.

Are you an astronomer too?

I study sociology. I didn't think he'd mind me using the telescope to make observations of the village. But he did. He broke off our engagement.

Wouldn't it've been easier to do your observations down here?

You miss things. The pattern. And particular events. I saw a suicide. Someone put an electric heater in their bath. They were very relaxed. They lay down in the bath with their eyes closed and held the heater above them with both hands for a long time. I was about to run to the phone when they dropped it into the water and the light went out.

Why are you having the party if the doctor doesn't want to get married?

Maybe he'll change his mind. Did he say anything to you?

No.

Angela laughed so loud that a chicken which'd found something juicy near her feet ran away in terror. Oh dear. You know how to cheer a woman up, don't you?

No.

Dinner was the ravioli they hadn't eaten before, fried

slices of beef and salad, and the pears, and wine. The old Madonna concert was playing quietly on TV.

They blocked the cistern, said Massimo.

Nobody spoke for about five minutes after that, they ate, slicing, spearing and chewing, to the tap and squeak of fork prongs on china.

So get them to unblock it, you old goat, said Paolina. We need rain.

Maybe Alan'll bring it, said Angela.

They all looked at Alan the rainmaker.

See what I can do, said Alan, grinning.

What can you do? said Massimo.

Nothing.

Hn. Massimo harpooned a trapezoid of steak. We'd be better praying.

Oh yeah? said Angela.

To the Virgin.

Do you have a virgin in the village? said Alan with interest.

Some half-chewed steak went up Angela's nose.

The Virgin, said Massimo, not a virgin, The Virgin. The Madonna of the Smile. When the truly devout make an offering to her, her image smiles.

Life is a mystery, observed Madonna from the lounge.

How much would it cost to make her laugh? said Alan.

It's not the offering, said Massimo, it's the faith.

Couple of chickens would probably do it, said Paolina.

Mum! said Angela.

Not to make her laugh, to make it rain, I mean.

What, does she eat chickens too? said Alan.

No, but the priest does, said Angela. He passes them on to God.

Your shame'll kill you before He does, said Massimo.

Can the priest fix it with God? Couple of chickens seems cheap.

Cheap? said Paolina. Listen to him. You try living on an invalid's pension.

I don't know, said Angela. Depends on whether you can bribe God in the first place.

Shut your mouth! said Massimo. What's your astronomer doing about the rain, eh? What's your scientist doing? He spends his time staring at the moon instead of worrying about the ground that's got to feed him! He should be down here working out a way to make the clouds burst on us instead of raining on the heathens over the hill. I tell you I see more sign of God's work in Albari than I do of science. Why should I even believe your astronomer exists when he never comes to the house? I leave half of last year's wine at his door and he never comes out to meet us, he never shows his face. I don't ask him for miracles. I ask him to honour his promise to my daughter, but I'd be better getting the chance of a smile from the Virgin with my wine than making my offerings to him. You give me a choice of who to believe in? Why should I believe in an invisible man instead of an invisible God? Eh? Eh? Eeeeeeeeeeh . . . Massimo fell off his chair into another fit. His eyes were screwed up and his teeth were bared, his fists were clenched tight, his forearms held up against his chest, bumping against it. He was fighting it this time. He hadn't finished. His speech or his dinner, again.

Why don't you go for a walk round the village? said Paolina to Alan.

Yeah I will, thanks. Alan wiped his mouth with a napkin and got up. Angela was down on the floor with Massimo, holding him.

See you later, Angela, said Alan.

See you, said Angela, not looking up. Alan went outside.

It was muggy: hotter out than in. The darkness wrapping the village was pierced by small, bright white streetlights. They made sharp lit spaces with the jagged edges of shadows curling back around them. Music came from somewhere down the road. A baby's cry and the warning shout of an old woman sounded from the same open doorway. Impossible to tell which came first or if the baby and the old woman spent their days anticipating each other. Three or four people in jeans and teeshirts sat on a wall, murmuring and laughing. It was too dark to see their faces.

Alan walked towards the music. The street was steep and narrow with houses rising up and leaning towards each other on either side. Half of the doorways had sentinels, a couple of old guys on chairs in vest and shirt and hat and big guts, or old women in aprons and headscarves, not saying anything, hardly even watching, just sitting there and passing the time away with dying. Some of them called Good evening to Alan as he went past. He kept on without answering at first, then started saying Good evening back. After a bit he said Good evening first, and half of them greeted him back and half of them went on sitting out the time till sleep as if he wasn't there at all.

The road led down to a square where a concert was in progress with a few hundred people watching. A four-piece band was playing some boppy keyboard-heavy number Alan'd never heard. A six-year-old girl had got up on stage, a platform at one side of the square, and was doing all the moves from the old Madonna concert. She rubbed the palm of her hand down the inside of her groin, she grabbed her hair behind her head and ran her fingers through it and did pelvic thrusts. The audience was delighted.

Alan spotted a bar on the far side of the square and moved towards it. There was a line of cars parked outside. One of them looked like his. It was the same colour. The driver's side passenger window was taped up with a sheet of polythene. It was his.

Alan went up to the car, looked around, put his hands on the roof and peered in through the glass. No-one there. Nothing of Mike's or Deirdre's, a few things of his in the back.

There was a table in the bar from where he could watch the car. He ordered a coffee, taking his cash down to 9,000. It was coming up for 10 pm. The bar was almost empty. Three teenage girls who'd been eating ice cream left soon after he came in, and there was a drift of guys in and out to lean on the bar and talk about football and what shite the concert was compared to last year. They drank beer mostly, looked at Alan when they came in, said hello and ignored him. Outside on stage someone was crooning a slow number. Some of the audience were singing along. The song ended and there was a barrage of cracking sounds around the square: fireworks went up. There were screams and cheers. Deirdre walked out of the crowd, holding the car key in front of her. Alan stood up as she fitted the key into the lock. He felt dizzy, and some chemical flooded his chest which'd be banned if only it could be synthesised. She looked over the roof and saw him. Her eyes dropped, her mouth opened slightly and she looked no happier. After a moment she withdrew the key and, looking down at the ground, walked into the bar.

Alan held out his hand, palm-up. Deirdre put the keys into it and sat down.

Thanks, said Alan. I guess I'll see you sometime.

Don't go, said Deirdre.

No. I will.

Where?

I'm staying with a family here.

Oh. Nice.

It's work.

Oh.

Are you OK?

Uhuh. Fine.

Mike?

Fine. Everything's fine.

Good. I'll see you then.

See you.

It's better if I go.

Uhuh.

You don't like me. I don't like you.

Right.

Are you sure you're OK?

I said so, didn't I?

Are you crying?

No.

D'you want a drink?

No.

Alan went to the bar and got another coffee and a whisky. He put them down in the middle of the table and sat down opposite Deirdre. She was wiping her nose with a paper hankie.

How's the car? said Alan.

Fine. Deirdre took a sip of whisky and put the glass back. You didn't think I could drive.

No. It never occurred to me. Where did you go?

Away from you.

Yeah.

Sorry.

Don't say sorry all the time. It's the worst thing about you.

Sorry. Deirdre finished the whisky and moved on to the coffee. Alan watched as she tilted the cup. Her fingers were shaking.

Got any money? he said.

No. Have you?

Three and a half. I'm supposed to get paid the day after tomorrow. Where's Mike?

God knows. Or maybe not: Mike thinks that God doesn't know. He's looking for paradise. That's what he said. He said a lot of things. He kept quoting *Paradise Lost*. Not quoting, he hates that word. He says quoting is what dilettantes do. You have to know a book well enough to compose it all fresh in your head every time, he says, and then it's speaking the words, not quoting. Did you read it?

I was supposed to. I didn't finish it.

If you ever meet him again don't tell him that.

Where is he?

Somewhere in town. He followed us. He followed you I think, not me. I wanted to get away from you and be with him. I wanted to take him home. You don't know what's in my mind, what I remember about him from before, do you? When his certainty was about me instead of about angels and professors and demons. Me, me! When I was the aim and I was the journey's end. He looked at me then like he looks now at things nobody else can see. You remember that, when he seemed to be staring at nothing? Six months ago I came across him sitting like that, and he came out of it as soon as he saw me. It was me he'd been seeing. Now he stares the same way and I'm there next to him. So the latest thing is he's gone off to look for paradise. OK, sure, he's insane. We were heading out of town. It was dark. He looked out the window and said to me to stop the car. I did, he got out and walked away into it. The darkness. Speaking about destruction and salvation. I didn't even go after him.

How did you know I was here?

I didn't. I saw the posters for the exhibition at the observatory. I didn't fancy the road up the mountain at this time so I thought I'd stop here for the night.

Alan stood up.

Where are you going? said Deirdre.

The church, said Alan. D'you want to go?

Why?

Why not? They've got a virgin there.

They left the bar and crossed the square. There were still a lot of folk from the concert milling around. The crowd thinned out closer to the church, which was down a side street opening out into another, smaller square. Steps about twice as high as Alan led to heavy old wooden doors starred with iron spikes. Light from inside rimmed a small door set into one of the big ones. Alan took hold of an iron ring, twisted it and opened the little door. A blast of stone-chilled air raised the hair on his bare arms and he shivered as they went in. There was a hallway and more doors. They went through to the main vaulted space, a hall of gold, saints and candles, decorated with ornate patches of darkness. Deirdre crossed herself.

Behind the pillars to one side two nuns were winching the Madonna of the Smile off its plinth onto something like a sedan chair covered with a white cloth fringed with gold. A priest was directing them, sometimes stretching out his hand as if to guide the swaying virgin, hung from chains, but never touching it.

What's going on? whispered Alan. Are they Satanists?

It's for a procession, you prat, whispered Deirdre. They'll take it round the village.

What, to make it rain?

How should I know?

You crossed yourself when you came in so you obviously know something.

It's automatic. What're you after in here? I don't like these places. I feel I should be wearing tights and perfume and waiting for hours for some rite to be done.

Two nuns don't make a rite.

Deirdre slid down onto a raffia chair and folded her face in her fingers, shaking her head.

Are you going to pray? said Alan.

What if I did?

Can I listen?

It wouldn't be out loud.

Right. I thought I'd make an offering.

I didn't imagine you believed in that.

It's not believing. I've only got three and a half left and I reckon a lottery ticket costs more than that so might as well, eh? It'd look good with the old guy at the house. Maybe if it rained then they'd give me extra.

Maybe, said Deirdre, staring at the altar. She turned round to him, suddenly focused. They're not just old though, are they? You're chasing someone in that house.

She's about to get married, said Alan.

I knew it. You're such a quiet cunning bastard. You would get into her panties as well, I can see it, for three and a half and a lucky shower. What's she like?

She's not stupid. She doesn't believe in the power of

virgins. It's bound to rain eventually, of course. Everyone here must be praying every night. Every night there must be some different old boy who gets out his special heavy duty rain prayer and whichever night the storm comes, it's him who takes the credit.

And every night some different old boy beats up his wife and kids, said Deirdre. Someone's bound to be bruised and bleeding just before the rain falls and the fucker looks up from the face to the drops on the windowpane and thinks to himself yes, I did it.

You sound as if you were there, said Alan.

Deirdre knelt down on the round red cushion on the floor, clasped her hands together and rested them on the back of the chair in front, bent her head down and closed her eyes. We never had to pray for rain when I was growing up, she said.

Alan took the 3,500 out of his wallet and went over to the priest. The Madonna was settled on the chair and the nuns were adding accessories of gold and damask.

Can I make an offering? whispered Alan.

Who to? said the priest, not whispering. He smelled of tobacco and old wardrobes.

The virgin, said Alan more loudly.

What kind of offering?

This, said Alan, holding up the folded notes in his hand. The priest took the notes, unfolded them and reckoned the value. He stuck out his lower lip, shook his head, looked at Alan, held the notes out to him for a second and withdrew them till they were held just above the swell of his stomach.

D'you have something to confess? he said.

Not to you, said Alan.

Son, you can't buy forgiveness, said the priest. He looked down at the slim grubby banknotes. Not at this price, anyway. Is this all you've got?

I was just wanting some rain, said Alan.

Rain. How much would you like? Forty days and forty nights or would a lesser deluge be enough for you? Why can't you get down on your knees and pray like everyone else?

I heard the virgin took offerings, said Alan.

She takes faith, worship and adoration, my son, said the priest. What do you want to do? Tuck it into her waistband as she comes past?

Never mind, then, said Alan, reaching out for the money. The priest moved his hand away and behind his back, lifting the tails of his cassock and slipping the notes into his back trouser pocket in one smooth movement.

Hey, said Alan. What are you, her manager?

The church doesn't repair itself, my son, said the priest. Your charity's noted.

OK, said Alan. So you'll put in a word about the rain?

I will. The priest shook Alan's hand, blessed him and winked. Alan walked away.

His guts dropped for a second when he couldn't see Deirdre praying. But she'd only got up and was waiting by the door.

How was your praying? he said.

I'm a con merchant, said Deirdre. There wasn't anything, just me kneeling and thinking.

They went outside and stood in silence in the square, about two feet apart, looking at each other. It was like tearing up blank sheets of paper one after the other and throwing them away, not even trying to write on them.

I'd better go, said Deirdre.

Where?

Is it all right if I sleep in the car tonight?

Uhuh.

Alan, can you lend me a few thousand?

I just gave my last cash to the virgin.

Oh. OK.

What happened to yours?

Mike's got it.

What? Fucking bastard!

I gave it to him! I'll sign on tomorrow.

Have you eaten today?

Deirdre shrugged.

You should have said. Come back with me. There's a skipload of party snacks in the house. They won't mind.

Will they not?

Of course they won't. If they do what's the worst that can happen?

They could beat us to death.

Right enough, they could.

They walked back through the main square. The band was packing up, taped music was coming from the speakers. They failed on the bass notes. It was nearly eleven and there were more people than before, in their best clothes. Children were running from family to family like rabbits in a field. On every side women were looking after them with doubtful smiles and turning back to men, single fingers flicking their hair away from their eyes, and old men were in groups, going through their sufferings and denouncing other men's sons. Alan found the street leading back to the house. It was dark and quiet after the square but not cooler, still hot. He looked up and saw the stars. They heard the crack of fireworks behind them and thin yellow light washed over the sky.

A dog barked in the distance. There was always a dog.

There's always a dog, said Alan. How come they wrote about nightingales? Didn't they have dogs in those days?

They spent more time in woods, away from people and dogs.

In a room in a building they were passing a pot came crashing down onto something, a cooker maybe. Two voices, a man and a woman's, rose and fell.

I used to share a room with my sister that had a window out onto the street, said Deirdre. Late at night you'd lie in bed and hear the voices coming and going as the couples walked by and whatever they said you imagined them better-looking than they were. Once I got up to look and the guy had eruptions all over his face and eyes about half an inch apart and the girl was a big fat thing with burn marks on her cheekbones. If you didn't look though you wanted to be outside, going past the windows in the dark, maybe hiding in other folks' gardens and looking in to see what they were doing.

We could do that.

I tried. I got frightened. They can come up behind you too easily. There's no protection. You see the family in their lounge watching TV and they look as if they know what they're doing. That's when you start looking over your shoulder and you want to be indoors yourself.

The door to the house wasn't locked. There was a small lamp on in the kitchen. The party food was laid out on the lounge table and the freezer on big plates covered in dishcloths. They stood still in the doorway for a while, listening, and went in.

Sit down, said Alan. He fetched a plate and piled a handful of sausage rolls, a small pizza, a cream horn and some bits of pastry dipped in honey on it. When he put it down on the kitchen table in front of Deirdre she took two sausage rolls and stuffed them in her mouth. She chewed, nodding and shaking her head and humming. Alan fetched a bottle of wine from under the sink and a couple of glasses. It was two thirds full. He filled the glasses to within half an inch of the top and sat down opposite Deirdre. He lifted his glass, said Cheers and drank half. Deirdre downed a third of hers and started assaulting the pizza even while she was still chewing the rolls. The cheese had hardened to a shiny hard plastic consistency and the dough'd gone brittle.

Not so good cold, said Alan.

It's great, said Deirdre.

The family's very hospitable, said Alan.

I can see that, said Deirdre. She finished the wine.

Alan filled her glass again, topped up his own and fetched a fresh bottle. He sawed the top of the plastic stopper off with a serrated chopping knife.

Try the cream horn, said Alan. It's delectable. He emptied his glass and poured himself another.

Deirdre finished off the pizza and the sausage rolls. She washed it down and took a bite out of the horn.

Very erotic, said Alan.

You're drunk.

I don't believe so, woman.

You're a cheap drunk.

Have another horn.

Is that all you can think about?

You've got a dirty mind.

Here, did they make this by treading on the grapes with their bare feet?

Yes. But they washed them first. They're exceptionally clean people.

Deirdre got up and walked through to the lounge, taking her drink with her.

Where are you going? said Alan, getting up and going after her.

None of your business. Deirdre was lifting the cloths covering the plates.

Alan drained his glass and looked into the bottom. There was a half-circle of dark crimson sediment oozing down and collecting in the lower edge.

I feel like smashing this glass, he said.

Deirdre took it from him and dropped it on the floor. It smashed and the intact bottom section rolled on its side towards the doorway and fell over. She smiled at Alan and pushed another cream horn into her mouth.

Alan sighed, went back to the table, lifted the wine bottle to his mouth and drank from it. The sour darkness of it was so good he had to fill his mouth with it, then try and fill his throat, and his stomach. He misfired and coughed and wine splattered from his lips and pierced the phlegm and went down his nostrils.

Deirdre was coming towards the table with the plate of cream horns. Have some water, she said.

No, said Alan, coughing. No water. Not till it rains.

Deirdre's heel snagged a curved bit of glass, curve down, and glided over the floor. She fell and the cream horns were projected over a wide area. Alan got up and put his foot on one of them. He stood still with the sole of his boot floating on a cushion of smeared filling and looked down at Deirdre. She was lying on her back with her arms by her side on the floor, soft side up. She was laughing. Her legs were drawn up halfway and turned to the side and her black cotton skirt had ridden up over her thighs.

I can see your knickers, said Alan.

Good, said Deirdre, turning over on her side and presenting her arse. Is that good for you?

That's great. I like it when they're caught in the cleft like that.

D'you want to keep them? I don't mind.

They're nothing without you.

God, you're sentimental! You're incapable of keeping up a dirty conversation. Can you pass me my wine?

Alan knelt down on the floor by Deirdre. Did you hear thunder?

No.

There was a piece of glass stuck in Deirdre's right thigh, about halfway between the hip and the knee. A dribble of blood came from it. Deirdre started to move to get up.

Wait! said Alan.

What?

Wait. Don't move.

Is it so interesting?

Wait. There's a piece of glass stuck in your leg.

I can't feel it.

It's not big. A triangle.

Why don't you take it out?

Deirdre's thigh was taut, white, smooth and freckled. The glass had to come out, of course, but as long as it was in there you had the anticipation.

I'm enjoying looking forward to taking it out, said Alan.

Deirdre laughed. Alan reached for the bit of glass, took it out of the cut and threw it away. He leaned forward and down, spat on the cut, wiped the blood and saliva away with the back of his hand and wiped his hand on his jeans. He looked Deirdre in the face. She looked him in the eyes. Alan pushed his left arm in between Deirdre's back and the floor and ran his right hand up the inside of her thigh, put his fingers into her panties and stroked her lips.

Where are you sleeping? said Deirdre.

I don't know, said Alan. I'd rather do it here.

I don't want to be fucked on a strange kitchen floor with bits of glass and pastry all over the place.

God, just you saying that gets me going.

Deirdre took hold of Alan's wrist, pulled his wriggling hand out of her knickers and got up.

Maybe there's a bedroom for you somewhere, she said.

Be quiet, then, said Alan. He took the wine bottle. They went to the spiral staircase and climbed up. Alan lifted his head to just above floor level and looked around a small dark room. Straight ahead was an open door, half glass, leading onto a balcony. Enough light shone up from downstairs to see another door on the right, slightly open. There was a wardrobe and a couple of trunks: no bed.

Alan climbed into the room as silently as he could with Deirdre following behind. He crept towards the balcony. A floorboard went down about an inch with a squeal like a pig at slaughter. He stopped for a second and moved on. He reached the balcony and walked into the new warm medium of night air. He put his free hand on the railings. There were leaves and tendrils there. He looked down into the garden and up at the sky and drank from the bottle. Deirdre was beside him, looking anxiously towards the lights of the village. He put his arm around her waist. She turned to him. He moved his face towards hers to kiss her and she turned away. He let go.

Sorry, she said.

I'm getting used to it.

You fucking bastard.

What?

Give us the bottle, eh? Alan handed it to her and she took a big drink and gave it back. He had a couple of swigs.

Look, he said. Can you see anything up there?

Deirdre looked up at the sky. No, she said.

Neither can I. That must mean it's going to rain, eh? Look! Look! Did you see that?

What?

Lightning.

Was it not fireworks?

No, it was on the far side of the hill.

Summer lightning.

Alan put the bottle down and stood behind Deirdre. He cupped the underside of her breasts and rubbed her nipples through the cloth with his thumbs. She leaned her head back against his shoulder. He moved his hand down and under her teeshirt to stroke her belly.

Wait, said Deirdre.

What?

Wait. Deirdre walked further along the balcony. It ran the length of the house. There were two more doors. The first one led to a small bedroom with a single bed made up. Alan went inside, sat on the bed and took off his boots and socks and teeshirt. Deirdre was still on the balcony. Alan went back out: she'd moved further along and was standing by the third door, looking in through the glass.

Hey! whispered Alan. Deirdre looked round. Come on. He gestured with his hand. Deirdre waved come on to him and pointed into the house. Alan walked along towards her. There was a roll of thunder from a long way off: he stopped and looked out towards the invisible hill. He went up to Deirdre and looked into the third room. He couldn't see anything. Another dog, or the same one, started yapping in the village.

I can't see anything, he whispered in Deirdre's ear.

Wait. Keep looking, she said. She took the edge of the slightly open door in her hand and swung it wide open, exposing the cooler darkness inside like an empty grave. They stood still and looked. Alan heard a faint whistling sound. Snoring! He looked at Deirdre and she looked at him at the same moment and they both pressed their lips together not to laugh. They listened for a while longer and picked out the sound of three people sleeping: one snoring, one breathing loudly, the other breathing quietly and turning over every once in a while. Alan still couldn't see deep inside the room but there was a shape closer to the balcony, within arm's reach. It was a four-legged table the size of a kitchen stool. On it was a white dial telephone.

Alan slowly sank to a squatting position, steadied himself with his right hand palm down on the floor and knelt in the doorway. He wiped his hands on his chest, leaving two trails of damp coolness, and nipped skin from his lower lip with his teeth. He moved his right hand behind the telephone, found the cord and tugged at it. There was some play. He took the cord in his left hand

and wound loose coils onto it with his right: three. He shook the cord off, let it drop and moved back a little on his knees. He wiped his hands again, licked his lips and took firm hold of the edges of the table. He lifted it off the floor and moved it a foot closer so it was halfway out the doorway. He shuffled away again: his back was against the railings of the balcony. He lifted the table again and put it down. He looked over at Deirdre, who was standing a few feet along the balcony, closer to the stairs, watching him. She looked worried. She nodded.

Alan breathed in deeply and put his hand around the receiver. He lifted it. The bell inside the telephone chimed once. Alan's heart started battering to get out. He breathed deeply, running his tongue round and round his lips till they stung. Still quiet in the bedroom. He waited a minute and put the receiver to his ear. The dialtone sounded like a factory hooter. He started dialling the thirteen digits of McStrachan's number. A preponderance of nines and zeroes: he hauled the dial round and let it go clattering back to the stop. It completed the thirteenth spin. Alan stared into the jumping, popping grains of darkness and heard the sound of the absent presence of the ether on the line. He swallowed. The number rang out.

Hello, said McStrachan.

It's Alan Allen.

Can you speak up?

No. It's Alan Allen.

Did you get it?

No. It's been stolen.

I know.

Why did you ask if I'd got it then?

It's been found. The police have it. In the town of Vladikavkaz. You just have to go and pick it up.

I'm not moving from here till I get my money.

I can't give you the cash if you haven't got the egg.

You'll not get it unless I get half of what you promised up front.

It's a deal.

Is it?

In your account tomorrow.

I'll check.

I should hope so.

What's this about a hospital?

I don't understand.

Last time I called. A woman answered and started going on about a hospital.

My sister. She worked in a hospital during the war and thinks she still does. Barking mad. It's an unusual case. She thinks the family estate is a coal mine. I should stop her answering the phone.

What kind of hospital? said Alan.

Who knows? Check your balance tomorrow and get cracking. McStrachan put down the phone.

Alan put down the receiver. The sound of the bell didn't seem so loud. He stood up, lifted the table and phone and with two careful steps returned it to its place. He looked at Deirdre, grinned and did a silent hipswaying victory dance. She beckoned him over and whispered in his ear: I'm going to kiss you now.

246

The phone began to ring. Deirdre gave a short high sound as if she'd been kicked and put her hand over her mouth. Alan found his left hand gripping his throat and his right wet on the cool metal of the balcony. Light blinded them from the room. Angela was by the light switch in an ankle-length white nightie, blinking Morse code as she looked at them. She picked up the phone.

Yeah, what is it? she said, rubbing her eyes with the heel of her hand. What're you talking about? I was asleep. I wasn't – That's shit. What're you watching the house for anyway?

There was movement from a double bed in the far corner of the room. Who is it? said Paolina.

You've been at the wine again, haven't you? Angela said down the phone. God, you're such a wanker. Listen, there's another couple on the balcony. It's true! D'you want to speak to them? Look through your telescope again. D'you really think I look like that, white and skinny like a zombie or something?

Fuck you, said Deirdre, making a move for the bedroom. Alan held her back with his arm across her chest.

I don't know what they're doing there! Coming to rob us, maybe? I told you, I was asleep. I'm telling you, look at him! Would I shag that? Would anyone?

She's out of order, said Deirdre.

I keep telling you! shouted Angela. It's got nothing to do with me! Yeah, right. Right. Yeah. Go back to your black hole. Marry that. Yeah, if your prick was as big as your ego you might just touch the sides.

Angela! shouted Paolina, getting out of bed. Angela put the phone down. Paolina strode towards her from the far corner and Deirdre went for her from the balcony with Alan holding onto her wrist, trying to pull her back.

You shouldn't speak to your fiancé like that! screamed Paolina.

I don't know who you are but nobody speaks about me and my boyfriend like that, said Deirdre.

I'm sorry, said Alan.

Angela sat down on her bed, slapped her hands on her thighs, shook her head and laughed. Oh dear, she said.

There was an explosion from the double bed. With a movement that didn't seem possible, like he'd clawed himself straight upright by his toes alone, Massimo burst from the sheets in striped pyjama bottoms and a white vest and stood there, legs apart, arms slightly away from his body, jaw moving from side to side. He was humming and chanting a single, loud, low note. His eyeballs were almost all white.

Dad, said Angela, getting up slowly and fingering the buttons on her nightie.

And she calls me a zombie, said Deirdre.

Shut up, said Alan.

Massimo began to lean. Angela and Paolina lunged for him. He propelled himself off the bed and smashed into the wall opposite, taking the force on his chin and upper chest. The women held him for a second and he broke free, charging into the wall on the other side of the room, hitting it with his side. The building shook. He threw himself under the bed, growled to a crescendo and tipped it over with a heave of his shoulders. Angela and Paolina stepped back. Deirdre put her thumbnail in her mouth. Tears appeared in her eyes. Angela turned to her and Alan. Help us.

Massimo rammed a full-length mirror in a wardrobe door with the top of his head. The mirror fractured with a smear of blood where the head had hit it. He stepped back, stunned, leaning further and further over backwards, and fell, landing on the floor on four corners of his body and arching his back. He rolled at speed towards the nearest wall. Paolina ran to him and tried to pin his shoulders to the ground. Angela, Alan and Deirdre came over. Alan and Deirdre took an arm each and Angela grabbed his ankles. Massimo's foot came up and caught Angela on the chin, knocking her head back. She clenched her jaw and forced the foot back down. When she opened her mouth slightly to draw breath, Alan saw blood between her teeth. Massimo arched his back, tried to writhe, and screamed.

There you go, said Paolina.

Hush now, said Angela. She turned aside and spat blood out onto the floor.

Massimo moaned and twitched for a time, growing more still. Angela moved forward on her knees, astride his legs, and lay down on top of him so that her head lay on his chest. She murmured to him, half-singing. Paolina let go of his shoulders, went out of the room and came back with a wet flannel. She began mopping his head. Alan and Deirdre let go his arms, stood up and backed towards the balcony. There was a hissing noise from outside.

It's raining, said Alan.

Good, said Paolina, without looking up.

Alan leaned out from the balcony and stretched his hand into the rain. He didn't feel anything. The hissing faded. There was a smell of watered life and a sound of crickets. The moon came out.

It's stopped, he said. Will it've helped?

No, said Paolina.

Deirdre went downstairs. Alan put on his boots and teeshirt and went after her. They cleaned up the kitchen, rearranged the cream horns on the plate, covered it with the cloth and left the house.

They walked back towards the car. The village was quieter and darker. No more fireworks, only the dog. The bar was shuttered and the stage cleared. The sound of the car doors opening bounced off the walls of buildings around the square. Alan sat in the driver's seat and started switching the lights on and off. Deirdre's knuckle rapped gently on the passenger window and he opened her side. She sat down.

What are you doing? she said.

Pressing a button and bringing a machine to life, said Alan, staring at the dashboard brightening and darkening. On and off. You can't go wrong.

There's plenty of petrol.

Alan took his finger off the switch and rested his forehead on the wheel with his eyes closed.

Are you going back? said Deirdre.

Alan turned his head to rest it on his side and looked at Deirdre. Worried. About herself, or about him, or hiding something. Her eyes were wide: she was looking beyond him. He sat up straight and looked out of the door window. There wasn't anything, the dark steel shutter on the bar, a motorbike, a stack of cardboard boxes. He turned back to Deirdre.

I thought you'd seen something, he said.

No. I was looking at you.

I thought maybe . . .

No, Alan, no. Honestly, I swear I don't know where he is.

How'd you know that was what I was thinking? said Alan, glancing round again, behind him as well this time.

It was obvious. How're you feeling?

It was going fine at the house until you turned up.

You didn't have to ask me back.

No, I did have to ask you back because I'm stuck with you. I can't understand it because you're in love with a psychopath, not me, but still I'm stuck with you. It's ordained, pre-programmed. It's genetic.

He's not a psychopath.

Alan started the engine and pulled away from the kerb.

Where are we going? said Deirdre.

Glasgow.

Alan found the road to the coast and headed for Salerno. He had trouble with the bends coming down through the hills. He came at them too fast and only stayed on the road by shooting across on the wrong side.

What's wrong? he said.

You're drunk.

Coming up to a village Alan swerved to avoid a car and ran onto the verge. He braked sharply, the car began to swing, he fought the swithering wheels with his wrists. The car scraped against a wall on his side and stopped. Alan wound down the window: it'd sounded bad inside but the car had barely kissed the wall, it was more paint-work than metalwork. He looked around. There was open ground, tufts of grass and dirt, ahead and behind: the open road to the left. The moon had come up and there was a fair amount of light. No-one could get in on his side or open the door with the wall there.

Good, he said. Let's sleep here. Tomorrow's Friday.

I want to go to the beach, said Deirdre.

PART FIVE

The wall kept them cool in shadow as the sun rose. Thirst woke Alan. His head hurt and there was no money. He tried to open the door: it wouldn't open. The wall stopped it. Condensation blurred the windows. Alan's mouth was like a shoe into which a foot with a thick dry sock fitted. He drew a vertical line through the wet on the side window and looked at the glistening spot on his fingertip. He turned to the bottom left hand side of the window and licked a broad upward stripe with his tongue, sucking at the glass. It cooled the tongue and moistened it but there was no satisfaction and a taste of stale rain.

He looked down at Deirdre. She'd put the seat back to the horizontal and was still asleep. He leaned over, pulled the far door handle and prodded the door open. He swung his legs up and over Deirdre, leaned forward to grip the outside edge of the car roof with his hands and pulled himself outside.

The sun steamed on the top of mist in a field of green shoots. Alan knelt down on the ground and felt the damp seep into his jeans. He ran his fingers through the grass and they became wet with dew but when he held them up in front of his face there were no drops on them, only a sheen.

He got back in the car, started the engine, and giving it big revs scraped it off the wall. He reversed back onto the road.

What's going on? said Deirdre, sitting up and falling down again.

We've got to get some money.

I need to get something to drink first. Deirdre was cranking herself upright, gritting her teeth as she wound the seat knob round with her hand.

We can't, we haven't got any money.

You don't need money for water. We'll stop somewhere and ask.

Why should they give us water for nothing?

Why shouldn't they?

Alan wound down his window and looked out at the scratch. There was a scored stripe of bare steel about two feet long and three inches wide and a slight dunt in the panel. Easier to recognise next time somebody stole it. They drove on towards Salerno. They stopped at a house on the way and Deirdre went to ask for water. She came back with a plastic litre bottle. They emptied it, 60–40, in a few minutes.

They could make a fortune bottling and selling stuff like this, said Alan.

It came from the tap. I asked them and they gave it to me.

It's true, it's hard when people help you who don't expect anything in return. Cause even so you think you'll have to pay later.

You think?

Yeah, I do.

They drove into Salerno and walked to the bank where Alan'd been the day before. It was a different woman. She didn't hum. McStrachan had put five million into Alan's account. Alan withdrew a million. He squeezed the thin cream-edged wad, twenty notes, between his fingertips, feeling the smoothness of the paper and the roughness of the fresh printing, and kinked it till it cracked. He waved it in Deirdre's face, grinning, and a smile passed through her worry for a moment.

Does this mean you have to go to Vladikavkaz? she said.

It won't take long.

You could put it back and not go.

We need it.

Do we?

Don't give me the happy hippy line. The car won't run on water and you won't either.

They checked into a double room in a hotel for 100,000 a night for the two of them. It was on the third floor. It had a beige fitted carpet and air conditioning and a pale blue quilted imitation satin bedcover on a broad firm double bed. There were white bath towels in the bathroom and plastic bottles of shower gel with the hotel logo on. Alan breathed in the smell of laundered airfreshened things and locked the door. Deirdre sat hunched on the edge of the bed with her hands clasped between her legs. She yawned, smacked her lips and kicked her shoes off. Alan sat down beside her, put a hand on her shoulder and a hand on her thigh.

I'm going to have a shower, said Deirdre, getting up. She went into the bathroom and locked the door.

Hey, said Alan.

He went over to the window and watched the dazzling roofs of the cars shunting past for a bit. He ran the palm of his hand over the warm brown veneer top of the TV, then sat down on the bed and took off his jeans. He let them slither onto the floor. He listened to the sound of the shower and put his fist round his straining cock. It was about set to sing like a kettle. Wait. He took his hand off it and lying stomach down on the bed went through a bag of his stuff he'd brought up from the car. Certain key things'd been lost at the astronomer's, like toothbrush and razor and the book he'd been meaning to get on with for more than a week now, *His Preaching Hands* by Giacomo Mansueto. It'd been good but the handless one had been taking a hell of a time to buy that loaf. Alan rolled over and stared at the ceiling. Water lashing her breasts. She'd be out any minute and they didn't have to go anywhere. He should've bought a toothbrush on the way up, and a paper. Yeah, and read about Gregor Ferguson and the town at peace.

Deirdre came out wearing a white teeshirt and holding a hairbrush. Her hair was wet. Alan grabbed her round the waist and tried to throw her onto the bed. She shook him off and took a couple of steps back.

Wait till my hair's dry, she said. Have you got a hairdryer?

No. Come on.

Deirdre turned away from him towards a mirror and started hacking her way through the tangles in her hair. Alan watched her for a while and went and had a shower. Under the water his hand kept straying down to his cock. Wait. What happened to sperm if they didn't get used for a week? Did they eat each other? Did it go off like yoghurt? Was it just building up in there?

Alan kept his hair dry. He came out of the jet, switched off the water and wrapped a towel round his waist. He cleaned his teeth with Deirdre's toothbrush and came out of the bathroom.

Deirdre sat on the bed facing him with her legs drawn up. She looked up when he came out. She'd put thin scarlet lipstick on and eyeliner. She had a black raw silk shirt on and a black velvet skirt, and black sandals tied with thongs around the ankles.

Are you going out? said Alan.

Why?

Dressed like that. Dressed.

I thought you'd like it.

I do.

Well.

Alan sat down on the bed and leaned towards Deirdre. He put his hand on her thigh.

What's that perfume?

Miss Dior. What's the matter? said Deirdre.

I'm thinking about what to do next. What do you want?

259

Whatever you like.

Talking about it doesn't work for me. You say what you like, you used to talk more.

Take off my clothes without unfastening anything and massage all my muscles, especially the shoulders and the legs, the calf muscles, they hurt, and my face. Go down on me for about an hour, and none of the dainty hummingbird type stuff with the tip of the tongue, you've got to do some sucking as well. After that you can put it inside me, but very accurate, and keep it up for another hour or so. And no letting it out when you come, I couldn't be arsed with another shower. Deirdre was looking into Alan's eyes. She smiled.

Has anyone actually ever done that?

No! Many have tried.

They tried and failed?

They tried and died. Deirdre fell back on the bed and drummed her fists on the bedcover, shaking her head from side to side as she laughed. I love *Dune*! she shouted.

Alan leaned over Deirdre, supporting himself on one elbow and stroking the skin of her neck with his fingertips.

Do what you can, said Deirdre.

Alan moved his face down over Deirdre's to kiss her. She turned her head sharply to the side and his mouth fell into the thin coils behind her ear. Alan clenched his teeth and placed his hand around Deirdre's throat, gripped, felt the pulse beat once and snatched his hand away. He got up off the bed.

What's the matter? said Deirdre, pushing herself up on an arm. Her hair fell down over her cheek and one eye, her eyes flicked down. She bit a fingernail.

You treat me badly, said Alan. I've driven you about, I've given you somewhere to sleep, I've brought you food, and you turn away from me like a shangri la saving herself for the leader of the pack. What do you see in someone who beats up old men for the sake of dead poets?

There's something I don't get from you, said Deirdre. I can't. It's not there. You don't know what it is. It's my fault. Mike loved the teacher and the teacher let him down. You're not like that. If you beat someone up it'd be because they were being a nuisance. Mike's going somewhere and you're going anywhere. He's way ahead of me, I know. I know I can't keep up with him. I can't help seeing how far ahead he is, but I can't help wanting to try to catch up because I know he doesn't like to be alone.

Is he alone? He never looked alone to me, even when he was by himself.

We used to have a cat and a dog at home, said Deirdre. The dog was this big furry hound, an Alsatian, that was always jumping up on you the second you came in the door. It'd lick your face and bark and wag its tail and make these whining noises in its throat like it was trying to sing to you. Even when you stopped paying attention it was always following you and watching you, waiting to be loved. You'd just have to glance over at where it was sleeping and its eyes'd open, its head'd come up, its tail'd start to go and it'd come bounding over. I hated it. But the cat – it'd eat the food you gave it, it'd sit on your lap if it was cold, it'd let you stroke it if it felt like a purr, but there was no gratitude. It wasn't dependent on you for anything. It didn't want affection, it didn't need it, if you wanted to love it, it was up to you. The cat had one great aim you could never discover and wouldn't've made any sense if you had. It concentrated on that. And it was always walking away from you.

Am I a dog? said Alan.

No. You're not a cat either. You're Alan Allen.

It's not my fault your boyfriend went fucking psycho on you. Why're you taking it out on me?

What do you know about what happened? Why d'you think I'm not still at the hospital? They don't like it when the nurses start sleeping with patients.

Alan looked at the door, went over and tried the handle. It was open. He looked out into the corridor. It was empty. He closed the door and locked it.

Why d'you unlock the door? said Alan.

Deirdre shrugged. I don't like locked rooms, she said. Listen, I thought we were going to the beach.

Alan put on his jeans. I'm going out now, he said. I'm taking the car. I'm leaving 100,000 for you and him on the desk. Don't touch my things. He went out. After a couple of steps he went back to the room. Deirdre was sitting in the same place. She looked at him.

What happened to the cat? he said.

It lost an eye in a fight with a raven. It got infected and we put it to sleep.

On the street Alan found a shop with a fridge filled with soft drinks and bought a can of Sprite. He asked the way to the council building. It wasn't a good idea to drive there, there was nowhere to park and the one-way system trebled the distance, but he'd said he was taking the car and he would. When he got there he shoehorned it between two Fiats and went inside. There was a woman sitting behind a counter.

Good morning.

Good morning.

I'm looking for Councillor Ferguson.

He hasn't been in today.

Will he be in?

There aren't any meetings. It's summer. They're all on holiday.

Where do they go?

The beach, the village and the country.

Councillor Ferguson – he's in town, isn't he? I read about him in the paper.

Our councillors are always in the papers.

There was a riot. A theatre got burned down. People were arrested.

Really? That's terrible. I must read about that. Which day was it?

No, if you haven't already . . . don't. It was exaggerated. It wasn't true. Parts of it weren't true. About the theatre particularly.

Burning down a theatre, what a shame.

No, they didn't. It was a misunderstanding.

How do you know? Were you there? It's true you can't rely on the papers.

Forget I mentioned it, OK? Have you got the councillor's address?

It was a heavy drive out to Gregor Ferguson's flat in traffic that basked in heat and fumes around locked junctions where drivers nudged forward on red and were blocked on green. The wheel was almost too hot to touch. Alan arrived just before 11 am. The councillor lived with his wife and baby daughter in a two-room flat on the fifth floor of a six-storey block built in 1960. The slam of the car door when Alan got out was a summons to twenty children, half of them barefoot, who gathered round with their fingers in their mouths and their bellies stuck out, swaying from side to side. Every few seconds one of them would go off like a mine, giggling and running to and fro between the other children. There was a smell of drains and the sun piercing the flocks of laundered sheets and socks overhead pulled dust off the street into the air where it shone like something precious. Half the cars parked there were leprous, rust-eaten, with wheels and panels missing, the rest were big, powerful machines ridden up onto the pavement. In the shadows beyond the bright dust and on shaded balconies old women watched.

D'you want your car cleaned? said a boy, jumping up and down in front of Alan.

No.

It's very dirty.

Alan shrugged and walked towards the entrance to the block.

Who'll look after your car? the boy called after him. It's dangerous here. We'll clean it for 15,000.

Alan looked over his shoulder at the children. The ring around the car was tightening. He went on inside. The lift wasn't working: he climbed five flights of stairs and rang the bell by Gregor Ferguson's door. A woman opened it.

I'm looking for Councillor Ferguson. Beyond the woman the councillor crossed the hall, glanced at Alan and moved on.

Yes, came his voice from another room.

The woman pulled the door all the way back and stood against the wall. Alan passed her. Thanks. He followed the councillor into a lounge. There was a suite and a coffee table and some bookcases and a TV and video. *New York, New York* was playing. Liza Minnelli was paused in the snow outside the JP's house, her lower lip vibrating as the tape head read her face fifty times a second. Gregor Ferguson sat in one of the armchairs in a teeshirt saying Geologists Do It For Ages, black shorts and trainers.

What's the problem? he said.

I met you a week ago. You lost a tooth.

That was a bad night. It was a bad weekend. The whole interglacial's been a bad era altogether. Rita! D'you want some tea? he said to Alan.

The woman put her head round the door. Could you get us some tea? said the councillor. He reached behind him for a packet of Marlboros and a lighter. Yeah. Very bad. You must've heard about the guy getting banged up. He's out now, they let him go. Folk are in a difficult mood.

What's his name?

D-D. Want one? That's a fucking relief, I've only got three left. That's what he answers to. If you ask him he says fill it in yourself. Damned, dead, destroyed, decayed, dreamed . . .

Dud.

Heh. I wouldn't try that out on him if I were you. Gregor Ferguson inhaled and put the cigarettes and lighter back where they'd been. He scratched his face under the beard. What is it you want? You don't live in my ward. You should be doing some fucking student summer job. So should I.

I'm trying to. I'm trying to do a job. Only I keep reading the papers and there's been a misunderstanding. I wanted to get it sorted out so's I can concentrate on this job. Just before I met you last Friday this woman I'd never seen before came up to me and started complaining to me about her housing problems. She thought I was you. I was in a hurry and she got a hold of my arm and I shook her off and she fell down. Then she had this toy theatre with her and it caught fire. A toy theatre. That was it.

The councillor tapped ash into an ashtray on the table and put the cigarette back in his mouth. The tip glowed. He looked at Alan through his thick spectacle lenses. It was hard to see the expression in his eyes. The door to the balcony was open on the far side of the room from the TV. Net curtains heavy with light rippled sluggishly in a slight movement of air. Liza Minnelli vanished in a storm of static as the video switched itself off. Rita Ferguson came in with a teatray and put it on the table. The councillor was still looking at Alan's face. He kept on looking and smoking while his wife laid out the tea things and poured the tea.

I'm sorry, said Alan. It was a shame she hurt herself and it was a shame the theatre got burned but it didn't seem serious.

Rita Ferguson left the room. Gregor stubbed out his cigarette. He put his hand in his pocket and pulled out a stone with sharp edges. He tossed it in the air a couple of times and threw it over to Alan. Alan caught it. It was red and looked like it'd just been chipped off a bigger piece.

We were up on the volcano first thing, the councillor said. Taking samples. Maybe it'll erupt again this afternoon. Then nothing would be fucking serious, would it? He laughed.

I don't even look like you, said Alan.

Who else knows about this version of yours?

No-one.

How do you know it happened like that?

I was there!

Yeah, but how do you know it happened like that?

I remember.

Memory's a very unreliable thing. See that rock there, that's reliable. It's better than a photo. It tells you what happened a million years ago. Lava cooled. But what's your memory? I could try taking a chip off it with my wee sampling hammer but all I'd be left with'd be a sticky mess and you'd never remember anything ever again. And another funny thing is if I came at you with the hammer and gave you a few taps on the head with it I bet you'd remember anything I asked you to remember.

He laughed again and fetched and lit another cigarette. Why could you not just have listened to Dora? Did you know she was called Dora?

No. Alan drank some tea. It was weak and he hadn't put sugar in it.

She was in trouble! said the councillor.

Yeah, but she was looking for you, it was nothing to do with me, and I was late.

You could have listened to her for a few minutes instead of shoving her onto the ground.

What good would that have done her getting a new house?

None whatsoever, you stupid cunt! said the councillor. In order to get her a new house you have to get a new housing policy which says everyone gets a house, and in order to do that you have to get money from people who have money, and in order to do that you have to get the police your side, and in order to do that you have to win an election or win a revolution and become the police.

There you go, then.

Yeah, there you go, there you go. The councillor

was jigging up and down in his seat. Ten minutes out of your life is too short a time to change the world so you tell the old lady to fuck off and go on your way. Rita!

Rita Ferguson appeared again. Uhuh?

Any biscuits?

No.

Too bad. D'you want to go out for a bit?

Yeah, why not? said Alan.

Gregor Ferguson went off to get changed. Alan took a couple of sugar cubes and crunched them. When the councillor came back he was wearing charcoal cotton slacks, a white linen shirt and a black acrylic bomber jacket. They went downstairs. Children slid off the car bonnet and roof and formed up a few yards away.

Will the car be OK down here? said Alan.

Did you pay them anything?

No.

Wo! shouted the councillor. A couple of the boys ran over and Gregor Ferguson put a note in their hands. Go to the beach.

They walked down a hill between more sixties multis shedding tiles and displaying satellite dishes, under a motorway ramp, down a street of shops with metal grilles on the windows, to a building site. Or maybe a demolition site. It was the corner of a block, cordoned off with red and white tape and stakes, with an old tracked bulldozer grunting blue diesel smoke and levelling off fresh earth streaked with white powdered masonry. Gregor Ferguson stopped by it. There were other groups of men and women and children on bikes and mopeds watching.

What was here? said Alan.

It used to be a theatre, said the councillor. It got burned down last week just before the main trouble with the police.

What happened?

Gregor Ferguson scratched his ear. You told me you were there.

That was another theatre. It was made of cardboard.

The councillor grinned. Cardboard, he said. Heh.

I had nothing to do with this.

Someone looking like me beat up Dora last Friday and torched the theatre. Some of the young folk used to go dancing there. It was good, it was dark inside, you could do whatever you felt like. They reckoned the police did the beating and the theatre both and there was a lot of trouble. People got taken in. People were charged. Damage was done. Maybe they'll put more money into the area. Maybe not. Maybe not enough damage. Maybe round two next weekend. Anyway I say you don't look like me, this isn't a cardboard theatre, your memory is utterly fucked and you didn't have anything to do with anything or anyone in this part of town, and it'd be best if you didn't have in future.

My memory can't be fucked, said Alan, licking his lips. How was the councillor not boiled in his own sweat in that jacket?

If not by nature, said Gregor Ferguson, then by the hand of man. I know someone who had part of a Latin motto carved on his chest last week cause D-D's mates thought he was involved. Come on, let's get back. Shit, too late.

An old guy in a flat cap and pinstripe shirt came over. He was almost bent double and walked with the help of an aluminium stick. His face was stretched in an eternal smile, cocked upwards in readiness to let you like him. He shook hands with the councillor and held out his hand to Alan.

This is Alan Allen. He's a tourist, said Gregor Ferguson. This is Marcello. He took out the Marlboros packet and rattled it. One left! he said. Here.

Marcello was still squeezing Alan's hand in his cold dry boniness. Look what they did! he said, pointing with his stick at the gap site. You see? Pigs! Tell them.

Everyone will know, don't worry, said the councillor. Come on. Marcello took the last Marlboro and Gregor Ferguson and Alan went back up the road. Just before they went under the ramp the councillor stopped and whistled up to the sky. A couple of guys with cigarette cartons in their hands leaned over the crash barriers and looked down.

How much? screamed the councillor. One of the guys held up two fingers.

One! screamed Gregor Ferguson. A packet of Silk Cut came down. They couldn't catch it, it landed in the dust. The councillor picked it up, ripped off the cellophane and drew out a cigarette. They walked on.

The trouble is, said the councillor, in some parts of town, this one for instance, there's more than one kind of police. If you don't pay your taxes they come for you eventually, right? There are some taxes you pay so's not to be arrested by the police with the uniforms and the flashing blue lights, and some you pay so's not to be shot by the police with no uniforms and no flashing blue lights. They work along the same lines, sometimes it seems as if they're fighting each other, sometimes they are. Most of the time they're just trying to organise the folk who aren't police. And if you let yourself be organised it can work well for you, but only if you've got cash in hand. To be organised without any cash is difficult. What's in it for you? Zero! So destroy! Bring the organisers down to your level! That's the trouble here. You'd think with all these police and organisers this'd be the most organised place in the whole fucking town but it keeps breaking down cause there's not enough cash.

What about you? said Alan. Are you police?

I'm a special category, said the councillor. He stopped, looked round, opened his jacket and gripping the zip pointed down at the waistband of his trousers. His belly pressed soft round a dark oblong pistol butt. He closed the jacket and walked on. It's registered, he said. Self-defence. But when the folk here who aren't police start fighting back against the people trying to organise them, they need to generate their own police. It's inevitable. Anarchy and communism start spontaneously generating police after an incubation period of sixty minutes. Good ones at first. Better it should be me becomes their police than D-D. Maybe not, though. I could work with that.

They reached the car. It was intact. The children

were smoking where they reckoned the old women couldn't see them.

What you remember about Dora and the theatre's got no relevance to the history of this part of town, said the councillor. So you don't remember it. Do you?

No.

Watch yourself. D'you know a mental case called Mike? He's been hanging round here, preaching. I don't like him. He's tangential. I don't like tangential people. They only touch you once but they touch you all the same and you never know where or when it's going to be.

I don't remember.

Here, I never said you had to forget everything. In fact I never said you had to forget anything. Forget I said that. Gregor Ferguson shook Alan's hand, gave him a single pat on the shoulder and went back into the house.

Alan walked over to where the kids were smoking, in the walled-round entrance to a basement. They were close together, not laughing. They hardened as he watched. In the web of smoke threads there seemed to be an arm too many and an odd number of dark eyes.

I'm leaving shortly, said Alan. Tell me one thing: where's the mad one? The stranger who talks all the time and doesn't make any sense?

The children murmured to each other, much older with the cigarettes than they'd been before, and told him. Alan got into the car and drove away. He parked underneath the ramp.

Away to the left the ramp was supported by three pillars about sixty feet high. Further on there were three more pillars, much shorter, and from there the ramp and the ground closed in on each other over a length of about thirty yards, the ground banked up in the last ten yards towards where it met the road. Mike was sitting right up at the apex of the triangle, his shoulders pressed against the concrete of the ramp and his head bent slightly forward. His chin was resting on his hands. Further down two guys of about fifteen stood with their hands in their pockets, looking up at him. They turned round when Alan came up, then turned back to Mike. Mike was talking.

. . . to make out that you're ugly but it's not you, it's external, it's where they've left you to live, said Mike. It's not that you're good. You're not virtuous, you're not kind. The teachers pretend you should be so's to trap you inside the impossible. I believed them once but I was wrong. Don't be wrong. Don't believe them. To believe them is worse than murder. It's even worse than trying to change the words which exist because they've been printed. When I say I believed them once that's for you to understand me, because there's no once. I'm at all times because my life and memory and what's been written are continuously present and the same thing. I'm at the beginning and at the end. I'm seeing him then. I'm hearing him then. Mike pointed at Alan without looking at him. He thought the teacher was God. I was the only one who saw God pretending to be a teacher. I see the form of him now, and I'm standing over the body where I struck it, and I'm taking flight out across the void, and I'm smiting that hypocritical angel Alan by a dark stream, and I'm looking down on fallen enemies in all future times. All future times. If you're with me you're guided. You're following a fixed rope through galleries where's no light. You can't go wrong. You might die but you can't go wrong.

Mike, said Alan, moving a few steps closer.

I could tell him what's going to happen, said Mike, reaching down and swinging the baseball bat up to rest on his knees. But he should have the illusion of free will.

What about Deirdre? said Alan.

Mike turned round to look at him. He looked as if he hadn't slept since they met, like his eyes were about to liquefy and slide down flat into the dark cups of skin beneath the sockets. His face was dirty, dust stuck to each layer of sweat which'd oozed out and then dried.

How is she? he said slowly.

She'd like to see you.

I can't see her, said Mike, looking at the ground and baring his teeth. I mean, I can't see her! She isn't there in the places where she might have been or might be.

You mean you don't remember her?

There isn't any memory any more. Just ises. One is after another all at once. It starts with heaven, as white as first and last pages, it goes through hell and chaos, it ends – I could tell you how it ends.

Mike. I know where you were. You need medication.

Deirdre can help you. She wants to, I don't know why.
I can tell you where she is.

Mike didn't say anything. His head sank down
between his knees though his eyes were still open. The
two guys stood looking from Mike to Alan.

Listen, said Alan. Here's the way it is. I'm not an
angel, I'm not a teacher, I'm not a friend or an enemy
of a teacher, I'm not working for the police, I'm not
working for the not police, I'm not a dog or a cat and
I'm not a satellite of frozen gas. I'm not good, reliable
or loyal and I'm not a bastard. I'm Alan Allen. I gave
you a lift. I'm in love with Deirdre. She's in love with
you. You're ill. She's in a hotel room in the centre. I
can take you there now. Are you coming?

I sit here until it gets dark, said Mike, lifting his head
up. I'm Satan the discoverer of tyrants. I see who stands
in the way of knowledge, who tries to hide truth behind
understanding. Wait with me and see what happens.

Have you been here long? Alan asked the two guys.

They looked at him for a few seconds. Maybe he'd
speak again.

No, said one. They both shrugged.

He a mate of yours? said the one who spoke.

Yeah, said Alan.

We're just waiting till D-D gets here, said the guy.
The silent one gave him a hard shove on the shoulder
and the pre-stab eyes.

Look after him, said Alan. Shrugs. He went to the
car and drove back to the hotel.

Deirdre'd gone out. She hadn't left a note. She'd

taken the hundred thousand but left her things. Alan locked the door, took off his clothes and took a pair of white cotton panties out of Deirdre's bag. They weren't fresh. He leaned his bare back against the cool wall beside the desk, pressed the knickers into his face and wanked himself off, not bothering about where the stuff landed. Afterwards he threw the panties away and sank down onto the carpet, still clutching the softening cock. He sat there in a blank state with his eyes closed for about five minutes. Then he got up and started tracking down the spots of spunk. Most of them had gone a good way, landed on the bed. There was a bit on the carpet. He soaked a face towel and cleaned them off. The fake satin bedcover didn't take to it well. It wasn't just the big, dark, damp stains but you could tell something would be left after the water dried.

Alan took a shower and packed the things he had into the carrier bag he was using. He wrote a note to Deirdre on a piece of paper with the hotel logo, telling her where Mike was. He signed off plain Alan and left another 100,000.

In the hotel restaurant he had a plate of linguine with clams and a glass of fizzy mineral water. The clams still had their shells on. They were tiny. After working the flesh out with the tip of his tongue from about twenty of them he tried chewing on one with the shell. The crunching of it felt like an accident. He rinsed his mouth out with the water and swallowed. He had to do it a couple of times before the fragments were clear. He had an espresso. It was 20,000 with tip. He drove out of town and found a place where they fixed glass. They repaired the window for 95,000. The car was whole. It was 4 pm. Alan was alone. He started the engine and drove on.

He made good time north, dreaming in the roaring flow between the crash barriers and a thick strip of dark pink flowers down the central reservation. He rounded Rome as the sun rolled fume-red along the edge of the world, but still bright: he had to pull the sun shield down with each turn of the road west, and stretch his neck to avoid being blinded. He was well on the road through forested flatlands with illuminated citadels by nightfall and passed Florence at 11 pm. He stopped once for petrol and bought a roll with cheese and ham and a bottle of Orangina. He finished it off in a couple of minutes and hit the exit still chewing, lumps of solid bread kicking their way down his gullet. He was high on the unlimited commodity of miles per minute. It was free falling down an endless grey shaft lit by the head-lights, it was accelerating up an endless winding grey trunk lit by the headlights, it was following a fixed rope through dark galleries lit by the headlights.

Just after 1 am Alan started to nod off on the approaches to Padua. He pulled off the motorway, found a deserted layby part enclosed by trees, and slept.

He woke at 6.30 am, yawned, rubbed his scalp, sniffed, tasted the bitterness in his mouth and wound down the window. He blinked at the morning for a few seconds, shook his head, went for a piss behind a tree, got back in the car, clipped himself in and started the engine.

He grinned, and straightened the grin out because he didn't know what it was for, but it came back.

He drove back onto the motorway. It was empty like a runway and looked fresh made in the first light. On a smooth straight downward slope he kept his foot pressed down on the accelerator till the needle trembled on 105 and wouldn't go any further. The traffic thickened and he pulled it back to 85. He stopped for petrol and a coffee at 7.30 am. In the cafeteria he could hardly make himself sit down. The coffee was too hot to drink. He drummed the point of the car key on the formica tabletop for a few seconds and swallowed it anyway, scalding the back of his throat. He got up and walked as fast as he could to the car, short of running.

He drove without stopping, threading through the tunnelled mountains. He emptied the tank in four hours and filled up again near Klagenfurt. He took a Picnic bar and a small box of pineapple juice into the car and finished them off in a couple of minutes once he'd moved up through the gears and was cruising. By 5 pm he'd reached Budapest. Without penetrating the centre he found a hotel, a five-storey block with an electric blue neon sign saying A-Hotel. The building looked like it had been wrapped in a single sheet of dull bronze which'd had small square window holes neatly punched in it. The neat punching and flush-fitting in smooth metal, veneer and fake marble was carried on through the hotel. It didn't appear to have been built so much as cut out, folded and wired up. Alan bought a toothbrush and toothpaste and shaving stuff in a shop on the ground floor and went to the restaurant. He had a glass of lager, spicy soup with cherry peppers, fried carp with fried potatoes, apple strudel and coffee, and another lager. It was good. He went up to his room on the third floor. The door opened with a plastic slot-in strip with holes neatly punched in it. He switched on the TV. There were nine ordinary channels and two pay channels, one with Tom Hanks and one hard core pornography. You got two seconds of hard core before the screen blanked and you were asked to pay. After about fifteen minutes Alan's thumb got tired pressing the buttons to and fro and by that time the porn had got gynaecological. He switched to Viva and opened up the mini-bar. He popped the mini-champagne and drank half from the bottle. It was sweet. He went to the phone. Maybe he could catch his parents before they started laundering the flags. He dialled Malcolm's number first. There was no answer. His parents weren't in either. He finished the champagne and fetched out a mini-Johnnie Walker, a mini-Campari and a mini-orange juice. He poured them all in the one glass with a couple of ice cubes. Not brown enough. He added another mini-whisky. That was it: the colour of shallow sea-water when you put a foot down sharply in the sand on the bottom and it billowed up in clouds. I thought we were going to the beach? Alan drank. He went to the bathroom and spat down the basin. He poured the rest of the drink down the toilet, flushed it and cleaned his teeth. He got into the shower. He came out, wrapped a towel round his waist and lay down on the bed. It was still light outside. He went to sleep.

Next morning he drove out through wide flat fields of grain on a single carriageway road lined with telegraph poles with storks' nests on top of them. The traffic was light. He overtook horse-drawn carts and trucks hauling loads of forty tons.

In the early afternoon with the petrol low the road deteriorated. The surface roughened and became dustier and more worn. Holes appeared. The white lines down the centre became fainter and disappeared for long stretches. In a village of a single street of low broad wooden houses painted blue, green or black, behind green fences and thick screens of fruit trees, with grass and a dusty path for a pavement, Alan swerved to avoid a turkey that came out onto the road. On the outskirts of the town of Mukachevo he found a petrol station. There were two sets of flaking red pumps with the quantity in litres given out shown in digits on a row of three drums. There were empty cars parked near the pumps and an old truck filling up. A couple of guys were standing by the sales point, which was a hut made of white bricks. There was a barred window and a hole a few inches wide to talk and pass money through. You couldn't see who was on the other side, there was a set of flowered curtains part-screening the window.

Alan went over to the hut. One of the guys was talking through the window in a voice too low to hear. Alan waited for ten minutes. Someone came up from behind them, spoke quickly into the window, passed something inside, went back to their car, took the nozzle from the holster and started filling up. Alan moved forward and leaned down so as to speak to the controller.

Can I get some petrol? he said. He could see an old woman's hands resting on a metal box with lights and switches. The woman's head darted into view and away again.

Only for coupons, said the woman.

Eh?

Coupons! Coupons!

I haven't got any coupons.

Then you don't get any petrol. Who's next?

How do I get coupons? said Alan.

You need a form! shouted the woman. Next!

How do I get a form?

They're available at filling stations.

Can I have one?

We haven't got any left.

How'm I supposed to get petrol, then?

I'll tell you one more time: you need coupons. Leave me alone. I'm not an information service.

Alan went back to his car. He leaned against it with his chin resting on his folded arms on the warming roof. There was a petrol reek and a smell of old vegetables and tobacco. The guy with the truck was smoking as he filled up a line of aluminium canisters with fluid. Alan watched him. After a minute he went over.

Is that petrol? he said.

What if it is? said the guy, not looking up.

Can you spare any coupons?

We don't have coupons. We get a service ration, said the guy.

How about some petrol?

How much d'you need?

Thirty litres.

What'll you pay?

Alan put his hand in his pocket and took out a thick red wad. He looked at the numbers for a moment.

500? he said.

OK, said the guy. Give us your canister.

I haven't got one.

The guy straightened up and looked at Alan for a second. I'll bring it over, he said.

After a few minutes the guy came over, waddling quickly with the weight of the bright silver canisters, one in each hand. He set them down beside Alan's tank.

Where's your funnel? said the guy.

I haven't got a funnel.

How did you get here? said the guy. He went and fetched a funnel and poured in the fluid. He didn't spill a drop. The fuel smelled good. Alan counted out fifty red ones and got back in the car. The sound of the engine and the sight of the petrol gauge floating over to rest solidly on F for full, it was like waking up after a dream where your legs'd been amputated and finding they were still there.

A few miles further on Alan pulled in at a barbecue. A couple of guys had set up a black rusting rectangular metal tray on spindly legs of iron and filled it with smouldering charcoal which they provoked once in a while with a squirt of vinegar from a squeezy bottle. They took lumps of pork from a big glass pickle jar full of vinegar and spices, skewered them and grilled them. They served them on paper plates with a hunk of stale white bread, ketchup and a bit of parsley. The pork pieces were an inch square with a crusted glistening block of fat that burst on biting and ran down the chin. It was 50, with 10 for a bottle of fart-flavoured fizzy mineral water.

The road wound on up into the Carpathian mountains, narrow and bad through pine forests, over a pass, down on the far side to apple and cherry orchards and cornfields and lime trees lining the verge with white bands painted round their trunks. Old women with headscarves and cotton print dresses tight around their fatness drove white geese along the roadside. Alan overtook trucks with sky-blue cabins and steel load carriers with single words stencilled on the side, Bread, Flour, Food, and a hunting green motorcycle with a live pig in the sidecar. It was a pale pink sow with a wet snout and two front trotters sticking out over the edge of the sidecar. She turned her head with an expression of interest to follow his car as it went past, calm, like her journey was going to last for ever and his was transient.

It got dark as he approached the town of Lviv. It'd been raining and the road was wet and sticky. The trucks ahead sprayed mixed oil, mud and water onto his windscreen where it dried and hardened before his wipers could clear it. He tugged at the windscreen wash stick every few seconds till there was no fluid left and the only visibility was a narrow strip between sheets of brown slithering down the glass as the wipers thudded to and fro. Ahead he could see two glowing red flying duck stencils cut out and stuck onto the rear lights of the truck in front. The ducks swayed to and fro. There were no other lights. Even Alan's headlights seemed to have lost their power. The road forked. Alan followed a sign pointing to Lviv and the red ducks flew off the other way.

The road narrowed and turned to cobblestones, ruts and potholes. Alan slowed down to second gear. The car lurched into a shallow pit filled with water and came out the other side. Alan stopped, left the engine running and the lights on and got out. He examined the headlights. They were crusted with a dry oil-based mud that made the plastic opaque. Alan fetched a rag from the car and scraped it off. It couldn't be wiped, you had to get at it with your fingernails through the cloth. Alan heard a murmuring and a rustling a few yards away. He stood up. When his eyes adjusted from the brightness of the cleaned headlights he saw a line of women dressed in dark clothes and wearing headscarves lining the road, watching him. Some of them had carrier bags.

Which way to Lviv? said Alan.

The women pointed back the way he'd come. That way, son, Lviv's back that way. Alan made out a concrete bus shelter with a mosaic of a dancing woman on the side. They were waiting.

Can I get some water here? said Alan. For the car.

The women murmured again. They pointed down

the road to a well. It had a roof, a pulley and a bucket on a rope. Alan filled the bucket and replenished the windscreen wash. He turned the car round, drove back to the fork and headed on. He reached Lviv in about half an hour.

He drove down into the centre of town, circled a steep, narrow, cobbled one-way system a couple of times, the suspension taking a beating from where the cobbles had sunk around tram tracks. He found a multi-storey concrete hotel at the top of a hill, looking down on a park. He paid 20 to put the car inside a chained-off area at the front and went inside. Two women at the reception desk were talking to each other. He went over, leaned on the desk and waited for them to finish. They went on talking.

Hello, said Alan after five minutes.

One of the women moved her body round on a swivel chair, still talking, and turned her head to Alan after about thirty seconds.

I'm listening, she said.

I'd like a room, please, said Alan.

No places, said the woman, and turned away.

Are you sure? said Alan.

I'm absolutely sure, said the woman, without looking at him. No places, no places, no places.

You must have something.

Young man, do we look stupid to you? I said no places. It's your problem. Leave us alone. Next time make a booking.

Alan went outside. The young guy running the car

park came over. He was eating sunflower seeds from a twist of paper, spraying out the black husks from his lips.

No places? he said.

Yeah.

Do you want a place?

Yeah.

Give us 100, I'll get you a room. Alan gave him the money and the guy went inside. After a few minutes he came out and beckoned to Alan. Alan went back to the desk and filled out a form and the woman gave him a room card. On the seventh floor there was another woman behind a desk, watching *The Sweeney* along with two men in emerald green shellsuits and a policeman sitting in big, low, soft, wrinkled vinyl chairs. Alan swapped the card for a key and got the room. It was 10 pm.

Alan switched on the television. There were five channels. He selected MTV. An old Human League concert was playing. There was a glass door opening onto a bare concrete balcony. Alan went out and tested the night. The air was warm, there was a smell of leaves after rain from the park, with a trace of kidney-scent. The lights of the town were scattered. A couple of churches were lit up. Red flashing lights defined a TV transmitter on a hill opposite. He went back inside. There were two short narrow beds with a folded blanket and a folded linen sheet on each. The sheet had been pressed and starched to a solid block, it unfolded with a tearing sound. It was a bag in form. Alan fed the blanket through a lozenge-shaped opening cut into it and laid the combination out roughly on the bed. He took off his clothes and went into the bathroom. The kidney smell was stronger. The shower hung from yellow-grey tiles like a chrome crook. There wasn't any hot water. Alan put his hand round the feed pipes: cold. He splashed his face and washed his hands. Kidneys. He lifted his hands to his nose and sniffed. It was the soap.

In the restaurant on the first floor a woman was on stage, singing What A Wonderful World, accompanied by a man on Yamaha keyboards. On a space in front of the stage a slim woman in a black velvet dress was dancing close with a man in a maroon suit. His thick hand rested on her bare back between her shoulder-blades. Alan ordered green borsch, sturgeon in a white wine sauce and cherry vareniki. They didn't have any. They brought what they had: slices of hard yellow cheese and ham, a sliced cucumber and a sliced tomato with a line of sunflower oil drawn over it, sliced smoked red fish, white bread and butter, fish soup and a hotpot of meat, potatoes and garlic. It was good. He drank a bottle of beer and they brought him a scoop of ice cream and a cup of tepid instant coffee.

He checked out at seven the next morning. He got petrol through a taxi driver at a filling station on the edge of town and headed on. The road was hard going. Once the tarmac gave out altogether, there was yellow mud and gravel for a couple of miles through a frozen project of bypass building. The road was lined with abandoned earthmovers and rollers. At the town of Rivne the way became easier. Alan bought a Picnic bar, a litre bottle of Coke and a tin of cashew nuts. He drove faster, it was a dual carriageway with a cable slung down the middle for a reservation. He ate and drank as he drove. By three in the afternoon he was in the forests round the town of Kiev, by four he'd crossed the river Dnepr and cleared Kiev and was on the motorway. It didn't last long past the town of Borispol. Alan filled up again at a dark green tanker parked by the roadside. He stopped at around 10 pm, just past the town of Poltava, walked around the car for a bit, drank some Coke and went to sleep.

Next day was fair and dry: he set off into the sun early, about six.

The land was bursting with green. Between roads and miles-wide fields of corn, leaves and shoots boiled like clouds, trees and weeds and bushes and grass choking each other, cleared for cultivated strips of maize and vegetables that the old women hacked at, feet planted astride in the earth and bent double. After the town of Khar'kov the land began to rise and fall, bigger than dunes, smaller than hills. Alan ran over a sand-coloured dog. He killed it. He felt the bump through the tyres, looked in the mirror and saw the life'd been crushed out of it in a moment. The dog'd dived under the wheels in the empty land on a road with few cars. Did dogs kill themselves? And so well?

It was an easy cruise down to the town of Rostov-on-Don. Alan bought fruit and petrol in a roadside market and made it to Rostov by 8 pm. He checked into another hotel with small narrow beds and a lozenge-shaped hole in the sheet. This time there was hot water.

Next day as it got dark he passed a police post by the roadside near the town of Nal'chik, a dugout with sandbags around it and a policeman with a helmet and a heavy machine gun inside. The gun was pointing the way Alan was going. Three hours later he drove into the town of Vladikavkaz. At the hotel the woman asked how long he was staying for.

One night, he said. She gave him a room card. The room was on the eighth floor. The bed was already made up. There was no water at all. Alan got a pot of tea and some sugarlumps from the concierge, drank a couple of glasses, watched the end of *Terminator II*, undressed and went to sleep.

He woke just after 7 am. He got a steady trickle of tepid water from the shower head. It splashed off his body and straight onto the floor, draining into a hole between the toilet and the basin. He washed himself with the kidney soap, shaved and wiped his face with a thin white towel like a napkin. The other towel was just big enough to wrap round his waist. He went out onto the balcony. In front of the hotel there was a shallow, fast-flowing river crossed by a footbridge, and on the far side a park. A couple of hundred yards downstream there was a red brick mosque. He got dressed: black jeans and a navy blue acrylic shirt with a couple of bars of the music to I'm Getting Married In The Morning printed on it in white. He combed his hair and left the room.

To the left of the lifts was a set of glass doors leading to the stairs and a set of big picture windows. He saw the Caucasus mountains. The blue rock and the patches of snow on the peaks took the red and the gold of the rising sun. The mountains ate the sky. Alan went through the doors and watched the mountains, tracing cliffs, cracks, ledges, and blinking and seeing the whole of it. He saw an outcrop of rock detach itself from a ridge and float off into space. There were two of them. They were police helicopters with humped brows, stunted wings and guns poking out of their noses. They flew towards the town and steered away before crossing it. Alan took the lift downstairs.

The restaurant hadn't opened for breakfast. Alan went back to his room and tried to phone McStrachan. A tired voice repeated a message: Number dialled incorrectly. Number dialled incorrectly. Alan called the operator.

Operator 25 I'm listening, said the operator.

I'd like to make a call, said Alan.

Number?

Alan told her.

When for?

Now.

Minute, said the operator. Alan heard voices in the background and a clattering and ringing. The operator came back.

Tomorrow, she said.

Tomorrow?

Tomorrow.

That's a long time.

D'you want to order it?

Eh . . .

The operator hung up. Alan went back down to the lobby. There was a doorman wearing a peaked cap with a yellow band round it, staring sleepily out of the door from a wooden bench. Alan went over to him.

D'you know where the police station is? he said.

The doorman looked up at him, and looked out of the door again without saying anything. A police convoy had drawn up outside the hotel: a Jeep, an armoured troop carrier with a machine gun in a turret and two trucks. Policemen in black berets and blue denims, with flak jackets and submachine guns, jumped out of the back, two by two. Some of them were wearing dark glasses. They started filing into the hotel and up the spiral staircase leading to the restaurant on the second floor. Alan heard them battering on the door of the restaurant.

The things you have to do to get breakfast in these places, eh? said Alan to the doorman.

The doorman watched the last of the policemen sprint up the stairs, three at a time, to the restaurant. The doors had been opened.

Is it like this every morning? said Alan.

Like what? said the doorman.

You think you're safe enough in a hotel, said Alan. Sooner or later you're going to have to go outside among the houses and the high flats and the police, but you can put it off for a while. You can hide in your room and watch TV. You can eat in the restaurant. You don't have to go back to the streets and shops and people. Only now it seems the police come to you.

Ah, go and get your breakfast, said the doorman angrily, not looking at him.

If anyone comes looking for me don't let them in, said Alan. He went up to the restaurant. A waitress standing by a desk just inside was staring at six tables of policemen sitting laughing to each other and rubbing their thumbs against their fingertips. As soon as she saw Alan she moved to block his way.

We're not open, she said.

What about them?

They're on police business.

I've got a right to breakfast too.

You don't have any rights. You're a guest. You should be glad you've got a room.

What if I sit down and wait?

I don't care.

Alan picked an empty table near the window with a tablecloth but no place setting. He watched waitresses bringing wedges of flat, round bread to the policemen, slices of hard sheep's cheese and sausage, saucers of sour cream and glasses of kefir, hard-boiled eggs, bread and jam and tea. The noise once they began to eat was like a disaster in a surgical instruments factory, the clatter of aluminium forks on china and teaspoons on glass and the spare magazines they carried in the pockets of their flak jackets and their guns swinging from their straps on the backs of their chairs. After about ten minutes

Alan got up and went over to one of the tables. He touched a blond policeman with a moustache and a red face lightly on the shoulder as he was raising a half-eaten boiled egg to his mouth and asked if he knew where the police station was.

The table fell silent. The blond policeman put the egg down on his plate, dabbed his mouth with a napkin and looked Alan in the face.

What? he said.

I'm supposed to pick up a stolen antique egg from the police station.

The policeman frowned. That'll be Captain Alan you're after, he said. He's out hunting today. As for antique eggs, why don't you try this? He held the half-eaten boiled egg up to Alan's mouth and put his hand on the back of Alan's head as the others round the table laughed like dogs. The policeman's fingers tugged at the hairs on the back of Alan's neck.

Come on, open up, he said. Alan tried to pull away with gradual force but the fingers wouldn't yield. He parted his lips and immediately the powdery yellow boiled yolk pressed through his teeth. He took the rest of it and chewed. The policeman let go and clapped him on the back and the table applauded in laughing frenzy. A chair was pushed against his knees from behind and he sat down. A bottle of arakas appeared on the table in front of him and a shower of small tumblers glittered across the cloth.

What's your name? said the blond policeman.

Alan.

I'm Alan, said the blond policeman, pouring brimful measures of liquor for them both. We're all Alans. I'm Lieutenant Alan. That's Big Alan, Fat Alan, Young Alan and – who are you again?

I'm G. K. Chesterton, said the last policeman.

Everyone roared except Alan, who smiled and rubbed the back of his neck. The lieutenant raised his glass towards Alan. Alan lifted his.

A guest is sacred, said the lieutenant, looking round the table as he spoke. He's sacred like your wife, like your children, like your land, like your home, like your father and mother and your grandparents, like your sisters and brothers and cousins and in-laws. A guest is everything an enemy isn't. The more you give a guest the better, but to have anything taken from you by an enemy is shameful. A guest can live in my house for a year and I'd give him clothes, I'd give him money, I'd give him my car, I'd give him my furniture, I'd let him marry my daughter. But if an enemy so much as takes a glass of water from my tap I'll hunt him down to the ends of the earth and cut his throat. Guests! The lieutenant clinked glasses with Alan. They all clinked with each other and knocked the drink back in one, except for Alan, who took a sip, saw the knocking back and finished the rest off before they noticed.

The lieutenant laughed, clapped him on the back, told him to eat some tomatoes and asked if he was married.

No. You?

Yes. With a son.

What about the daughter?

I don't have a daughter.

D'you have a car?

No. D'you? What kind? How much was it?

You said you had one.

The lieutenant didn't remember. He poured Alan another tumbler full. D'you like Black Sabbath? he said.

No.

Deep Purple?

I never got into them, said Alan. What about Captain Alan? Where can I find him?

He might be at the station. He might be out at the front.

The front of what?

There are some people who don't understand how to behave, said the lieutenant, smiling down at his drink, aware of the others watching and listening to see how he'd mystify the guest. They need to be taught they can't behave that way. They need to be taught who's in charge. It's something we should've done a while ago. Here, it's your turn. He flicked his finger against Alan's tumbler.

Alan lifted his drink. Tumblers rose round the table like they were pulled by a common string. Present times are hard, he said, and you can't expect anything from the future but travelling and travelling and getting nowhere. Only the richness of the past, with its infinite possibility, holds hope for a better life. To the past, whatever it may hold!

The policemen grinned and clinked tumblers and the

Alans drained their arakas. The lieutenant stood up, put on his beret, lifted his gun and shook Alan's hand.

Come and see us later, he said. We'll be out on the road north.

Thanks.

Swap you a grenade launcher for your car.

No, it's OK. Where's the police station?

The lieutenant told him and the police moved out of the restaurant, hoisting their weapons and gear like men strapping their genitals back on after removing them in order to play more calmly with children. Alan was left alone with the waitresses and plates of half-eaten food and silence. The police'd taken the drink with them.

Alan went out of the hotel, walked across the foot-bridge and through the park to a long boulevard with trees running down the middle and trams running down either side. The shops weren't open, there was hardly anyone about, though it was past nine. The traffic was police cars and armoured troop carriers. They drove fast and carelessly, like they weren't expecting to meet non-police cars. Most of the pedestrians were police, judging from the guns, even though they were wearing ordinary clothes, tracksuits and teeshirts and leather jackets.

It was a few minutes' walk to the police station. Around the door was a crowd of about fifty policemen in camouflage uniforms and ordinary clothes. Half of them were divided into groups of young ones listening to older grey-haired ones with moustaches explaining a situation. Others were sitting on the steps, smoking, forage caps pushed up over their foreheads and rifles across their knees, squinting up into the light at new arrivals. The group nearest the door were guards, they had helmets strapped under the chin, flak jackets, lace-up boots and pockets fat with magazines and grenades. They were ignoring the rest. Alan went to the guard nearest the door.

I'm looking for Captain Alan, he said.

He's not here.

Where is he?

Out on the edge of town. Up north.

How can I get there?

You can't. It's closed.

It's police business?

Yes, said the guard, looking at him for the first time. It's police business.

Something going on?

The guard shrugged. High spirits, he said.

Alan headed back to the centre. He passed the market and went inside. Most of the stalls were empty. A few people were selling bundles of parsley, coriander and spring onions, eggs, chickens and potatoes. A man in a bloodstained white coat was hacking a lamb carcass in two with an axe on a serrated stump of wood. Nearby a woman was selling snake meat. Alan went up to her.

How much? he said.

200 a kilo, said the cruelty woman. Look, it's good, fresh meat, no fat, no gristle, look at that, feel it, it's lovely. Excellent meat. You! She drew in all the air of the market for her outrage. The snake-murdering homosexual!

It's not my snake, said Alan. I gave you a false address. I lied. I don't think much of you for an animal lover, selling it like this. It must be a couple of weeks old by now. It's disgusting.

There was a smell coming off the meat, something like socks worn too long.

I'm not ashamed to be selling this meat, said the woman. I'm not a vegetarian. It's good stuff, very lean and tasty. It's all part of the general fund-raising effort.

What can you do with it?

Fry it, make soup, roast it. You could fry it up in a few minutes, it's that tender.

Could you make a curry?

I wouldn't know about that. Will you take some?

No.

The cruelty woman stood up. By the powers invested in me by the Society for the Prevention of Animal Cruelty, I hereby notify you of an intention to prosecute for wilful neglect and ill treatment of an animal to the detriment of its health.

It wasn't my snake, said Alan.

The woman sat down. Tell it to the magistrate. It's lucky for you the police are busy today.

Look, said Alan, if I bought the whole thing, would you just forget the case, seeing as it's not my snake anyway?

The cruelty woman laughed. Bought! she said. D'you think we can be bought so easily? That'd be convenient for you, wouldn't it, buying up the evidence at 200 a kilo?

Yeah, said Alan.

All twenty kilos of it.

Alan counted out 4,000 from his wad and gave it to the woman. Have you got some carrier bags? he said.

They borrowed the services of the guy in the white coat to hack it into two-kilo chunks and put it in four carrier bags. Alan left the market and headed back to the hotel. The heat and the dust were up and the bags were a terrible weight, the greasy plastic thinning and cutting into his fingers. The strain spread up from his wrists to his forearms, to his shoulders and blazed out across his back. He stopped to rest under a tree in the park and noticed the first of the dogs, a lean sand-coloured tyke the size of a cat with fangs like a vampire and huge glistening black eyes. He picked up the bags and pressed on with the dog trotting silently just at the edge of his vision. After a couple of minutes he noticed a couple more mongrels with the same pedigree, plus a sad old black creature with the body of a labrador and the legs of a dachshund and a bitch with sagging dugs almost trailing along the ground.

There were a few more people out and about by now, unarmed. As he crossed the bridge Alan passed a slim woman in a black silk suit with full lips and dark blinking eyes. She stared at him. He grinned at her and after she'd passed wanted to have stopped to speak. The vampire dog began to yelp and the others joined in as he approached the hotel. They started nosing into the meat bags, sniffing in such a depraved way Alan wished he could smell it through their noses. When he reached his car he opened up the back, put the meat inside and locked it. The dogs weren't sure whether to follow him into the hotel or loiter round the car. It was 10.30 am. Alan went up to his room and tried to call Malcolm. He got through.

Hi, he said. I'm sorry about last week.

That's OK, said Malcolm. He sounded like he was in a hurry.

I didn't mean it. No, I did mean it, but I shouldn't have said it out loud. Are you in a hurry? said Alan.

I've got a meeting. Where're you calling from?

Town. The hotel near the mosque.

Are you still trying to get to Glasgow?

Yes.

What's stopping you?

We used to be friends.

Yeah.

Listen Malcolm, I've got more problems than I did before.

You're not the only one, Alan, it's fucking unreal what's going on up there. There's women getting their throats cut and men getting raped. Snipers all over the joint.

Can I come and see you?

Why can't you keep your head down like the rest of us? You're safe so long as they don't try and make a policeman out of you.

Come on Malcolm, I'm pissed off here on my own. D'you want to meet for lunch?

No. I'll be at the Kazbek at noon. Wear a suit if you can, a jacket and tie at least. Malcolm put the phone down.

Alan asked the way to the Kazbek and drove there. He had on an old black linen blazer and a pink shirt with a dull gold tie that had a black grid pattern on it. He drove with the windows open but even so the stench from the rotting snake meat made the arakas remains churn in his stomach. The dogs galloped after the car for a few blocks before he got ahead of them. More dogs were waiting at the restaurant, which was on the central boulevard. He found a shaded parking space in a yard and kept the windows open a couple of inches.

The restaurant was in a cellar with walls painted white and low ceilings. The tabletops were made of beaten copper. On one wall there was a mural showing muscular policemen in tight-fitting mail shirts and conical helmets carrying spears, their faces stern in profile. The restaurant was empty. One table was set for a banquet: three glasses at each place, champagne, vodka and Fanta, plates of sliced smoked sturgeon and ham, saucers with dollops of red and black caviar with butter. The waitress seemed glad to see Alan.

I'm with the Malcolm Tummel party, said Alan.

Sit down, grinned the waitress, pointing to the set table. Alan took a corner seat: there were six places. The waitress came behind him, reached over his shoulder to pick up a Fanta bottle, opened it, poured orange froth into a tumbler, set the bottle down on the tablecloth and stalked away. Malcolm came in with a woman: they sat down opposite Alan.

This is my friend Alan, said Malcolm. This is Tanya, Paula's cousin.

Hi, said Alan, shaking Tanya's hand.

Pleased to meet you.

You're looking smart, said Malcolm.

So are you. How many of those suits have you got?

I bought them in a sale.

And that dress is amazing.

I like to dress light in summer, said Tanya.

How's Paula? said Alan.

She's gone home for a while, said Malcolm.

Oh.

The waitress came and did the Fanta routine for Tanya and Malcolm.

You're still here, said Malcolm. He spread some butter and red caviar on a piece of brown bread and took a bite. Here, you might as well open this. He handed Alan a bottle of champagne.

Yeah, said Alan, twisting the wire cage off the cork through flaking silver foil. Two weeks now I've been driving and I'm still here. I don't want you telling me I'm wasting my time, though.

I wasn't going to.

Alan had his thumbs on the plastic cork. He saw Tanya hunch her shoulders and protect her face with her hand. He pointed the bottle towards her and felt the cork begin to move. Malcolm reached over and pushed the bottle upwards. The cork banged out and cracked against the ceiling.

Sorry, said Alan quietly to Malcolm. Malcolm shook his head and waved his hand.

Why sorry? said Tanya, holding out her glass and

looking directly into Alan's eyes. Alan filled it with champagne, then his and Malcolm's.

To the prevention of accidents, he said.

Acquaintances, murmured Tanya when they clinked glasses. The champagne was sweet.

I wanted to see you, said Alan. No special reason except it's been a while. Did you finish your dissertation?

Uhuh.

Good?

Yes. It says that the now isn't a point, it's a field, and that some people have bigger fields than others.

Good bread this, said Alan.

I love red caviar, said Tanya.

Have you read Malcolm's dissertation? said Alan.

No, it's too long. I heard his songs though. Tanya looked at Malcolm and without looking at her Malcolm squeezed her bare thigh.

What about your business? said Alan to Malcolm.

Terrible, said Malcolm. Everything was fine till this shit with the councillor and the theatre and that boy getting killed. We were all set to put a hundred boxes of toothpaste into the shops till it came to a head last night. It'll be over soon but the partners aren't happy.

Toothpaste?

Yeah, people need toothpaste.

Is there money in it?

Of course.

D'you want to buy twenty kilos of prime quality meat?

No! Malcolm laughed. You sound like that old animal

rights woman down the market who's been trying to flog a dead snake for the past fortnight. He looked at his watch.

It's OK, I won't be here when they come, said Alan.

I wasn't meaning anything, just checking the time.

Done any more gigs?

A couple.

Two guys in green suits with leather jackets on top came into the restaurant. They came over to Malcolm. There was handshaking and kissing and one of them had a murmured conversation with Malcolm. They put a hand on each other's shoulder and spoke into each other's ear, eyes swivelling free of their thoughts. The two guys walked away. They weren't the ones Malcolm and Tanya were waiting for.

What boy was killed? said Alan.

I don't know. Some boy. The one whose mother started all the trouble. They found him under a tree yesterday morning.

D-D?

Who?

He had asthma.

That's one way to cure it, isn't it, ventilation by bullet.

Who did it?

How should I know? Do you care? Thought you were leaving.

I will get to Glasgow, said Alan. I'll do what I have to do here and then I'll drive on. Time's not the only thing.

Of course not.

Though you're looking well on it. Here, let me leave something. He put 500 on the table and stood up. Malcolm picked up the cash and offered it back to him, shaking his head.

I can afford it, said Alan.

I know, but there's no need.

Alan took the money and put it back in his pocket. He shook Malcolm's hand.

Bye, he said. Give my love to Paula.

I will. You thought I was better than I was, didn't you? You're disappointed.

I haven't the right. It's shameful but there are people you're forced to like whatever they do. As soon as I get fixed up in Glasgow I'll have you come over and cook for you.

Malcolm smiled. Glasgow, he said, glancing at Tanya. He shook his head.

I'll cook for you there, said Alan. He left the restaurant and fought his way through the dogs to the car. There were about twenty of the bastards, all starved, stunted mongrels. He caught one of their snouts in the door when he tried to slam it shut. He felt the door bounce off the thin furry jaw and heard the dog scream in pain. He closed the door and drove away in a hysteria of barking. The snake-meat stank.

Alan drove out along a broad highway lined with trees and came to a junction part blocked with man-high cubes of concrete. He drove round them and passed a red brick factory building. The road curved and began to climb; there was a wooded hill in the distance, and a vertical column of black smoke. Immediately ahead was the Alans' police unit, one of the armoured troop carriers drawn across the road and the Alans leaning against it, smoking. G. K. Chesterton was squatted down on the tarmac stripped down to camouflage trousers and a striped vest, spooning meat from a can into his mouth. Alan drove up and parked close by. He got out.

Where's Captain Alan? he said.

He went to do a reconnaissance up ahead, said the lieutenant, drained of the joy of breakfast toasting. Then he grinned. Still looking for eggs? He reached down and threw something at Alan, who caught it. He felt a cold, heavy shape in his hand with something like an earring swivelling from it. It was a grenade. He threw it back to the lieutenant with a spasm of his forearm from the elbow and wiped his hands on the sides of his trousers, shivering. The lieutenant pretended to fumble it like a hot potato and the police roared before he clipped it back onto his flak jacket.

D'you mind if I go on ahead? said Alan.

The policemen looked around, at each other, at the ground, in the air, shifted their gunstraps, sniffed, cleared their throats. It's dangerous, said the lieutenant.

Snipers, said G. K. Chesterton, licking his spoon and throwing the empty tin over his shoulder into the ditch at the side of the road.

It's a question of clearing up a case, said Alan.

The policemen laughed, snorted and shifted weight uneasily like horses presented to a novice rider.

I'm asking you as your guest, said Alan.

The lieutenant's mouth pinched, he straightened up and banged three times on the side of the troop carrier with his fist. The engine throbbed and black exhaust jetted from its outlet pipes. It moved jerkily forward off the road.

Thanks, said Alan, and drove on slowly. In his mirror he saw the carrier reverse back into place.

About half a mile further on he came to where houses were burning. A track led off the road into a group of about fifty houses. A couple were on fire, five or six were smoking and another dozen were shells, the glass gone from their windows, soot-licks black from the windowframes, shiny tin roofs buckled from the heat. Alan drove up the track till he came to a parked police car with its blue lights flashing. He stopped and got out. He raised his voice and said was there a Captain Alan anywhere.

Yo, called the captain from the gap between two homes. One of them was undamaged, the other had a small fire on the go in the front room. Every few seconds burning wood cracked like a cap gun. The captain came out towards Alan. He had on an old set of camouflage fatigues fastened up tight at the neck. He had an automatic rifle in one hand and a metal bucket sloshing in the other.

Here, he said, holding the bucket out to Alan. Try this. Alan took it, stepped forward and flung the contents through the window. The fire roared up and the whole room, floorboards, walls, ceiling, ignited and ran with flames. Alan dropped the bucket. The captain came up and stood beside him with his hands behind his back, looking into the inferno. He shook his head.

Listen, he said. Can you hear it? That hissing? There was water in that petrol. You can't trust anyone. I almost put it in my tank as well.

Where are the people?

Ah, said the captain, smiling and tapping Alan on the collarbone with his forefinger. That's a good question. Let me ask you something. If the police came round to your house, would you run away?

It depends.

Heh heh. Come on. The captain tapped harder.

I don't know.

You wouldn't, because you've got nothing to hide. These people ran away. Only before they ran away, they set their houses on fire. Look at this place. He pointed at the building Alan had just thrown a bucket of petrol into. Nice house, isn't it? Bigger than mine. You might wonder where they got the money for all that furniture. Then they think nothing of setting a match to it. The captain tapped his eyelid. With my own eyes, with these eyes, I saw the man who lived here throw a bucket filled with petrol through the window.

Maybe they were frightened after the boy got killed.

Oh! The captain pointed his finger at Alan's face. That was why we came here, wasn't it? About the boy. Inquiries! And they started shooting at us. Where'd they get the guns from, eh?

I've got to be getting on. I'm Alan Allen, I'm here to pick up the antique that was stolen . . . Alan saw something moving on the ground at the edge of the next house along. It was a woman crawling jerkily through the dust. Alan went over and squatted down beside her. She had two black eyes, they were puffed and swollen and she could hardly see out of them, her cheeks were bruised, there was a cut across her forehead and a lump of matted hair and dark oozing matter on top of her head. Her floral dress was ripped at the neck and the hem, and streaked with soot and dried blood. There were more bruises on her legs. She was wearing Eeyore the donkey slippers.

Are you OK? said Alan.

The woman coughed and spat. She turned the thin white slits of her eyes towards him. Yeah, fucking brilliant, she said.

God, is that Mrs D-D?

They killed my son.

Let's not be having any of that kind of talk now, said the captain. Everything's got to be investigated properly.

He's dead, isn't he?

That's not to say they killed him.

Who?

You see the problem, said the captain to Alan. You can't get a straight answer from these people.

You need a doctor, said Alan to Dora D-D.

Help me up, eh? she said.

Alan put his hands under her armpits, raised her up on her legs and propped her up against the wall. She twisted her face and gasped and coughed.

All right? said Alan.

Uhuh.

He let go. She collapsed in a heap on the ground and struck the dust lightly with her right fist a couple of times. I'm sorry I can't offer you a cup of tea, she said, but they've burned the fucking house down, haven't they?

I'm not going to warn you again, said the captain, standing with his boots a few inches away from Dora D-D's face. You'll not be making those allegations until there's been a proper enquiry.

We need to get her to hospital, said Alan.

Oh! said the captain. The mental hospital. That's where they found your egg. One of the patients stole it.

This isn't the time, said Alan. Let's get her into one of the cars.

One of the cars, repeated the captain, frowning and scratching his chin.

Is there any water? said Dora D-D. She coughed again and spat.

Is there? said Alan.

Yes, said the captain. Go and get some. There's a well over behind the third house along.

Don't go, said Dora D-D.

I'll just be a minute.

Don't go, eh?

Alan went off to look for the well. It was where the captain had said it was, in between two cherry trees by a small plot of maize. There was no winch, just a steel bucket with a length of orange nylon rope fastened to the handle lying on its side next to a shaft topped off with a three-high square of white bricks. Alan picked up the bucket and dropped it down the shaft. There wasn't a splash, there was a dry pat. Alan tugged at the rope a couple of times; the bucket seemed to be resting on something solid. He hauled it up; dry. He looked down into the well. Black darkness. The earth could fall down around him and the walls close around his body, the earth the dam and his body the finger, holding the flood of darkness back.

Alan walked back to where the captain and Dora D-D were. The captain was lighting a cigarette, the gun held in the crook of his right arm. He shook the match out with his free hand, threw it away, deftly switched the automatic to his left hand and dragged hard on the cigarette, looking up the track towards the hills. Dora D-D was lying on her back with her legs flat on the ground, one forearm held up, the other across her chest. A dark stain spread down from her neck like a bib over her dress and was drying on the skin of her neck. Alan went closer. Her chin was down over her throat but you could see the beginnings of a straight deep cut under the clotting blood.

Alan went over to the captain, who had his back to Dora D-D. The captain had a bayonet in a leather sheath on his belt. Alan stood a few yards from the captain, standing in his line of sight.

Did you find the water? said the captain.

No.

No? That's too bad. The well was full yesterday. Alan

watched the captain, who dropped the cigarette in the dust, bent down and tore up a handful of grass. He held the gun between his thighs, spat on the palms of his hands in turn and rubbed them with the grass.

What happened to Mrs D-D? said Alan.

What, something happened? said the policeman. He threw the grass away and went over to the body. He prodded Dora D-D in the shoulder with his toe and shook his head. You turn your back for a moment, he said. He looked at Alan. What are you doing here? On the face of it it's a clear enough case of suicide, but there's going to have to be a full police investigation into this. You should leave.

What if it was the police who did it?

If it was the police we must have known what we were doing, mustn't we? It'll all be analysed in due course.

Oh God, said Alan.

The captain looked irritated. His fingertips strayed to the hilt of the bayonet. I don't like your tone, he said.

It's someone I know, said Alan, and covered his face with his hands just as Mike's baseball bat cracked onto the side of the captain's head. He took his hands away and saw the captain kneeling on the ground with his eyes closed like he'd fallen asleep praying. A little blood trickled out of his ear. Mike stood behind him with his legs wide apart, teeth bared and clenched, holding the bat with both hands. He was staring at the head he'd just hit. After a moment he prodded the captain between the shoulder blades with the blunt end of the bat and he fell forward onto the ground.

It's no good counting on the old victories, said Mike to the not moving officer. The written words one after another. The calculated triumph on the final page at the end of time. I'm already there. I'm on every page and in every word, and the words are becoming one. The future is me dismantling teachers and writers and peeling away the words until there aren't enough of them to hide the light. It's so easy! He laughed. If you'd known how easy it was you would've destroyed yourself as soon as you knew what you'd become –

Where's Deirdre? said Alan.

– where you all are, said Mike to the officer, speaking on through the interruption without paying any attention. You're all connected. The teachers, the writers, the books and the verses. I can see you all together as clearly as I can see the dirt on a window.

There was a creak and a crash from the burning house as a roof-beam came down. Mike! said Alan, more loudly. Hey! Prince of Darkness!

Mike looked up, serious, gravely serious, so heavy and dense with gravity that nothing light could escape. Don't call me that, he said. He moved towards Alan, bent forward slightly with both hands on the bat held horizontal. Alan walked backwards.

Mike, where's Deirdre? he said. Is she OK?

Not everything's clear, said Mike. You're a blur. I can almost see through you. Are you in my way or not?

Not, said Alan. He reached his car and opened the

door. A warm thick stench flowed out. Mike straightened up.

What's that? he said.

Meat, said Alan.

What kind of meat?

Snake meat.

The serpent! said Mike.

Do you want it?

Let it go! Mike had let the bat fall to his side. He
was almost in tears.

Alan opened up the back of the car, took the bags
out and put them on the ground in front of Mike.

There. It's yours, he said.

Mike dropped the bat and thrust his hands into the
bag. No, he said, crying and sniffing. He started taking
the chunks of meat out and setting them on the ground.
Alan watched for a while. He put his hands in his pockets.
The stink wasn't so bad in the open air. Mike was trying
to re-create the form of the original snake by putting
the parts together in their proper order. Soon he was
going to find out the head was missing.

It's different, said Mike in a broken voice. He sniffed
and wiped his nose with the back of his hand.

Different from what?

It's not the way it's being.

You've got a hell of a thing about tenses, haven't you?
What way's Deirdre being? Having been being been?

I'm the serpent coming to her and she likes it. I'm
not the serpent now, so why's it here?

Alan sat down sideways in the driver's seat of the car

with his legs out the open door. That was a book, he
said. Your brain's fucked up and scrambled it all. He heard
the sound of an engine from up the track. There was a
lorry coming down from the hills about a mile away,
kicking up dust.

That was in the garden, then, was it? said Alan.

Was?

Sorry, is.

Yeah.

Where is it? Where's it happening? Could you show
me where the garden is?

You're not there.

What about free will?

The truck came squeaking and rattling into the
village. It had an olive green cab and an open wooden
trailer at the back. It was half-filled with armed men.
Alan didn't recognise the driver. Next to him in the
cab he saw Deirdre and on the outside Gregor
Ferguson, dressed as a policeman, with a red armband.
The truck stopped by the body of Dora D-D and the
unconscious captain. Gregor Ferguson jumped down
from the cab. Deirdre climbed down behind him. The
councillor looked round, squatted beside Dora D-D,
stood up, looked at the captain and turned him over.
Deirdre walked towards Mike and Alan. Alan stood
up. Without looking into his face Deirdre put her arms
round him and pressed her body against his. Alan hesitated a second and put his arms round her. She was
wearing knee-length denim shorts and a black teeshirt.
How thin and warm she was.

Have you been with Mike? said Alan.

Yes, said Deirdre, but he hasn't been with me.

Was it bad?

Yes. It was bad. Deirdre looked down at Mike hunched in the dust pressing two hunks of rancid flesh together. He was hissing. They've been trying to catch him, the councillor's people. They were keeping me, thinking he'd come. They've been calling him a bad influence, and harmful to the cause, and a police provocateur. They're saying it was his fault the boy got shot and this trouble started.

It started a long time ago. It was my fault.

Don't be stupid. None of this is anything to do with you. It doesn't touch you. You should get in your car now and drive out of it.

Did no-one ever suggest he was just insane?

Deirdre stepped back from Alan and shoved him hard in the chest. He staggered back a few steps. What? he said.

There's no just insane, said Deirdre. That's what you've never understood. You're afraid of Mike for the same reason the police and Gregor Ferguson and the professor are afraid of him, the same reason the boy who got shot loved him. He's inspired and he acts. The rest of you are groping around in the dark and he's following something, and everyone can see it in him, and they either trust him or they hate him.

Why does he keep hitting people?

You always ask why as if you'd ever know. You've never got anything out of these whys. You see knowing something like solving a puzzle, and he's trying to destroy the puzzle.

To get to what?

If I knew I'd be with him.

Down in the dust trying to reassemble a putrid snake.

It's easy to take the piss at times like this.

I'm a driver ferrying great souls about, said Alan. Sometimes I look over my shoulder at what they're up to in the back seat. Sometimes it looks like fascists back there.

Deirdre looked down at Mike. She didn't say anything for a moment. Then she said: He's not organised enough to be a fascist. He hasn't got an organisation. People follow him but he doesn't lead them. He's by himself.

Alan watched Gregor Ferguson and three men wearing tracksuit bottoms and teeshirts lifting the captain to his feet, propping him up against a wall and shaking him by the shoulder. His head lolled from side to side with some movement of its own. Another three guys came walking fast, almost running down the track; one in an old brown suit and a fawn shirt, the other two younger, with shellsuits, both carrying rifles. They were the ones who'd been with D-D outside the off-licence. The councillor stepped back from the captain out into the road, and walked towards them with his hand held out. The trio ignored him and went over to Mrs D-D's body. The one in the suit stood over her, looked at her for a couple of seconds, then grabbed at his head with his hands, squeezing it tightly, fell down on his knees, bent so that his face was touching hers and made a sound like a roar and a moan. It had the noise of a furious mute in it, a baby crying to be fed, a threat to the takers of her life that they should give it back, the promise of suicide and revenge and the resolution to empty the canister of grief till the fist was banging on the bottom to get the last drop out. The corpse changed from a stiffening yellow thing to a killed loved woman. The councillor and his people looked at each other and looked away, looked at the ground. None of them wanted to cry. Alan felt his own eyes pricking.

This is all shite, he said to Deirdre, who was still watching Mike. People are getting killed here. I'm going to the mental hospital. That's where the egg is. We can leave Mike there and I'll take you on to Glasgow.

Always leaving people, murmured Deirdre, staring at the snake.

Christ, I wish I could.

There was a reordering around Gregor Ferguson, the captain, and the body. The truck reversed round sharply with clashing and shrieking of gears. Mrs D-D was wrapped in a blanket and passed up to the back of the truck. The councillor pulled back one guy who'd been pressing the muzzle of a pistol hard into the captain's throat and had just cocked the gun in his face. The gun was already cocked and a cartridge flew out onto the ground. A small boy appeared and snatched it up. They tied the captain's hands behind his back with a length of cable trailing from a telegraph pole and set him down on his knees so he was facing the open trailer of the truck.

The councillor came over to Alan, Deirdre and Mike.

I thought I told you to stay away from here, he said to Alan.

I'm here on unrelated business, said Alan.

Did you see what happened to the woman that got killed?

I was behind those houses –

Did you see what happened?

No.

Then shut the fuck up. He turned to Deirdre. I'm holding you personally responsible for your Charlie Brown there, he said. I don't want him wandering. I'll be back to deal with the pair of you once I've finished with the suspect.

Listen to you, said Deirdre. Chief Inspector Ferguson.

D'you think? grinned the councillor. He slapped Deirdre hard across the face and she fell down. He walked away, looking back over his shoulder once. You've got to learn to take it if you're going to try dealing it out that way, he said.

Deirdre got up and Alan grabbed her arm. She shook him off and brushed the dust off her shorts. She didn't make a move to go after Gregor Ferguson.

The councillor hauled himself up onto the back of the truck. Will the court please be upstanding? he said. The captain managed to struggle to his feet before anyone could get to him. Gregor Ferguson checked his name, age and address and said: You're charged that on or about the past few hours you did wilfully and without due cause murder by throat-cutting Mrs Dora

Lisa D-D, in violation of common law. How d'you plead?

Not guilty, said the policeman.

Who presents the prosecution case? said the councillor. I do. Thank you. Sir, it's the prosecution's contention that the prisoner was involved in looting and burning homes in this district when he was disturbed by the victim. He beat and sexually assaulted her and in cold blood murdered the only witness to his crimes. Thank you. Thank you. Who represents the accused? I do. Thank you. Sir, at the time of the events in question, my client was carrying out in all good faith orders which he had himself issued for restoring order in a particularly difficult neighbourhood. It's my submission that the unfortunate woman died, most likely by her own hand, as a result of the turmoil and confusion which always surrounds these episodes, and that the true victim of this sorry affair is my client, who was simply doing his job of putting the law into effect. Thank you.

There was muttering among the councillor's people. Move it, shouted one of the men.

Shut your face or I'll clear the fucking court, said Gregor Ferguson. Can we call the first witness? Councillor Gregor Ferguson. Prosecution. Thank you. Can you show the court what you've got there. Thank you. A bayonet. Does it belong to the accused? It does. In your expert opinion, are the wounds suffered by the victim consistent with the use of such a weapon? They are. Thank you. No further questions. Thank you. Defence. Thank you. Councillor Ferguson, is there the slightest trace of blood on the blade of this bayonet? No. No further questions. Thank you. He could have wiped it clean. I didn't ask that question. Strike that from the record. Would the accused please take the stand? Prosecution. Thank you. Tell the court what happened.

I was discussing housing problems with a well-known member of the community, said the captain. I went for a smoke and when I came back she was dead.

No further questions. Thank you. Defence. Thank you. Captain, we've heard a lot in the course of this trial about the law. Which law are we talking about?

The law of the people who pay us, said the policeman.

No further questions. Thank you. I call upon the prosecution to make its final submission. Thank you. Sir, the guy's a butcher. Look at the state of this place. It's a pre-planned police terror operation. He's guilty. Who else could have done it? A life for a life. Thank you. Thank you. Defence? Thank you. Sir, my client's a happily married man with three lovely children who's devoted a lifetime's work to the public service. A riot's a riot but the fun's got to stop somewhere. What d'you want, mob rule seven days a week? I'd like to add that in the event of charges being dropped my client's willing to serve in his professional capacity any legitimate self-proclaimed authority in this area, including the elected local councillor Gregor Ferguson. Thank you. Thank you. I'll now retire to consider my verdict. Have I reached a verdict? I have. Will I state my decision to the court? Not guilty.

The councillor's people rushed the truck and Gregor Ferguson fired shots in the air. There was a sound from the direction of the town centre like a woodpecker heard on the far side of the forest on a still day. Alan looked round. The Alans' troop carrier was moving up the track towards them. It was still a good way away. Following on behind were police on foot, wearing helmets.

It's time to go, said Alan. He got into the car and started the engine. Deirdre took hold of Mike's wrist and tried to pull him towards the car. The woodpecker sounded again. Orange stars sailed overhead, trailing pencil lines of dark smoke. Alan saw Gregor Ferguson fall and the truck started to move, men scrambling aboard. One of them turned, sighted carefully and shot the police captain in the back as he ran away. Deirdre was having trouble with Mike.

Let him take the snake if he wants, said Alan.

The flies, said Deirdre.

There was a sound like scattered applause ringing up and down the street.

Mike! shouted Alan. Back to the garden!

Deirdre led Mike to the car and they began to move off up the track. Deirdre slammed the door shut and Alan tried shifting up a gear and accelerating. His head banged off the roof and he slowed down. There was no way to go any faster than 25, round the holes and deepest ruts, without getting stuck or beached or fucking the suspension.

He looked in the mirror. They were putting distance between them and the troop carrier, gaining on the lorry. Alan signalled to overtake and crawled past the truck on a patch of hard-baked grassland.

The track rose up into the forest, oaks and horn-beams and walnut trees. After a couple of hours, no more than forty miles, they crossed a ford, Alan drag-ging the car over the stones in an overthrottled first gear, afraid of any obstacle that'd stall him and strand them in the river and somehow lock the moving parts, send water to drown the delicate engine. The water curved into the air off the wheels like swans' wings. The river was fifty yards across, but at its summer low and less than a foot deep at most and gravelled on the bottom. The car did stall trying to climb the steep bank out of the river on the far side, front wheels up and rear wheels in the water. The windows were open and in the silence before Alan started the engine they heard a cuckoo call through the trees, wood pigeons, and gunfire in the distance, or maybe a real woodpecker. Alan revved up and tried to mount the bank; the wheels lost their grip and spun free in the damp soil. He reversed back into the river, hearing the water breaking gently round the wheels, gave it big revs and brought the clutch up. The car charged the bank, struck the packed earth hard on with the front suspension and lurched over onto the level. A few seconds later there was a flapping beating sound from under the car. A puncture.

They got out, Alan loosened the bolts and jacked the car up, the jack sinking a little into the ground but holding firm.

Look, said Deirdre.

Alan stood up with the four heavy black rusted bolts in his hand. A couple of hundred refugees were wading across the ford, along with two Ladas and a Zaporozhets with their own weight in furniture and mattresses lashed to the roofs. Some of the refugees had handcarts. There were children with sacks on their backs, mothers with children on their backs and old women holding shopping trolleys over their heads to keep them out of the water. The Zaporozhets and one of the Ladas made it up the bank, slithering and swerving, with seven faces pressed to the windows of each one and the baggage swaying to the rhythm of gravity. The other Lada fell back into the water, the wardrobe tore free from the roof and mattresses followed. A crowd of people waded through the water to push the car up the bank and save the goods. They tied the sodden mattresses back on and hauled up the wardrobe, one of its door mirrors smashed, and the car crawled on.

Alan took off the damaged wheel and fitted the spare. The refugees walked past them without saying anything, though they did look. A ten-year-old boy went by panting a Roxette song to himself. Alan tightened the bolts and jacked the car back down. The three of them got in and Alan tried to drive on. The wheels spun again. After they'd spun three times in the damp, deepening groove they were making, Alan said Mike and Deirdre needed to get out and push. Before they could get out, six men from the refugees pressed up against the back of the car and shoved. The car floated forward. Alan tried to give them money but they refused.

He offered to take a couple in the car and they said there was no need. They walked on with the others and in fifteen minutes they'd left them behind.

After another hour the track merged with a metalled road and they passed through a village where a wedding feast was going on in the front garden of one of the houses. Beyond the village a stone wall came out of the trees and ran along the edge of the road. It went on for about a mile before they reached a stone gatehouse in the form of a small fortress, flanked by stone unicorns on pillars. The gate was solid steel, painted green, with a smaller door set in it. There was a sentry box, with windows, and a policeman sitting on a stool inside. Alan got out, taking the keys with him, and spoke through a hole a couple of inches across cut into the sentry's window.

My name's Alan Allen, he said. I've come to pick up a stolen antique egg.

Allen, said the sentry. He ran his finger down a list of names and numbers written in an exercise book with thin, stiff, grey pages. There's nothing here. Who was it you were after?

I don't know. The police said the egg was here.

The sentry picked up a phone. Reception? There's an Alan Allen here about an old egg.

Antique.

Yeah. Does anyone know about that? Uhuh. Uhuh. OK. The sentry put the phone down, took a slip of paper and scribbled something on it. He poked it out through the window.

Room 307, third floor, he said. Give me the paper when you leave and I'll let you out.

Thanks, said Alan, taking the slip and turning for the car.

Hey! said the sentry.

What?

You can't take those two in the car with you. They'll have to wait for you here.

Alan asked Deirdre and Mike to get out.

I'll be two minutes, he said through the driver's window while the gate was opening. Mike looked less sad. He'd begun to frown and his lips were puckering. He kept looking over his shoulder at the sun like he thought it was following him. Deirdre held Mike by the wrist and looked at Alan with a good smile and worried eyes.

Can you keep a hold of him? said Alan.

Deirdre shrugged and grinned. I don't know, she said. Take care in there.

Why?

Deirdre looked worried. The smile came back on top of it. I do like you, she said, and me liking you has got more to do with being human than me loving him. That's the honest truth, whatever else I said. She leaned forward and kissed Alan on the lips.

I'll be two minutes, said Alan. He drove through the gates.

The main part of the mental hospital was a six-storey staple-shaped building in off-white brick. Alan parked next to a Lada in the forecourt, a paved area with strips of rosebeds and a dry, grubby fountain painted white and blue. A couple of guys in blue pyjamas and slippers were sitting on a bench watching him. He walked into the lobby. It smelled of disinfectant and urine. A guy slid across the floor on his slippers like a cross-country skier. His eyes were closed and his arms crossed across his chest. A policewoman rose from a desk with a bunch of keys as Alan approached.

The one for the egg? she said.

Yes.

He followed the woman to a steel door. She unlocked it and swung it open. On the other side was a man wearing a short white coat and a cylindrical white cap.

Room 307, she said.

Let's go, said the man. The door closed behind them. They went to the stairwell and up three flights of stairs.

The lift's broken, said the man.

They reached a double door covered in thick wire mesh. On the far side was a long corridor painted light green and floored with brown tiles. A man in pyjamas was running up and down it, screaming or else imitating the sound of a submarine klaxon. There were benches bolted to the floor along the wall. Alan could see a man with a black storm of hair and yellow skin angrily playing with himself, three men leaning forward to hear a fourth who was making a speech beautiful in the delicacy and precision of the gestures he was using, and two men playing chess. At least five others sat by themselves, not moving, staring at a fixed point in space.

The man in white unlocked the door. They're harmless enough, these ones, he said. The room you want's over there. He pointed.

What about you?

I'll wait here. Just give us a shout when you're ready to come out.

Alan went down the corridor. He heard the rattle of the mesh behind him as the door closed. The klaxon man flew past him. The door to room 307 was open by a few inches. Alan went in and saw McStrachan sitting on a stool by the window. The stool was chained to the wall.

Who're you? said McStrachan.

You know who I am, you fucking bastard.

No . . . have you got a slip?

Alan showed him the piece of paper. McStrachan took it, read it and folded it in four. Alan! he said, getting up, shaking Alan's hand and pushing the great jaw to within a millimetre of his forehead. You must be glad to see me.

About as glad as I'd be to see a shite on a cheeseboard. Alan looked around the room. It was painted a dark glossy brown. There was a bunk with a coarse, dark grey blanket on it, a cupboard with a Davy lamp on top, a stained hole in one corner, a bucket of water, a shelf with a couple of candles, a picture of colliery winding gear, and a stack of books: *Wealth of Nations*, *Humphry Clinker*, *Roxana*, *Life of Johnson*, *An Enquiry concerning Human Understanding*. There was a small square table with a pile of dog-eared blue jotters on it, a jar filled with short blunt pencils and a dark blue cube-shaped leather box, hinged in the middle. Alan unfastened the catch and opened the box. Inside, held in a fur-lined pocket, was a painted egg. The end was painted black. On one side was a depiction of the visible moon, on the other the face of a woman. Alan closed the box and handed it to McStrachan.

Here's your egg, he said. What about the rest of my money?

McStrachan laughed. The windowpane shivered behind the bars. What about your going to Glasgow? he said.

Just give us the cash, eh?

It'll be transferred like the last time.

It's your redundancy money, isn't it? What'd you spend it on this for?

You needed work. I don't know what you mean by redundancy money. I reap a handsome income from my estate, or would if it wasn't for circumstances like the smoke and the fire and the flooding. They tell me the roof's in danger. It's not a problem. There are time share opportunities, clay pigeon shooting, I could introduce pheasants. It's true there aren't many places for them to hide and the beauty of their plumage might spoil with the dust. Would you like some coffee?

Yeah, all right.

I'll just go and fetch some from the kitchen.

Alan went over to the window. You could see the wall stretching away into the distance on either side, no end to it. Over by the gatehouse Deirdre and Mike were standing where he'd left them. Then the two of them started walking off the road into the woods.

Alan turned and went to the door. He looked up the corridor in time to see McStrachan showing the piece of paper he'd given him to the nurse, who opened the mesh door, let him through and locked it.

OI! screamed Alan and pelted towards the door. The sound of it coincided with the shriek of the klaxon man, who found himself running alongside Alan. He stopped and stared as Alan grasped the mesh with his fingers and shook it.

Wo! shouted Alan. He kicked the mesh and rattled it. After a few minutes the nurse came back and stood looking at him, a few feet from the door, with his hands on his hips.

Come on, this isn't your first day here, he said.

Just let me out, eh? said Alan with a dry mouth.

We told you someone was going to come and take it away from you, said the nurse. You shouldn't have stolen it, you know that.

D'you not recognise me? said Alan.

The nurse frowned. Who are you? he said.

I'm Alan Allen. I just came to get the egg off McStrachan.

The nurse nodded and looked around him. Yeah? So if you're Alan Allen, who was it just left with the egg?

McStrachan!

I see. And you just gave him your pass out?

He took it!

The nurse licked his lips. Why don't you just wait in your room for a bit? he said. I'll ask someone to come. He walked away.

How long? called Alan.

Soon! shouted the nurse without looking round.

The klaxon man had resumed his running and screaming. A couple of the still men followed Alan with wide, grave eyes, like politicians at a ceremony they felt obliged to honour even though they didn't believe in it. He went back to his room, took one of the jotters and sat down on the stool by the window. In the courtyard he saw McStrachan get into the Lada and drive out through the gate. He opened the jotter. It was filled with neat pencil drawings of mine shafts in plan, cross-section, elevation and artist's impression. The mines had been transformed into split-level shopping centres in which shoppers crawled along on their hands and knees, pushing trolleys loaded with groceries along rail lines winding through the tunnels.

There was a knock on the open door. A man in a white coat over a black suit and tie and carrying a brown folder came in with the nurse.

Hello, hello, how are you today? he said, coming over and holding out his hand. Alan didn't get up and didn't shake the hand. Not good, he said. I'd like to leave now.

Of course. And you are . . . ?

Alan Allen.

Of course. You know who I am, don't you?

No.

Come, come, Mike. Dr Belanbekov?

My name's not Mike, it's Alan.

I'm sorry, of course. Can we . . . yes. The doctor opened the folder and fumbled through a few papers, not reading them. He closed the folder and held it against his chest with folded arms. He pushed his glasses up his nose with his middle finger, cleared his throat, whistled a couple of bars of the theme to *La Dolce Vita* and drummed his feet on the floor.

How long have you been Alan? he said.

Always.

Always. I see. Always. And McStrachan?

A completely different person.

And Mike?

I do know a Mike. Also a completely different person.

And the person who came here just now?

That was me!

I see. And now he, or you, have left.

That was McStrachan. Alan's teeth ached from pressing them together.

The doctor looked at the male nurse. You see? mouthed the nurse. The doctor nodded, took a blue Bic pen out of his breast pocket and tapped it between his teeth.

The trouble is, we remember the patient in this room as Mike, he said. Then there was a certain incident, a series of incidents, with a female nurse.

Deirdre?

Ah! said the doctor, grinning, straightening up and pointing the pen at him. He's making the link. He remembers.

But I'm not Mike.

We remember you as Mike. That's what you're down as in our records. Then Deirdre had to leave – you remember that?

I wasn't here.

No . . . shortly after that you began referring to yourself as McStrachan. You read a lot. Talked about the
coal industry. Ring any bells?

That was somebody else.

Right . . . and now you're Alan.

I always have been Alan.

Obviously. Obviously. And you didn't collect the egg
because . . . ?

I've been stitched up from the beginning. D'you think
I look like them?

I can't remember. I haven't been up here for a while.
I just know we've got a male patient registered under
the name of Mike in this room, and he's never been
released.

Have you got a geriatric unit here? said Alan. Have
you got a patient called Sim?

No.

Why not?

Why should we?

I'd like to see him, that's all. I shouldn't have left him
like that. I wanted to be on my own with Deirdre.

There you are, said the doctor. It's coming back. Of
course, we wouldn't want you to start abusing the sports
equipment again.

Shut up, said the nurse. Don't remind him.

You were the one who taught them to play baseball,
whispered the doctor.

I should have walked out of the car there on the
motorway, left them, like an angel, said Alan.

What's he saying?

Ssh.

But you can't be an angel unless you're insane like Mike.

We never said you were insane, Mike. That's not a word we like to use.

All the angels are insane because they can't lie to themselves. If they're going to Glasgow that's what they'll do, and if they're going to travel for weeks after an egg that looks like the moon that's what they'll do. They can't want both. They can't be hungry for money and careless about getting it, they can't be trying to get somewhere just so's they can leave it and go back to where they came from, they can't be with the woman they love just so's they can long to be with their friend and be longing to be with her.

Alan hardly noticed when the hypodermic needle slipped into his arm. He went on for a bit and then the waves throbbed through him and he went under.

When he woke up he was in the bunk with the blanket creased over his legs. There was a blue light from the window filling the room. It was either dusk or dawn. The birds were so loud: what was the point? Dawn, then. He looked at his watch. 6.25. He sat up and felt a loose, greasy presence over his body. Pyjamas. There was no light switch in the room and it was dim. The door was locked. He looked round for his clothes. They weren't there. His wallet and car keys were missing. He could see from the window that the car was still where he'd left it.

Alan pissed in the pit and felt a terrible thirst. He looked in the bucket, sniffed it. It smelled OK but what guarantee was there that McStrachan hadn't topped it up with some of his own?

The light came on and someone began walking down the corridor, rapping on the doors and unlocking them. Alan went out and called to the nurse with the keys, a woman.

Hey, I want to get out of here today. The klaxon man burst out of his cell and began running up and down the corridor, screaming.

Exercise after breakfast, said the nurse.

Can I see the doctor? The one who came yesterday?

I'll put your name on the list. Mike, isn't it?

Some of the other patients were washing. Alan took his bucket and stood in line in a room with taps and basins and soap. He emptied, rinsed and refilled the bucket, drank some water from the tap and washed his face with the soap. Kidneys. At seven they went downstairs to a canteen for breakfast, under supervision of three nurses. The main item was pancakes, rolled up and filled with something. Alan took a couple and bit into one. The filling was cold porridge. He spat it out and took the rest, stale brown bread and glasses of tea. There were no forks or knives, only spoons. After breakfast they were led out to a paved wired-off compound behind the hospital with benches and flower beds where they could wander around for a couple of hours. Alan saw the nurse who'd first let him in to see McStrachan.

This is a mental hospital, right? Alan said to him.

Right.

How can I get out?

Show us you're OK.

What's wrong with me?

Personality disorder. Multiple personalities. You started calling yourself McStrachan, now you're Alan.

So if I was Mike, and I was behaving myself, you'd let me go?

Of course. Next time your family came to visit they could take you away.

When do they visit?

They never have so far, not since they brought you here.

When I was McStrachan, you let me use the phone.

The nurse looked around and leaned close to him. That was while you had money, he murmured, and moved away.

They went back to their rooms. Alan learned he had an appointment with the doctor just before lunch. It was 10.30 am. He sat on a bench in the corridor and watched the klaxon man running up and down. After a bit he got up and began jogging down the corridor in the opposite direction from him. He built up speed to match the klaxon man; the klaxon man broke stride and stopped, looking at him from under his eyebrows, breathing hard, hostile. Alan stopped. The klaxon man began to run; Alan ran towards him. The klaxon man screamed; Alan screamed. They passed each other and ran to the far end of the corridor, turned and ran back. Alan caught the klaxon man's eye as they crossed again; the hostility

337

was fading, he was watching Alan like a dancer watching his partner. They ran up and down, screaming twice on each length. Alan screamed once as he passed the last radiator on the right towards the window and once when he got to the second bench before the mesh door. By the third run pride in their team work had entered the klaxon man's eyes; by the fourth, an eagerness to be judged well by Alan; by the fifth, a confidence that he was better at it. Alan was tired. He sat down to rest at the window end of the corridor. The klaxon man ran a couple of steps further, stopped, stared at Alan, licked his lips and sat down sharply on the nearest bench with his fingers tapping at the edge of it. He looked down at the floor and looked over at Alan, and got up; he saw that Alan didn't get up, and sat down again. He threw his head back and made his klaxon sound, looked at Alan again. Alan shook his head. The klaxon man rubbed his nose with the back of his hand, stood up, sat down and began to cry.

Alan got up and started to run and scream again. The klaxon man stopped crying after a while and watched Alan but didn't move. Alan went into his room and drew hills and birds on McStrachan's notebooks until they came to get him. He looked back down the corridor as the wire mesh door closed; how quiet it was, but much as before, the lone masturbator, the orator and his audience of three, the two chess players and the others sitting by themselves, not moving, staring at a fixed point in space, except there were six of them now instead of five.

They took him to the patients' library on the second

floor and told him to wait. There was no-one else there. There were four bookcases, mainly with scientific texts, pragmatic philosophy, maths, physics, cookery, natural history. There was no history or biography and the only art books were strictly realistic. There was a twelve-volume encyclopedia in which every entry referring to historical personalities had been cut out and replaced with the same essay on personal hygiene. There were a couple of shelves of fiction. They didn't have *His Preaching Hands* but they did have *Bandicoot Bebop*. Alan took it down and turned to the last page.

He read: Frank thought about what the old man had said that night when the rain came down without limit, before the river took him, roaring down the valley with the voice of a fresh-woke dragon hurtling to sate itself before the long sleep resumed. They found farmers and boys aplenty in the days after, hung on branches and beached up on the shore, all swelled up and stinking, but Frank got fished out and the old man hit a deep dark current rushing him below the surface, over the bottom, through the rocks, till his corpse was folded into the cold salt tendrils of the sea and run swiftly down to fathoms the fish hook and the diver never saw. Even in the rain his hands had been warm under Frank's arms as he held him up above the waters, screaming at him, lit up inside by the grandeur of his coming death.

Two things you don't ever get away from, Frank, that's true love and your own self. The rest's scenery. You go all across the country and it don't matter, you can't cut 'em out.

The old man had been right, Frank knew, and that seemed to matter more now than whether he'd set those fires or not. The old man had been shaped by time and desire and hadn't sought himself in wearisome journeying over the gaudy illusion of a travelled world.

Frank got up off the porch seat and walked to the steps, looking over at the woods on the far bank of the river. He switched off the light and the oscillating moths vanished. The trees aspired to secrecy under the moon as it crept from cloud to cloud. There was a smell of ham and corn from inside the house: Meonie was waiting. Frank took off his shoes and socks, went down the steps, walked through the grass and came to the riverbank. The smell of the kitchen was gone. He took off his clothes and stepped into the river.

Alan closed the book and put it back. The windows of the library faced onto the other side of the hospital, away from the gatehouse. Beyond the exercise compound was a park, crossed by a road lined with trees, leading to a wood. There was no sign of the wall.

The library door opened and the doctor came in carrying a plastic bag. He came over to the window and leaned against the wall, facing Alan.

What's up? he said.

You took some things of mine, said Alan. My clothes, my car keys, my wallet. I'd like them back.

Didn't we get you to sign for them? said the doctor. No.

Everything's safe enough. You're a dangerous and

unpredictable individual, Mike, and we can't just give you back these things and let you go roaming around.

I don't want to roam around, I want to drive a bit in my own clothes in my own car with my own wallet in my pocket. It's not like I'm going to leave the hospital grounds. It's rehabilitation.

I see. It's against the rules. I don't know if I've ever mentioned this, Mike, but we don't get paid much here, the prices, it's terrible, these are hard times. Hard times. Anyway.

Alan lowered his voice. The reason I was asking about the wallet, right, is that I've no idea exactly how much is in it. What I'm saying is somebody could take cash from it and I wouldn't even know that something was missing. If they were to take, say – how much do you think?

Two thirds?

I don't think they'd risk taking that much. But if they took half, I wouldn't even know.

Half, eh? said the doctor. He shrugged. You'd better have it back and check, then. He handed Alan the plastic bag. If you knock three times on the outer door the policewoman'll let you out. Be back by five tonight and don't try and leave the grounds. They're big but we've got dogs and if you're not back in time we'll send them after you. I know you've been doing your best to seem lucid since Allen came for the egg but we can't afford to lose you. Look at it from our point of view, Mike, we need to keep our numbers up. The budget's on a per head basis.

The doctor left the library. Alan took his clothes and shoes, his wallet, already lightened of half the cash in it, and the car keys out of the bag. He got dressed, put the pyjamas in the bag and went downstairs. He knocked three times on the steel door and the policewoman opened it. She looked at his face and nodded him through. He went out to the car, got in, started it, and leaned back and listened to the sound of the running engine for a couple of minutes.

He drove round the hospital block and found the road which led through the park. It was a strip of tarmac without signs or markings, wide enough for a single vehicle. It went on for half a mile before broadening as it passed an artificial lake, then narrowed again and wound steeply downhill through a forest. After two hours Alan came to a main road with a white line down the middle of it and cars and trucks travelling in each direction; he turned left and after four miles pulled in at a petrol station. He filled the tank and bought a packet of cashew nuts, a Topic bar and a can of Vimto.

Is it far to the edge of the grounds? he asked the cashier when he paid.

What grounds?

Is it far to the wall?

What wall?

Never mind. It was almost 3 pm. Too late to get back to the hospital by 5 pm. Alan drove on.

At midnight he reached the town of Mineralniye Vody. Next morning he began travelling again, in the same direction. He went on for four days, sleeping in the car each night, and at the end of the fifth day, driving on a smooth six-lane motorway, saw towers against low hills on the horizon. It was the town of Glasgow.

Alan drove into the centre and at 5.30 pm, with the sun slanting through frosted glass and gouging a white-hot strip across the bar, went into a pub. He climbed onto a bar stool and ordered a pint of lager. Behind the bar was a woman of about Alan's age wearing a white shirt with the sleeves rolled up and a long white apron. She handed him the drink.

Thanks, said Alan. Is it far to the wall?

Which wall?

Is there more than one?

I reckon there must be.

Yeah. Listen, you're not short-handed at all are you these days?

No, sorry. We were looking for someone a couple of months ago but we took a trainee on.

Trainee, eh?

Uhuh.

I need to find a place to stay.

I've got the *Evening Times* here if you want it, said the woman, reaching down and holding out a folded paper.

No, no, it's OK, thanks. Alan blocked out the sight of the paper with his hand, trying to make it look as if he was waving the woman away. Maybe later. Is there anything there about the councillor and those people getting killed?

Probably. Who got killed? Why don't you have a look? The woman nudged it along the bar top.

I will later, thanks, I will. Yeah. I just arrived. I've been sleeping in the car for the past five days.

Uhuh. You look a bit rough.

Is it OK to park outside?

The woman looked at him from a few feet down the bar where she was slotting wineglasses into a rack over his head. No, she said. It's no stopping there. They'll tow you away. I'd think seriously about moving it while you're still fit to.

I came through from Edinburgh.

Uhuh. I usually take the train myself.

They stopped talking for a time. There was the sound of the glass stems on wood and glass, a fruit machine honking and cheeping, traffic outside and a pack of dogs barking in the distance.

Can you hear dogs barking? said Alan.

The woman frowned, listened and shook her head. Nope, she said.

Good, said Alan. I thought I heard barking. He drank a couple of mouthfuls of lager and reached for the paper.